Mending: New and Selected Stories

For Joan —
and our shared
love of New Mexico

Mending

NEW AND SELECTED STORIES

Sallie Bingham

Sarabande  Books
LOUISVILLE, KENTUCKY

Managing Editor
Sarabande Books, Inc.
2234 Dundee Road, Suite 200
Louisville, KY 40205

Library of Congress Cataloging-in-Publication Data

Bingham, Sallie.
Mending : new and selected stories / by Sallie Bingham.
    p. cm.
ISBN 978-1-936747-00-9 (hardcover : alk. paper) — ISBN 978-1-
936747-01-6 (pbk. : alk. paper)
I. Title.
PS3552.I5M46 2011
813'.54—dc22

                                    2011006208

Cover Art: *Red Studio #3* by Derrick Buisch, 2010. 24" x 24", oil on
canvas. Permission provided courtesy of the artist. Photographed
by Eric Tadsen.

Cover and text design by Kirkby Gann Tittle.

Manufactured in Canada.
This book is printed on acid-free paper.

Sarabande Books is a nonprofit literary organization.

The Kentucky Arts Council, the state arts agency,
supports Sarabande Books with state tax dollars and
federal funding from the National Endowment for the
Arts.

For Ann Arensberg, Anne N. Barrett, and Cyrilly Abels

CONTENTS

ACKNOWLEDGMENTS

The Touching Hand and Six Short Stories, by Sallie Bingham (Houghton Mifflin Company, 1967).

The Way It Is Now, stories by Sallie Bingham (The Viking Press, 1972).

Transgressions, stories by Sallie Bingham (Sarabande Books, 2002).

Red Car, stories by Sallie Bingham (Sarabande Books, 2008).

"Mending" was published in a textbook anthology, *Imagine What It's Like, a Literature and Medicine Anthology* ed. Ruth Nadelhatt, Biographical Center of the University of Hawaii, 2008.

"Mending" is also included in an anthology from 1977, ed. Linda Hamalian and Leo Hamalian, Dell, *Solo: Women on Women Alone*.

"Selling The Farm" originally appeared *The Arkansas Review*.

MENDING

On Fifth Avenue in the middle fall, the apartment buildings stand like pyramids in the sunlight. They are expensive and well-maintained, but for me their grandeur stems not from the big windows with the silk curtains where occasionally you can see a maid dusting with vague gestures but from the doctors' names in the ground-floor windows. Some buildings have bronze plaques for the doctors' names beside the entrance door. Whether those doctors are more magical than the ones who are proclaimed in the windows is one of the puzzles I amuse myself with as I ply my trade up and down the avenue.

My trade is not what might be expected from the height of
my red-heeled sandals or the swing of my patent-leather bag.
I am, after all, a good girl, a fairly young girl, although I have
a few lines and a tendency to wake up at five in the morning.
Taxi drivers still comment on my down-home accent, and
although for a while I tried to dispel that impression by buying my clothes at Bloomingdale's, I have given up the effort.

My trade is doctors, and it is essential. I have a doctor for
my eyes and another for my skin; I have a special man for my
allergies—which are not crippling—and I also have a special-
ist for the inside of my head. For a while it seemed that my
head was as far as he would go, with an occasional foray down
my throat. Finally a choking sensation forced me to cancel my
appointments. I suppose I should not expect anyone to take
that at face value. He was a very handsome man; he is still,
and it is still painful for me to imagine the man whose lap I
longed to sit on presiding behind his profession, gazing with
those curious green, unshadowed eyes at the women (why are
they all women?)—the young ones, the old ones who hang
their coats on his rack and sling their bags beside their feet as
they sit down, with sighs, or in silence, on his couch.

My childhood was made to order to produce a high-heeled
trader in doctors on Fifth Avenue, although my childhood
would never have provided the money. My mother was blond
and a beauty, and she had a penchant for changing men. My
favorite was a truck driver from Georgia who used to let me
ride with him on all-night trips down the coast. Mother didn't
approve of that, but it took me off her hands. He would sing
and I would doze in the big, high cab, which seemed to me as
hot and solid as a lump of molten lead—as hard to get out of,
too, as I discovered when I tried to open the door. Oh, that
truck cab was ecstasy. That was as close as I could come. My
mother lost interest in him when I was six and replaced him
with a white-collar worker. She thought Edwin was a step up,
but for me, he never had any kind of appeal; he was the first

of her men to carry a briefcase, and I learned an aversion then I have never been able to overcome to men who tie their shoes with very big bows and carry cow-smelling leather briefcases.

There were many others after Edwin, but they washed over me and I do not remember disliking them at all. They did not make much of an impression, as my mother would say; that was left to my first doctor, a personable Cincinnati gynecologist. My mother, who had settled in that town with a railroad man, made the appointment for me. She wanted me to know the facts, and she did not feel up to explaining them. Of course by then I knew everything, as well as the fact that if you turn a boy down, he will suffer from an excruciating disease. I did not really need to know that to be persuaded, since the interiors of those 1950 Chevrolets smelled just like the cab of Ronny's truck.

The gynecologist armed me with a strange rubber disk that flew across the room the first time I tried to insert it. The second time I was successful, but I was never able to find the thing again. It sailed like a moon through the uncharted darkness of my insides. I knew it was not right to have a foreign body sailing those seas, but it took me a month to summon the courage to call the gynecologist. I was so afraid he would be disappointed in me. He rescued the thing the next day as I lay down on his long table; he was disappointed, and the thing had turned bright green.

After that my mother married an Air Force man who was going to be stationed in Honolulu. I still think of her little black boots when I think of brave women leaving for parts unknown. She tripped up the steps to the airplane, an indomitable little mountain climber, with tears in her eyes. The Air Force man was in tears, too, and smiling as though their future lay shining on the tarmac. There was no room for me in that arrangement, and so I was farmed out to my mother's only prosperous relative, a hard-working doctor who lives in Greenwich and had the luck to marry my aunt.

I was nineteen, too old to be educated, too young to be employed. It made sense for me to do what I could to help Aunt Janey run her large house. There were people to do everything that needed to be done, but no one to organize them. Often the window washer arrived on the same day as the man who put up the screens, or the children needed to be picked up at friends' just as Aunt Janey was going to bed with her second cousin. (He was no relative of mine: another briefcase man.) So it was vital to have someone she could rely on to make telephone calls and draw up schedules.

Since I was not being paid in money but in good food and a fine room with roses on the wallpaper, Aunt Janey felt responsible for finishing me. She had been a brilliant woman once, and she still had her books from those days. She wrote my assignment every morning while I started the telephoning. I had to do it before I could do the bills. I can't say the reading meant a great deal to me, but the swing of the sentences—*Jane Eyre*, for example—seemed to carry me out of my ordinary way. I had thought that life was quite plain and obvious, with people coupling and breaking apart like the little snot-colored dots I had seen under the microscope in fifth-grade biology. The only lesson I had learned so far was to stay out of the way of those dots. After I read about blind Rochester's cry, I began to want some of that for my own.

I had not been demanding until then. No one could have complained that I made a fuss over a quick one in the back hall—that was the furnace repairman—or took it more seriously than the roar of the crowd at a construction site. I was never a prude, and my body did not do me that kind of helpful disservice. At home, in the upper South, in the Midwest, in Florida, they talked about boobies or the swing on my back porch. Greenwich is more refined, even New York City is more refined, and the repairmen used to praise my eyes. When it came to seeing one of the men twice, I would shy away, not only because I was waiting for the voice across the miles but because I did not want to spend any time with a man who might begin praising my eyes and then go on to feeling things himself—I did not mind that—but then would expect me to feel things, as well.

In feeling, I was somewhat deficient. It had not mattered before. I could remember the smell of Ronny's cab and glory in it, but I was not able to enjoy the particular flavor of a man's body. A naked man, to me, was like a root or a tuber. I can't say I was afraid. But I never could see the gleam, the light before the dawn, the pot at the end of the rainbow when a naked man stood in front of me. It seemed to me that women were seemlier, more discreet, without that obtrusive member I was always called on to admire. I could not touch it without conscious effort, and that showed in my face. For a long time, it did not matter to me, but it mattered to those men. They wanted me to admire, they wanted me to feel something. Even the man who came to prune Aunt Janey's forsythia insisted that I had to feel. "What's wrong with you?" he complained, when we were lying under the bare branches of the big bush. I knew he was feeling that it was somehow his fault.

I have never wanted to hurt anyone. I have wanted to help, if possible. And so I decided I would stop going out with men.

The trouble was that I wanted a pair of arms. I need a pair of arms with a pain that even now I can't bring myself to describe. That, of all things, I had carried out of my childhood. When my mother was between men and feeling the ache, she would call me into her bed and squeeze me until suddenly she would fall asleep. I was more the holder than the holdee. It did not matter. The warmth of her thin arms, the wrists hardly wider than milk-bottle necks, the bones as fine as glass splinters, would last me through the next day and the next. Chronic cold was one of my chief complaints. But after she had held me, I didn't even need to button my school coat. I would walk down whatever gray street we were living

on in whatever more or less depressed small-city neighborhood in whatever indistinguishable section in the middle of
this country, with no scarf over my head, no gloves on my
hands, and the wind that comes from the Great Plains or the
Mississippi or the Rockies or some other invisible boundary
lifting the ends of my mouse-colored hair like a lover. Of
course the trick was that my mother didn't expect anything
of me, except not to wet the bed. She didn't expect me to feel
anything in particular or to praise the way she looked in her
nylon slip. She gave me the warmth of her long, skinny arms,
and I gave her the warmth of mine, and before I was ten years
old, I was addicted.

When the new man moved in, I had to spend the night in
my own bed with my fist in my mouth, not because the sounds
they made frightened me—they were no more frightening
than the chittering of the squirrels in the little city parks—but
because there was no more warmth for me. Mother got into
the habit of buying me bunny pajamas and a woolly sweater
before she installed a new cousin.

After the forsythia man and my decision to do without
men, I started to get cold in that old way. Aunt Janey noticed
the gooseflesh on my arms one morning when I brought
up her breakfast tray. She made me sit down on the satin
blanket cover. "We haven't had a talk in I don't know how
long." She was the prettiest woman I'd ever seen—the best,
the brightest, with her jewelry box turned upside down on
the pillow and her list of the day's duties, prepared by me,
balled up and thrown on the floor. I could think of her only
in silly ways—still that's the best I can do—because when I
think of her eyes and the way her lips curled when her second cousin rang the doorbell, I know I will always be lonely
for her. So I describe her to myself as a fickle woman who
cheated on what my mother (who never had her luck) called,
reverently, a perfectly good husband, and fed her children
peanut butter out of the jar when I made the mistake of leav-

ing a meal to her, and was happy. So happy. Outrageously happy. She had my mother's long, skinny arms—the only family resemblance—and although she very seldom held me in them, I knew she had the same heat. The difference a diamond wristwatch and a growth of fine blond hair made was not even worth thinking about.

(And he, the second cousin, did she make him groan with happiness, too? She used to come downstairs afterward in her Chinese kimono with her pearls hanging down her back, but I never saw much of him.)

We had our talk that morning. It was fall and Jacob the gardener was burning leaves. I insisted on opening the window, although Aunt Janey hated fresh air, and so I was able to flavor her words with the leaf smoke. She told me that I was unhappy; and there was no way I could deny that. So for once she took the pad and the telephone book and asked for the telephone, which had a crook on the receiver so that it could perch on her shoulder. And she began to make appointments.

She had noticed my teeth, she said between dialings. Was there an implication about my breath? She had noticed that I squinted a good deal over the print in the telephone directory, and so she was sending me to have my eyes checked. She was also not certain that I should be as thin as I seemed to be growing, and so she was making an appointment with her own internist on upper Fifth Avenue. Unfortunately in his office I felt my old enemy, tears, rising like an insurrection of moles, like a walking army of termites. When I cried on the leatherette chair, the doctor, who was as friendly as the repairman my mother had left after six months of too much loving, suggested that I ought to go and see the other kind.

That was all right, too, as far as I was concerned. I was ready to take anyone's advice. It did not seem possible to go through the rest of my life trying to get warmth from the eyes of construction workers; it did not seem possible to go on spreading my legs for men who took it personally that that part—"down there," as my mother called it—had no more feeling than the vegetable it so closely resembles: a radish, fancy cut.

The next waiting room was soft and beige, like the tissuey inside of an expensive shoebox, and I could have lain there forever, till the robins covered me with magazine leaves. Of course I had to get up and go and lay myself down when the time came—why this eternal lying?—on an even softer, browner couch in a smaller, safer room. I asked the doctor right way to let me stay forever. He held my hand for a moment, introducing himself, and my cold began to fade. Can it fade from the hand up and will the heart in the end be heated, like a tin pot on a gas burner turned high? I had always assumed that my body warmed up independently and that my heart, at the end, would always be safe and cold. He did not want anything from me—you can't count money in a desperate situation like this—except my compliance, so that he could try to help. And I believed him.

My mother would have said there is no such thing as a disinterested man; she would have gone on to add that since he had green eyes, he must have other things in view. He did have green eyes, pale, finely lashed, and a pale, tired face. He seemed to have spent himself warming people up. By the second session, I hated the idea of any particle of him going to other people, and I ground my teeth when I passed the next patient—always a woman—in his little hall. I wanted him all to myself and it seemed to me that this was my last chance. My day was flooded with sights I had never seen in my life, views of my lean body folded up on his lap or the back of my neck as I knelt to kiss his feet. I had been cross and mean all my life and now, like a three-year-old with a lollipop, I was all syrup and sunshine. Shame had no part in it. As I went my rounds to the other doctors, letting them fill my teeth or put

contact lenses in my eyes, as patiently as I have seen horses
stand to be bridled and saddled, I imagined myself in my
doctor's arms. Of course, he did not respond. How could he
respond? He wanted to help and, as he explained, holding me
in his arms for a while or even for fifty minutes could not do
me anything but harm. It is true that afterward I would never
have let him go.

I thought I could push him. After all, other men had
always wanted me. So I started to bring him little presents,
bunches of chrysanthemums from Aunt Janey's garden, jars
of my own grape jelly, poems on yellow paper that would
have embarrassed a twelve-year-old. He made me take them
all away, always neutral, always kind, always ready to listen,
but never won or even tempted. My wishes were making me
wild and I wanted to gather myself up and wrap myself in a
piece of flowered paper and hand myself to him—not for sex
or compliments, but only to be held.

Aunt Janey caught me crying after three months of this
and offered a trip to Paris as a distraction. I told her I couldn't
go because I couldn't bear to break a single appointment with
my doctor; she was taken aback. We had a long talk in the
late-night kitchen where Uncle John had been making pan-
cakes. She told me that analysis works, but not in that way.
"I can understand you wanting to go to bed with him, that's
what everybody wants, but I can't understand you letting it
get so out of hand."

"I don't want to go to bed with him," I said. "I couldn't
feel him any more than I could feel the furnace repairman. I
want him to hold me on his lap and put his arms around me."

"Yes, that's childish," she said, tapping her cigarette out.

"If I can't persuade him to do it, I'll die. I'll lie down and
die." It was as clear to me as an item on the grocery list.

"You will not die," she said firmly. "You will go to Paris
with me and we will shop for clothes and visit the museums
and we will find you a nice free man."

"With green eyes and rays around his eyes and long hands with flat-tipped fingers?"

"That I can't promise," she said. "But he'll be free."

"I won't go if it means missing an appointment."

She started to figure how we could leave late on a Friday and come back on a Sunday, but then she saw it was no use and decided to go for a longer time with the second cousin.

So I was left alone for two weeks, except for Uncle John and the children. He was gone most of the time, coming back at night for his ginger ale and his smoked salmon and a spot of conversation before the late news. He wouldn't let me fix real coffee in the morning; I think, being old and tired, he was afraid of the obligation. (The quid pro quo, my mother called it; nothing was free in her world, especially first thing in the morning.) The two girls spent most of the day in school and when the bus brought them home, I would have our tea picnic ready and we would take it out to the field behind the house. Late autumn by now and not many flowers left to pick, so we found milkweed pods and split them into the air. The little girls sat on my lap, either one at a time or both together, and when I kissed them, their hair smelled of eraser dust. I was in pain because the hours between my appointments were the longest hours of my life, and yet I never saw anything as beautiful as that field with the willows at the far end and the two little girls in their navy skirts and white blouses running after the milkweed parachutes.

By then I had discovered that my doctor had a wife and three children, and they all loved one another and managed well. More than that he would not tell me, and I was forced to believe him. After all, the owners of pale green eyes and flat-ended fingers tend to find the wives and get the children they can enjoy, the way a girl I met in one of my many schools knew exactly—but exactly—what to say to win a smile, and what flavor of milkshake would bring out the angel in her.

As my mother used to say, "Those that know what they

want, get it." But she had feeling all over her body, not just lodged here and there in little pockets.

Meanwhile my doctor was trying to take the bits and pieces I gave him and string them together to make me a father. I had never known or even asked which one of the cousins was my father, and so I gave him all the pieces I remembered from the whole bunch of them. Ronny and his truck. He had thick thighs that rubbed together when he walked and made him roll like a seafaring man. He liked to hold me between the thighs and comb my hair. Edwin with his briefcase that reminded me of my doctor's (although Edwin's was more expensive) and which, he once told me, held a surprise. The surprise, it turned out, was my cough medicine. Louis the railroad man who said he would take me with him on the train except that white girls brought bad luck; it was just like in the mines. The Air Force regular who yelped with joy and hugged me the day my mother said she would go to Honolulu.

My doctor wanted to know which one was my father, and he proposed that I write my mother and ask. I wrote her because I did everything he even hinted at and I would have as soon slit my own throat. Word came back a week later; she thought I had known all along. My father had been a Kansas boy stationed at Fort Knox one summer when she was working at a diner called the Blue Boar. I remembered then that she had always kept a picture of a big-faced smiling boy on the mantelpiece, when there was one, or on the table by her bed. She said he had been killed in Korea.

My doctor did not try to do much with that scrap. Probably my father never even saw my mother's big stomach; if he had, he might have told her what to do about it, as a farm boy familiar with cows. So we had to start all over again with the scraps and pieces, trying to undo the way my memory simplified everything, trying to get behind the little pictures I wanted so desperately to keep: the shape of men's hands and the ways they had let me down.

We were still at work when Aunt Janey came back from Paris and she made me get on the scales that first evening. I told her the work we were doing was wearing me down; it was like ditch digging, or snaking out drains. She knew I was better, and she told me not to give up now with the end in sight. I wasn't sure what she meant, but I knew I had to keep on. There was some hope for me somewhere in all that. At my doctor's, the sweat would run down my face and I would have to pace the floor because there were months and even years of my life when all I could remember was the pattern a tree of heaven made when the sun shone through it on a linoleum floor. My doctor thought some of the scraps might have forced me into bed, but I only remember being tickled or chased with the hairbrush or locked in the car while they went into a road house. Nothing high or strange but only flat and cold. Something killed off my feeling, but it wasn't being raped by Ronny or Edwin or any of the others. Mother had sense enough to find men who wanted only her.

I told my doctor I believed I had been an ugly, squalling baby who kept my mother up at night, screeching for more milk. That was the only thing Mother ever said about me, and she said it more to criticize herself. She hadn't had sense enough, she explained, to realize I was hungry and to give me more bottles. Instead she slapped me once or twice. That wasn't enough to kill off much feeling, although it is true that if I were asked to draw a picture of myself, I would draw a great mouth.

By then I was almost in despair about getting what I wanted from my doctor, even a kiss or a lap sit or holding his hand. I kept having faith in him, the kind he didn't want, the kind that keeps you from eating and wakes you up at night. That faith woke the saints with visions of martyrdom and woke me with visions of lying in his arms. I kept believing that nature and its urges would triumph over the brittle standards of his profession; I kept believing that his calm

attention was the marker for a hidden passion. I also believed
that if he would take me, I would begin, magically, to feel. Or
lacking that, light up like a torch: joy, like Aunt Janey with
her pearls hanging straight down her back.

But he would not.

So for me it was a question of quitting—which of course
I would not do, because at least during the sessions I saw
him—or of going on with the work, keeping to the schedule,
getting up in Greenwich in time to dress and catch the train.
It was a question of opening my mind to the terrible thoughts
that flashed through it like barracuda through muddy water.
It was a question of making connections between one thing
and another that did not come from the expression in his
eyes—the looks I called waiting, eager, pleased—but from
some deep, muddy layer of my own, where the old dreams
had died and lay partially decayed.

The result was that I lost what ability I had. The children
went back to eating peanut butter out of the jar although I
had gotten Aunt Janey to lay in a supply of bread. The little
skirts and tops we had bought at Bloomingdale's began to
stink with sweat, and I stopped washing my hair. It did not
seem possible to stand under the shower and come out feeling
alive and new. It did not seem worthwhile even to try.

I didn't care anymore about getting better—that was a
sailing planet—but I did care about the little fix of warmth I
got from sitting next to my doctor. I cared about his words,
which were for me and not for all the other women, and after
a while I began to care about the things he said that hurt
me and seemed at first unacceptable. There were, in the end,
no answers. Yet he seemed to see me, clearly, remotely, as I
had never seen myself, and he watered me with acceptance
as regularly as he watered the sprouted avocado on his win-
dowsill. Is it after all a kind of love? By January, I was back
inside my own bleached mind; I knew it the day I went out
and bought myself a bunch of flowers.

Aunt Janey washed my hair for me and insisted on new
clothes and a trip to Antigua; when I said I would go, she
hugged me and kissed me and gave me a garnet ring. Uncle
John told me I was looking like a million dollars, and the little
girls, who had been scared off by my smell, began to bring
their paper dolls again so that I could cut out the clothes. I
was still, and always would be, one of the walking wounded;
I was an internalized scab, and when I looked at myself in the
mirror, I understood why people call naked need the ugliest
thing in the world. I broke two appointments with my doctor and went to Antigua with Aunt Janey, and one night, I
danced with an advertising man. I was no queen, but I was
somebody, two legs, two arms, a body, and a head with a
mouthful of choice words. I wouldn't sleep with him because
I knew that I wouldn't feel a thing, but the next day we played
some fine tennis.

When I came back to New York, the pyramids on Fifth
Avenue were no longer shining. The gutters were running
with filth and melted snow, and the doctors' names in the
windows and on the plaques were only names, like lawyers'
and dentists'. My doctor was on the telephone when I walked
in, and I looked at his free ear and knew he would never be
mine. Never. Never. And that I would live.

New Stories

FOUND

THE DINING ROOM HUNG SUSPENDED from the arches at its three tall windows, opening onto a wintry garden. The big table in the center of the room floated in spite of its weight of wine glasses—empty at lunch, but still Jean insisted on placing them at the top right corner of the coffee-colored lace mats. The table hung from the chandelier whose candle cups held electric light bulbs that glared in the middle of the January day.

The children who were not really children but three lanky half-grown youths (the real children were closeted with their governess upstairs) lounged at their places, creaking their spidery gilt chairs. Saturdays revolved around lunch because both parents were briefly at home.

The two tall brothers clinked their empty wine glasses with their spoons; they knew something about drinking. The sister sat primly.

Jean thumped soup bowls down in front of them. The thin clear bouillon jumped.

"A little more gently, please, Jean," the mother said from the funnel collar of her plaid suit.

Jean did not acknowledge her request, whisking away at once to the pantry, the swinging door sighing behind him. No one knew what language he spoke. He was supposed to be Corsican and had come with the house, which the embassy had rented for the family, sight unseen. The mother had only stipulated the number of bedrooms.

"Children, you should know our ambassador to Italy has been recalled," the father said from his pale-blue silk breast pocket handkerchief. "You may be asked about it next week at school." He might have known that his eldest son seldom went, sleeping until the maid came, insistently, to make his bed; that the younger had failed his midterms and was kept on only out of fear of embarrassment (it was an American school, after all, an outpost in foreign if not actively hostile territory); and that the girl, sitting so primly, spoke no French and could not have answered questions from the mob of Parisian girls at her convent school. She had been transferred to the convent after seeing two boys fighting with knives at the American School — anything, she'd told her mother, would be better than that: the mucous and blood and, even worse, the sobbing.

"You are all citizens of the world, now," their mother had announced from her pearl necklace when they had shambled onto the liner for France; nevertheless, everyone had been fearful of her going to the convent school, speaking no French, and having no religion.

("Do they really want to go?" some petty St. Louis neighbor had asked, exhaling disapproval with her cigarette smoke, a question that should not have been asked and so merited no answer.)

Now the younger of the two brothers drawled out a question while plumbing his soup for something solid. "Why'd they recall her?"

The girl remembered that they had been talking about an ambassador.

Jean was bringing in the bread.

"She was taken ill," the father said from his narrowly striped tie in the voice he used to close a subject.

"What was she taken ill of?" the eldest boy asked with a submerged sneer.

Their mother answered promptly, "Arsenic poisoning, from the paint that chipped off her bedroom ceiling. Poor Claire."

Someone snorted, probably the eldest. Jean plumped the bread basket down in the center of the table where it was difficult to reach.

"Butter," the mother asked piteously, but they all knew from the way Jean turned away that he had no intention of complying.

The girl was thinking of the name, Claire. She had read the name in a story about St. Francis. She wondered if this woman, this sick ambassador, had been some kind of helping saint.

She knew the bedroom with the paint flaking off the ceiling. It would match her parents' bedroom with perhaps a little yellow added by the Roman sun.

She thought, Then we might be recalled, too, if somebody got really sick. But it did not seem likely. They were all, her mother said, healthy as horses.

"Didn't do her job before the elections," the snorter said sideways so as not to provoke an answer. "Let the Commies get back in."

It was another statement that merited no response. They all spooned their soup. It was not very hot, and there might be nothing much coming after it. Food was still rationed, although the war had been over for five years, and the PX where the mother shopped out of necessity was more poorly provisioned—all cans!—than a bad-neighborhood market at home.

The girl was wondering if she was supposed to know what the Commies were. She had learned not to ask. She was not expected to be ignorant.

"Communists," the younger brother whispered. He was sometimes kind.

Usually she could find something in a word that helped her to its meaning—an echo of another word, perhaps. But this time she ran through the possibilities without learning anything: come, communal, union. She began to perceive that this was another of those words no one discussed because they all feared it. It was like a disease no one mentioned because that might make it contagious. Fear, their father had said in one of his speeches, fear is the greatest menace to what we are trying to accomplish here, in France, and the girl made the connection: to mention something dangerous is to spread it, like the plague. She felt, for the moment, satisfied.

"I thought they'd keep her in Rome because of her friendship with the Pope—she's an RC, children," the mother explained. The girl knew the initials were a kind of soft drink, and once again she was baffled.

"The Pope's turned out to be a weak reed," the father explained, "absolutely useless to us in this case, as he was during the war."

The girl had seen a portrait of a pope at the convent school—a stretched-out, greenish figure in a red robe—and so she could imagine quite easily that under that robe there was only a reed.

"I don't know what Henry Luce will make of it, though,"

the father went on to the mother, privately, this time, since the three could not be expected to understand. "He was awfully set up by her appointment."

"Maybe his rag will turn against the Dems," the snorter said rashly.

The father turned to stare at him. "It couldn't be turned any further than it already is."

The snorter was abashed, and began to wipe his mouth with his napkin as though, the girl thought, he could wipe away his unwise words.

"They're both quite common," the mother concluded, "like their magazine," and signaled to Jean to take the soup bowls away.

He rattled them onto a tray perched precariously on a corner of the table. On other Saturdays, Dominique in her small white apron had helped him, but Dominique was gone for reasons the girl imagined although she kept them to herself. Once, in the kitchen, she'd seen Dominique sitting on Jean's knees.

That provided the clue. Common was a certain kind of behavior, and in a moment of wild imagining, she saw the sick American woman perched on the Pope's red knees.

Jean hauled in a heavy silver platter with a mound of meat on it and slid it across the table to land in front of the father. He asked something no one could understand, then offered the father a long leather box, opening it to reveal a knife and fork of superior size.

The father stood to carve, turning up his white cuffs, but the meat was obdurate and made him sweat. He swiped at his face with his blue silk handkerchief, then bent to the task again while Jean stood to one side, watching. The father tried to slice, then went to hacking, and the portions Jean passed around the table were rough and ragged. It was lamb, nearly red, a strange sight.

"I'm writing my menus for them in French, with the

dictionary," the mother said. "It doesn't make a bit of difference. They fix what they want to fix." The girl remembered seeing the cook, a column standing over her stove. It did not seem likely written words could reach her.

The meal ended quickly and they all went their ways, the tall house absorbing each one. Upstairs, with the governess, someone was crying.

The girl found her roller skates in the closet under the stairs—the stairs where she'd seen her parents' dinner guests, going up and down. She carried the skates out to the sidewalk. The iron gate clanged behind her and she dreaded ringing later to rouse the concierge to let her back in, but there was no way around it. She had to get out, into the air.

It was still foreign air, gray and dense.

Since they had always lived in the country, she'd never had a place to learn to skate; dirt roads wouldn't do. Now she lurched and stumbled, her eyes on her toes. The skate wheels made a fearful noise on the rough cement. At the corner, she nearly collided with a couple and felt their stares. She was too old, she knew, to be learning to roller-skate.

She pushed on toward the massed dark greenery of the great park. Its depths held a lake where she'd once rowed the children in a wooden boat rented for the occasion. She had never rowed before, but she learned quickly although the rough wooden oars blistered her palms.

She planned to skate all the way to the lake. Stares pursued her as she stumbled across the avenue.

In this country, she was strange, as was the rest of the family. They were not strange, at home. There were loungers there, like her brothers, sad children, and even a few tall, thin, pale asparagus-girls, devoured by unanswerable questions: what is life?—that kind of thing.

Here, families were tight knots, and each twist and turn of each knot was like all the others. And they were dark—so dark! Not dark-skinned, of course; that was at home. But dark-haired, their sleek, soft short hair often covered by scarves, veils, tight hats. They had dark eyes that were peering, intent, and did not reward curious glances. Their clothes were dark, too, shriveled-looking, the women's skirts not even covering their pale, pointed knees.

She knew they had seen things and done things she could never imagine. She remembered the bullet-pocked walls of the government building that ran along the Boulevard of the Saint in the Fields, and the bunches of flowers, left beneath inscriptions where people had been shot. MORT POUR LA FRANCE. She could almost see the bodies lying along the sidewalk as she skated, but not really. She had never seen a dead body. It seemed a grievous lack.

Lately she'd begun to understand why the girls at the convent school teased her, or simply stared. She was too yellow and gold, and she knew nothing. Sometimes they gathered around her in the muddy courtyard and asked her questions she couldn't answer, so she said yes, or no, at random; she knew those two words, in French. Usually her answer drew a trail of laughter.

She entered the deep foliage of the park, skating toward the pond. At the school, Mass was said twice a day, morning and evening — a mysterious meal. The students hurried to the chapel across the courtyard in the freezing dawn and dusk. Inside, they were shepherded in waves by a nun to the altar; when she clapped her hands, the wave, briefly, knelt. The girl glared in concentration at the girl nearest her, imitating each move. "You must pretend," her mother had told her. "You must fit in."

Next each wave was herded onto benches facing the altar, where a priest intoned. He stood with his back to them; she seldom saw his face. His eyes were fixed on the big gold crucifix with the naked man nailed to it; she tried not to look at the blood, glittering in the light of many candles.

The words were in Latin, a language she understood a

little, gratefully, from school at home: Gallic wars. This was of course different. At one point, they all lightly struck their chests. Then the priest raised a disk and a gold cup.

The chapel air was dense, stuffy; a cloud of nuns breathed at the back. Not the scrubbing sisters in their long coarse aprons, but the queen nuns in tall white headdresses and long, rustling skirts. Sometimes the girl felt so faint she thought she was dying—the plumes of incense seemed to smother her— but she never fell down, as some did. Her pride sustained her; she would not be carried out. And the business never lasted very long. Afterward they were herded back into the blue dawn or the gray twilight.

Now she was skating past a great white statue of a naked man. Sooty rain had streaked his shoulders and thighs; he wore a massive grape leaf. His meaty hands, dangling by his sides, reminded her that she was very hungry; the lunch had been even less satisfying than the lunches at school—the only meal she ate there, since she was not a boarder. Her mother had drawn the line at that. How grateful she'd been, after catching a glimpse of the file of beds in the dormitory, the freezing bathrooms with their battery of sinks, and tubs in closets.

But she did eat lunch there during the week, or at least she tried to, at a long table in the refectory while a nun read aloud to the clink of spoons. Lunch was usually soup with things floating in it. Baskets of torn bread were passed savagely up and down; at four o'clock, more bread appeared, layered with slabs of bitter chocolate. While eating, they were not allowed to talk, a great relief.

She saw the pond through a break in the trees. After one look, she turned back. Without the children, she realized, the pond held no attraction. Now she began to skate faster; the light was going down, and she remembered that she was expected to go to the dentist that afternoon. She didn't remember what time.

Skating back, faster and smoother now, the vibrations from the wheels on the rough sidewalk ran from the soles of her feet to the crown of her head. She was flying, faster than she had ever imagined going.

In front of the iron gate, Jean stood waiting, his hands on the top of the big black American car that had come across on a freighter. (French gas was too weak to power it up hills, and when it quaked and wavered, her father cursed under his breath.) She wanted to apologize to Jean for keeping him waiting but had no words. She clattered into the back seat—he'd opened the door without looking at her—then bent down to unfasten the skates with the key she wore on a string around her neck.

The car moved forward.

She liked looking at the streets through the thick glass windows that seemed to strain out detail. Hardly anyone was walking under the empty trees. Buses rolled by lighted up like aquariums, faces floating in the cool, inside glow. And the strange little cars were scurrying along like beetles; she rode high above them.

She heard Jean's deep sigh as he mashed the brakes at an intersection; then he said something under his breath, probably a curse. She knew what was wrong: the chauffeur, Phillippe, had been given the day off in order to get married. That seemed reasonable; he would be back on duty early the next morning. But Jean was not pleased. He wore Phillippe's black visored cap at a strange angle, pushed back on his head.

On the big avenue that led to the arch with the flame, they stopped at a red light. A few walkers crossed in front of them. One turned back. A face was pressed to Jean's window, a thin face, very white. Fingers flailed against the glass and the mouth was shaping words.

Jean snapped his head around, frowning at the face. The light changed and they started forward. The woman dropped away like a rag.

She wanted to ask what the woman had said. This was not the first time a stranger had approached the car, and she knew it had something to do with the license plate and the small, bright American flag planted above it.

She'd overheard her mother complaining, "We saved their necks during the war, but now. . . ."

"It comes at a price," her father had said. "In the end nobody really wants to be saved."

Not sure of the link but sensing its relevance, she remembered the conversation at lunch about the American ambassador in Rome, and wondered if she looked as dark and solid as her father's colleagues, standing shoulder to shoulder, drinks in hand, under the living room chandelier. But that look depended on their suits, the shoulders stiff and long with padding—women didn't wear such clothes—and on their barking laughter that penetrated to her blue octagonal room on the second floor.

Because it had been a dressing room, the blue room was meant to share her parents' bathroom, but that would never do. Instead, she hurried across the marble hall, morning and evening, to the loungers' disorderly bathroom, rushing in and locking the door. Often one of them began to pound before she was finished, and they claimed she left unmentionable things on the floor.

A darker quarter of the city closed around the car after it passed across a bridge guarded by marble horses. Jean stopped before a narrow house in a narrow street. Elaborately, he climbed out and opened her door. She was grateful not to look at him, not to have to see his displeasure.

Her mother always told Jean when he should come back after her fittings. Her French was equal to that. But the girl didn't know how to say anything. She made a face at Jean, imploringly, hoping he would wait, but he had already turned away and was looking over the top of the car. Then he closed her door with a smart snap, climbed in and sped off.

She searched her pocket for the scrap of paper with the dentist's name. When she took the scrap out, she felt her five coins, cool and reassuring.

His office was on the second floor of the silent little house. She rode up in an elevator like a cigarette box. It stopped on the second floor, and she waited for the gilt gate to open, finally realizing it was waiting for her to open it herself. It had a powerful spring that pressed against her as she passed. She kneed it aside as she would have kneed an unruly dog.

She rang, and a young woman in a black dress swiftly opened the door. She took the girl's coat, and then led her into a room with a window and a dentist's chair.

She sat down and began to wait for the dentist to appear. He came in the door without speaking. She watched his white cuffs as he arranged his instruments on a small tray. Finally she looked at his face. He did not look back. She understood that her mother must have told him she spoke no French. His face was as closed as though she were dumb, rather than wordless.

He was supposed to see how her teeth were doing now that her braces were gone. The orthodontist at home had snatched them off because, he said, there was no one in France who would know how to attend to them. (Attending to them meant having them tightened, excruciatingly, every other Friday.) He said the French were very backward about correcting teeth, as the girl had observed every time one of them opened his mouth. Their teeth hardly looked like teeth, yellow and crooked as kernels of corn — something to do with their wartime diet, her mother had said. The orthodontist had insisted that all his work would be undone if the girl went to France, but her mother had refused to be swayed by that. "After all, teeth are not the only consideration," she had said, leading the girl to speculate about the others.

Now the French dentist was examining her teeth with his little metal probe. Her head was comfortably fitted into the padded brace, and the big chair enclosed her like a shell. She closed her eyes, contented. He didn't hurt her.

As he scraped her teeth, only her tongue was uncooperative, blocking his tool now and then.

After she spat and rinsed her mouth, he motioned her up out of the chair. The woman appeared, handed her her coat, and escorted her to the front door. Behind, the dentist was smiling; she felt it, even though her coat. Somehow, even without words, she had pleased him.

The little elevator was waiting for her.

Downstairs, she pushed open the door and went out into the fading afternoon. She had no idea how long she'd sat in the chair.

Standing on the sidewalk, she looked around. The narrow street was walled with small buildings, two or three stories high. She couldn't tell for sure, but they seemed to be houses. However, no one came, or went, through the front doors and there were no lights in the windows. She began to wonder if the houses were deserted.

The air smelled grainy with coal soot.

Half a block away, on the corner, a green awning stretched part way across the sidewalk. There was writing on the awning, and she realized that it must be some kind of shop.

As she waited, the streetlamps came on with a flash that settled into a dim glow. The ornamented tops of the buildings melted into the darkening sky. The streetlight above her head was humming to itself in a rising and falling tone, almost like a song.

A light came on in a window across the street. She imagined a woman inside, beginning to cook dinner. She would lay out carrots, turnips, and onions and begin chopping. The carrots would still have their earthy beards. Water would begin to boil on the stove. She remembered a visit they had paid to a French family; those children had had plain water in their soup bowls. Seeing that, she had wanted to cry out, and stand

up from the table; her bowl was full of vegetables in a thick
broth. But she had gone on spooning. "Family hold back,"
her father had explained, later. There had not been enough
soup for everyone, and guests always came first.

She began to shiver. Darkness was falling, solidly. The
sky above the rooftops had turned black.

Hearing a metallic rattle, she looked down the block and
saw a man lowering a grille over the shop window.

Panic seized her suddenly with its iron claw. She ran
toward him.

He turned, surprised. He was a round cabbagey man in
a long apron.

Her hands fluttered up, her mouth opened. Then she
rushed in the shop door before he could close it.

A sparrow woman sat on a high stool behind a counter
with a cash register and a pyramid of glass ashtrays. She
stared at the girl.

"Please — "

The man in the apron came in behind her. He stood with
his arms folded.

It was some kind of café. She saw a few tables, all empty.

The woman asked her something. The girl shook her
head and spread out her hands.

Then she said, "Perdue. Je suis . . . perdue." They were
her first French words.

They conferred briefly, and then the man in the apron
waved her toward the door. She thought he was going to lock
her out but he nodded and smiled, reassuring her.

He followed her onto the sidewalk and began to gesture
and speak. Eventually she understood that he was pointing
at a sign with a picture of a bus on it. She'd noticed them
all over the city and seen the big groaning overloaded buses
pulling up.

She ran across the street and stood by the sign in a
circle of yellow light from a streetlamp. He watched her for

a moment and then went inside. Later he came out with the woman, locked the door, and went away with her, arm in arm.

Planting herself, she began to wait. Buses come. Buses always come. She felt in her pocket for her coins.

Finally, at the end of the block, a bus came lurching. She realized it might not stop for her and stepped into the street, holding up her hand. It was a gesture she'd seen the men in dark suits make, to interrupt each other.

The bus wheezed to a stop in front of her and the doors opened. She climbed up, fumbling for her money.

The bus was packed with dark forms.

The driver turned his face to stare at her. His hand, on the long lever, closed the door behind her and the bus started, with a jerk. He nodded at the coin box.

She dropped all her money in. He looked at her oddly.

She wanted to sit down, she wanted to fold herself into the dark mass of strangers.

The driver was still looking at her.

"Rue," she said. "Rue Alfred Deodangue."

He nodded, and handed her back two of her coins.

As she sat down, she remembered the poison paint flaking off the bedroom ceiling in Rome, sending the American woman home. With a stab of shame, she remembered that she had hoped they might also be recalled. Now, settling into her seat and beginning to study the street signs, she knew she did not want to be recalled.

The arm of the stranger next to her was solid and still. After a while warmth began to seep into her side.

Let us stay a long time, she prayed, until I can put it all together—the words, the streets, the woman with her face pressed against Jean's window.

It might even be possible to ask questions now that she had some words. She imagined asking one of the jeering girls in the convent schoolyard why she hated her, what she had done. Perhaps it would turn out not to be hate at all but only some kind of game. If it was a game, any kind of question could be asked, because games were always about asking questions: "Red Rover, Red Rover, who will you send over?"

She had always been good at games, chasing the ball across the half court and lobbing it into the net or sprinting down the soccer field ahead of everyone else.

Thinking about games, she prepared herself for her stop, recognizing the avenue the bus was rolling along. She stood up, leaving the still presence beside her. Stepping to the front of the bus, she waited for it to ease almost to a stop at the sidewalk. She'd seen how it was done—this jumping down from a bus that hadn't quite stopped. She primed herself and jumped.

Well, she fell, but it didn't matter. She got up at once as the bus wheezed off.

It was just a question of learning their rules. At school, she would remember to wear white gloves the next time grades were announced and to stand up from her desk with her arms folded on her chest when her mispronounced name was called.

Running home—it was late after all, and dark—she considered the question of asking questions. She sensed an opening, as though her French words had breached a low, solid wall.

The concierge let her in, looking at her curiously.

"Bon soir," she said. There were two more.

The big stairs seemed to reach for her, as though they had been waiting. She ran up, her footsteps muffled by the thick runner that was held at each tread by gold bars.

At the top, she nearly gave up and went into her blue room as she always did. But she was still aware of the opening, although it already seemed to be closing. She wondered briefly if it could only exist outside the house.

As long as it was still possible, she pushed her way through the dimness—lights hadn't been turned on yet—and knocked on her parents' bedroom door. It seemed unlikely that she'd ever done that.

She heard her mother's startled voice and went in.

That lovely lady, her mother, was sitting on the satin stool in front of her dressing table, decorated like an altar with candles, silver boxes, and trays. She turned, looking alarmed, and the girl saw her silken leg in the opening of her dressing gown. She was getting ready to go out — her evening dress lay on a chair — and the girl knew she had very little time.

"I took the bus," she said, and gasped with surprise at herself. "Jean didn't come."

"Well, that is something," her mother said, smiling. "That is really something." The girl didn't know whether she meant that Jean had not come or that she had taken the bus.

"I was thinking of a question," she said, twisting her hands. Her mother had turned back to the mirror and was dusting her nose with a feathery thing that shed powder everywhere.

"What question, darling?" her mother asked.

"How was that woman, that ambassador, poisoned?"

Her mother laughed. "You're still thinking about that?"

"I really want to know," the girl said desperately. There was so little time. Soon her mother would rise, drop her dressing gown, and lower the big dress over her head. Then she would pack her little purse, slide on her shoes, and leave.

"Lead in the paint that flaked off her ceiling," her mother said. "I thought you heard that." She was applying a coat of red lipstick.

"But I don't understand," the girl said, and now she knew she was talking about many things. "Did she sleep with her mouth open?"

Her mother smiled. "She may have," she said sagely. "She may have, for all we know." Then she stood up to get on with the rest of her dressing.

The girl went away. She didn't particularly want to watch

her mother don the big dress although she knew she would look beautiful in it.

She went into her blue room and turned on a lamp. Above her head, the paneling of the octagonal walls reached into the darkness, topped with swirls. She stood studying that. The room had been designed for something else, something she would soon understand.

"It is hardly a room for a child," her mother had objected when they moved in.

"A boudoir," her father had said quietly.

There was no other room available.

I will stay here until I understand, she thought, sitting down on the bed. I will stubbornly stay until I find all the words and all the connections and all the rules of their game.

SEAGULL

"LISTEN," SHE SAID, LEANING ACROSS THE TABLE and laying down her fork, "if this is about money, I'm leaving." She began to gather her coat around her shoulders.

"It's not about money," he said. "How could I invite you to dinner and the theatre and ask you for money?"

She hesitated, one arm in her sleeve. "You're edging toward it."

"How?"

"As soon as you started talking about trying to raise money for your play."

"That was innocent," he said. "Believe me. You're in this game, too; I thought you'd understand. Getting a new play on its feet — I thought you'd be sympathetic."

"I'm plenty sympathetic," she said, "but I have my own projects."

"I know."

She stared at him, assessing. Apparently he had researched her. It was easy to find what she'd done: two respectable off-off-Broadway productions, mounted by a company she'd helped to finance.

She regretted, now, that she hadn't done her homework. All she had to go on was the way he looked, on the other side of the café table. He was thin, tall, his background, whatever it was, hidden by decades of living in the city; she was thin, tall, sharp, her background still hovering in her Midwestern twang, worn proudly, like an award, although she, too, had lived in the city for decades. Both were theatre people — playwrights, occasionally directors, actors in their own or other people's productions, but invisible, really, in the crowd. And of course there was no money — never had been, never would be. Feeling cheerful, she'd say it kept them honest — theatre people, her tribe.

But he was black. That was a distinction.

After ten minutes of talk, she knew they'd both come to the city years earlier, expecting a special destiny. No one could have told them it had not worked out the way they had expected because they knew it had worked out, but that their expectations had been slightly, perhaps fatally, off. So they had already in that first ten minutes established a base and a sort of harmony, and then he had started off in another direction with his play, the production mired in financial problems.

"The sources I've turned to in the past have dried up," he said now, satisfied that she had let her coat fall to the back of her chair, taking her arm out of the sleeve, although she hadn't picked up her fork; her tuna filet lay exposed on her plate, rapidly chilling. "With what's happened to the economy, even the foundations are pulling back, and the two or three patrons" (he couldn't help giving the word an ironic tinge) "have cut back, as well—and it's a crucial time for me, I need to do this show now, before we have a change in administrations."

"Really," she said, relenting a little. She was not uninterested although she was dubious.

"It's explosive material, but it'll lose its bang after January. My best work so far," he added quietly.

Her opposition seemed to have died and so he set to work, pick and shovel. It was what he usually did, it was his job, as much as the writing of his plays. He didn't resent the need to lay out his plans, precisely and powerfully, and felt after all these years that the labor of raising money for his productions sharpened his appetite and gave him new reasons to go on. He was educating his patrons (the word had no ironic tinge now), he was bringing them into a world that still in spite of its tawdriness was magic.

She hadn't given him much time, rushing into the restaurant late and then looking surprised, in spite of herself, when she saw him. They would need to be finished with dinner and paid in forty-five minutes, to get across the street to the Booth Theatre on time. And neither of them was ever late to a play. They associated that with amateurism, loudly chatting visitors from the suburbs who didn't leave enough time to park their ridiculous cars.

She lifted her fork and pressed the tines, tentatively, into her tuna. "How's your fish?" he asked, hoping for a little air.

"I don't know, I haven't tasted it." She shot him an imperious glance. He could have strangled her; did she think he was one of those hapless waiters who ask the crucial question too soon? Then he checked himself. He often asked the crucial question too soon.

Not this time. Too much was riding on it.

He'd found her by chance because he was working part-time in the box office and had recognized her name when she called to order a ticket and, greatly daring, had called her back (her telephone number was part of her order) and asked her to join him for dinner and the play. "You shouldn't have to go to the theatre alone," he'd said, realizing from her startled silence that this was a new thought but not an entirely unwelcome one.

"I go to the theatre alone all the time," she'd said, opening another door for his implication: a woman of a certain age, living alone in Brooklyn, riding the subway to the downtown theatres and in spite of herself beginning to worry during the second act about the long, late subway ride home.

He studied her, realizing that, between bites of her tuna, she was studying him. What he saw didn't correspond exactly to what he'd imagined when he'd recognized her name; she'd had some success ten years earlier with a one-woman show. He remembered the newspaper shot from that production—a woman smiling energetically—and something of the story: how she'd been working on the piece for years, mentored by several serious contenders, picking up an MFA in theatre somewhere and then seeming to burst on the scene full-blown. But the one-woman show had been followed by silence, although he knew she'd continued to "contribute to the life of the theatre"—that meant money—as well as commuting into Manhattan for classes and plays. The story. All of it easily found, and he'd found it.

She saw something less defined since she'd never seen Jeffrey's name in the theatre section, which she still read assiduously as though it decided fates, as it had at one time. His name had been there, a time or two, but inconspicuously, when he'd directed something that bombed in Chelsea or understudied in a little show that managed to run on Perry Street for nine months. That was five years ago, and nothing much since, which was the reason for the part-time job at the box office.

He was in his early forties, she guessed, in good shape, never a leading man but now maturing into a skilled character actor; he was ready for the parts he had been waiting for when casting directors passed him over for the romantic lead. He was ready for the characters he had tailored in his own plays, which other actors had never found a perfect fit. She could see that; she could see that he fit, especially now that black actors were once again being cast occasionally in white parts, or parts that had always been assumed to be white, by nature. It might be that he was a better actor than playwright, even more likely that his real strength was as a director but knew that field was more surely closed. She thought she was probably a few years older.

"How did you know my name?" she asked, lightening a little as she ended her scrutiny.

"From *Woman in Love*."

"But that was a long time ago."

"I keep up," he said modestly. "You made quite a splash, back then."

"I hit the crest of the wave," she said, equally modest, although both of them suspected that modesty was not their strong suit. "Nobody's interested in one-woman shows anymore."

"Or one-man," he said, to set the record straight.

She glanced at him, and he wondered if he had run up against an opinion, a hard one, with edges. But she only said, "Did you do those, too?"

"Not my kind of thing."

"So what turned you from writing plays to directing?"

"Did I tell you I directed?"

"No, but I gathered." She smiled. "You have that manner."

"What is that manner?" He was amused, in spite of himself.

"I think you think you have authority." She gave the word the same ironic tinge he'd given to the word *patron*.

"Authority." He thought a bit before answering, realizing that this was a challenge, her gauntlet laid down. With some women, this was the way they began to flirt, although he did not think flirting was what he wanted. But it might provide a way in.

"Of course I don't plan to direct my own play," he said, to prevent her jumping to the conclusion. They'd both seen efforts spoiled by the over-involvement of the writer. She knew that. She was smart, sharp, he thought, in the spiked way of theatre women in the city, women who'd struggled for a long time and survived.

"Well, you know enough about the scene to know you should be asking for money from someone else, some talented young producer." She would have liked to add, "no doubt black," but resisted. He didn't seem to have any race identification and the time of those fights was long over. "Much more realistic than going around raising money from people like me."

As she said it, she saw he didn't believe her. In addition to her two plays, he'd seen her name listed here and there as a sponsor of little hole-in-the-wall shows, the kind of short run she felt sure he was contemplating for his play—equity minimum, rarely reviewed.

"I believe in this play, I'm willing to try any way I can to get it on," he said.

"There're some ways not worth trying."

"Probably a waste of time but—"

"No," she interrupted him. "Shameful."

Her eyes were light brown, almost yellow, and since she didn't take care of her eyebrows, her eyes seemed set in a colorless waste. He knew suddenly that she'd given up trying to find acting parts. "Can't you imagine how I feel?" she went on softly, intently. "I'm your peer, I'm a fellow playwright, but you couldn't care less about my work"—she held up her hand to prevent him from objecting—"you haven't asked

me a single question about myself. Can't you imagine how
I feel?" Now her voice rose, and someone at the next table
glanced at her.

"I suppose," he said as calmly as he could. "I suppose I
can imagine it."

She was still staring at him. He ate some of his potatoes
without tasting them. He'd called her on impulse; it was
something he'd never done before, and he suddenly remembered how her Midwestern twang had seemed, when she
ordered her ticket, to open possibilities. He would never have
called her if she'd sounded like a New Yorker. "Where do you
come from?" he asked, moving his hand along the tablecloth
to grasp his glass of wine.

"Indiana," she said, relenting, "a long time ago," and her
hand, matching his, moved toward her glass. "I've lived in
the city or at least in the boroughs since I graduated from
school." She gulped her wine.

He didn't need to ask which one. She had the implacable
air of privilege; it would have been Yale or an equivalent
although he couldn't think at the moment of an equivalent.
Certainly nowhere in the West or the South.

"Were you born here?" she asked in her turn; they were
moving onto neutral ground, and Jeffrey realized that she
was not intractable. It was even possible that she was embarrassed by her outburst.

"Right up in Harlem." It was what she expected. "Single
mother, all that."

"Don't use that as an excuse," she said briskly. "You
might end up president."

"So might your daughter," he said recklessly, trying to
even the ground.

"I don't have a daughter."

"I mean a young woman of that generation."

"I don't think anyone will risk it after what the Senator
went through last spring."

"You do have to be tough," he said. She was tough, he knew, but not in the way he'd expected; she had resources, but they were not spread out to be viewed, they were not her wares. He'd never met a woman with resources who did not spread them out, disparaging them, maybe, but knowing their draw. It was possible, he realized, that she believed she had another draw. But he could not be sure.

She was a realist. Surely she was. Otherwise it would be very hard to negotiate.

"Do you enjoy producing?" he asked.

She smiled. "Yes, my own work, but I can't afford it."

He knew that was not true. She was keeping a drop cloth over her display.

"I like that dress. A very nice color," he said, although until then he hadn't noticed. "Green is a good shade for your hair."

"No use, Jeffrey," she said, smiling. "I know what looks good on me, I don't need to be told."

There was the rock again, the foundation stone. "I'm not trying to flatter you," he said.

"I know, and anyway, you couldn't. We only have a few minutes—tell me what you want, stop beating around the bush."

He nearly gasped. Suddenly, she was coming forward, even rushing at him. "I want your help," he said, before he realized that she might misunderstand. "I want money," he explained, and felt a rush of shame.

"I know you do." She folded her napkin neatly. This was what she'd suspected from the beginning. She knew this situation as well as she knew the feel of her coat lining, the beige silk that hung over the back of her chair. "Go ahead," she said evenly. "Tell me your plan. You must have a plan," she added when he was silent.

And so he began. He had to. There was no option. And at the same time, he felt a great wash of sympathy, as though he'd found something in his path, unexpected, soft, wounded, and was about to step back to avoid crushing it, but did not.

The details now, all of them, were laid out. She listened without expression.

He did not believe this was the conversation she had expected when he called her up to make the date.

She would never admit that, now, and yet her vague, smiling fantasy of what he might have wanted hung in the air like a trailing bit of steam.

He summed up, sighing, in spite of himself. "That is what it would take." He had the specifics in mind; it only took two or three minutes to list them: the costs, in general terms, of a six-week run, Equity requirements, the audience he hoped to reach and how he planned to reach them. It was a template, and she knew that. There was nothing new in it although it was well-grounded in the experience they both shared.

"Isn't there another way to go about it? Selling tickets that way seems not to work anymore," she said, getting up as he waved at someone for the bill. "Everything happens on the net." She put on her coat while he was paying. "The audience has changed," she added, "and your ticket prices seem high."

He hurried after her. There was so little time. Her back was unexpectedly broad in her coat.

"We'll use the Internet, too," he assured her, holding the restaurant door for her to sweep through—and she knew how to sweep, he saw that.

"I should hope so," she said over her shoulder. "Print advertising—"

"Theatre audiences are older, they still look at the listings."

"Not for limited-run engagements way downtown that may never get past the previews."

He did not reply. That was just another dig, her due, he supposed. Nobody liked being asked; it seemed to devalue them, whether they gave or didn't was immaterial.

They were waiting to push through a crowd crossing the

street to the gold lights of the theatre marquee. In spite of
all their disappointments, the sight of that marquee and the
crowd streaming toward it excited them.

But then she took the shine off. "My fifth *Seagull*," she
told him.

"I've only seen it twice."

She began to name the productions she'd seen, the famous
Russian one, the new translation with a hot British director, the slipshod amateurs in a summer theatre on the Cape.
Meanwhile he guided her, palm under her elbow, across the
street and through the crowd.

It was what she expected. He was fairly sure of that.

They waited in line at the will-call box until a man in carefully rolled-up sleeves and a vest handed them their reserved
tickets. She seemed surprised that they would be sitting side
by side.

"How did you manage that? I thought it was sold out,"
she murmured.

"I have my ways." There were some advantages to his
part-time job.

He saw she was wondering if they were comps. "You paid
and I paid," he reassured her. That was not the sort of doubt
he wanted to raise.

They swam through the crowd, as used to it as sea crea-
tures to drifting weed. The waters parted before them; he
found their seats without assistance. He took the aisle. They
were good seats, more than he would have been willing to pay
if the ticket hadn't provided him with this opportunity.

The girl in black was on the stage. He hadn't had time to
look at the program and so didn't know her name, but there
was the famous line, "I'm in mourning for my life."

He glanced at Helen. Of course she was wearing black,
too. In this city it meant nothing.

He wondered suddenly if she wanted sympathy. That
had never occurred to him before, especially after he'd seen

her broad back, her shoulders like shelves, jutting. But now he heard her sigh, lingeringly, drawing it out, and although it might only mean she was relaxing—and she was settling into her seat—it proved his intuition correct. He remembered, suddenly, a summer when he'd been sent to visit an uncle in Jackson: the long bus ride, the slow lowering of the land that seemed to him—a small boy—to be running downhill to an invisible sea, the crowd of black people, as thick as in Harlem, at the bus station where he'd seen his uncle standing without expectation or surprise as though he stood there all his life. And then the long days. He'd felt sorry even for the dogs, lounging under the porch, scratching fleas.

There was no comparison, of course. Yet he felt the same inexplicable temptation to step back to avoid crushing something soft.

The play progressed. He'd had a long day. Before the end of the first act, he put his head back against the seat and dozed.

He jerked up at intermission as people began to climb over his knees. She was looking at him with her jagged smile. "So you don't care much for the play? Or is it the production?"

"I was remembering," he said, unshelled by his sudden waking. "I was feeling sorry."

"For what? Or for whom?"

"For you," he said, shaking himself awake. "It doesn't make sense."

She didn't answer, looking across the crowded theatre as though she recognized someone. Then he saw she was studying the gilded mermaids that decorated the long-unused balcony where the black casings of the lighting system protruded like snouts.

"Never mind," she said, which didn't seem a response to what he had said.

They fell into silence. It was not uncomfortable. She continued to scan the theatre, taking in its recently re-gilded ceiling where amorphous gods and goddesses reared and plunged. He felt relieved of the responsibility of talking to her. It was almost like being at home. His roommate expected nothing in the way of words, which was a relief for a man working in the theatre.

The sharp edge of his wish, of what he'd been determined to get from her, dulled, as though rubbed against a stone, and he felt sleepy, again, and wondered how he was going to stay awake during the long second act.

The audience was crowding back in. He stood up to let several large people pass. It struck him that he was small compared to most of these people. It was an odd thought.

Then it was necessary to look, at least briefly, at that seagull, stuffed and mounted in a glass case on the stage, surely the most ridiculous representation of a symbol he'd ever seen, and to hear the girl on the stage lamenting.

They were all lamenting for their lives, but how hideous it was to have that stuffed, yellow-legged bird in its glass coffin held up to represent them.

"At least grant us the privacy of our disappointments," she said, as though trespassing on his thoughts.

But it didn't feel like trespassing. It felt like something soft.

Then it was over, and they were shuffling into their coats. "Walk me to the subway," she said as they poured out with the crowd.

This time he didn't put his palm under her elbow. "I'm sorry I asked you for money," he said as they followed the swarm down the sidewalk.

She looked at him, surprised. "But I'm giving it to you," she said. "Why should you be sorry?"

He was silent. People jammed past them. At the entrance to the subway, she turned and gave him her hand. "Goodbye," she said. "I'll put the check in the mail tomorrow." Then she went, swooping down the long dirty steps.

SELLING THE FARM

IT WAS BEAUTIFUL. IT WAS ALSO, STILL, enormous, Shirley thought, sitting behind the wheel, her older sister Miriam beside her, neatly buckled in. Shirley had parked her hybrid by the old farm gate that still scraped the ground as it had every time their father jumped out of the car to open it, years and years ago, with the two sisters in the back seat and their mother cow-patient in front, waiting for him to jump back in and drive them through. After church, it would have been, Shirley thought, after a visit to the aunts in town, after a rare excursion to a state park to mark a holiday. The gate

had scraped whenever she opened it to drive in with an armload of groceries, a stiff supermarket bouquet to cheer their
mother. All that had stopped with her death; Shirley had not
opened the gate since the funeral.

It was locked now with a big new padlock.

"I had no idea," she said, looking helplessly at Miriam.

Miriam shuffled through her big black bag, coming
up with a bit of paper. She handed it to Shirley, who took
it, climbed out of the car and began to wrestle with the
combination.

After a minute Miriam rolled down her window. "You
need help?"

"No!" The lock gave finally. Shirley dragged back the
gate, then climbed in again behind the wheel.

"At least we don't need to lock it till we leave—nothing to
keep in, or out, now," she said.

Miriam didn't answer.

On the other side of the gate, the long rolling cornfield
that had bristled with dry stalks at this time of year had been
leveled. The bulldozers, having finished their work for the
day, were drawn up in a row, bright yellow and massive along
the side of the old tenant's cottage. It was falling down. The
roof had caved in, and the modest white posts on the porch
were sagging.

"Those posts were still straight last time I saw them,"
Shirley said into the silence that had opened between them
as soon as she'd turned off the highway onto the old two-lane
road, recently widened.

"Where?" Miriam craned her neck, surfacing momen-
tarily from what their mother had called a brown study. She
had been on the edge of it and sliding when Shirley picked
her up at the hotel.

Shirley pointed. "We used to sit on that porch swing
when we went to play with Johnny's kids. Once I swung so
high I touched the ceiling with my toes."

"Wretched old place. It always smelled like mice droppings. Johnny's wife—what was her name?"

"Susie," Shirley said. "Susie Taylor. She said she was related to that Civil War general."

"Unlikely. Anyway, she was no kind of housekeeper. I always thought she drank, hid the bottles behind the stove. I peered when she wasn't looking."

"My, you were suspicious."

"Realistic," Miriam said, her voice crisp as her profile. Hawk-nosed, like their father, the effect was softened by her small pointed chin, as though, Shirley thought, the upper half of her face had been designed for something grand, the prow of a boat, perhaps, but then the maker had thought better of it and given her a girlish chin. Not that the effect had really been diluted, at least in terms of the way Miriam led her life—as far as she knew, Shirley added to herself, in the interest of fairness. She saw her sister once or twice a year, and their rare communications were courteous and vague.

"When did they bring in the last crop?" Miriam asked.

"A month ago, after you sold the place. Johnny called to let me know."

"Johnny on the tractor and all those local kids he collected?" There was no nostalgia in Miriam's high clear voice, the voice that, carefully developed, had led her all over the world.

"A bunch of Mexicans, this time. All gone now, vanished into some illegal immigrant hell."

"Johnny?"

"He's gone too. Packed his pickup, loaded his wife, and drove off without even saying goodbye."

"Probably already had another job lined up," Miriam said.

Shirley imagined how Johnny would describe himself to a potential employer—twenty years running a farm, a few cattle, corn and wheat. Then, as she bumped over the rutted road, she thought of how she would put her own possibilities into words: wife and mother, dedicated community volunteer who still baked her own bread. As for Miriam, she would describe herself, Shirley thought, as a magnet for music lovers with a soprano voice that still in the lighter repertoire continued to be sought after, although now most of her commissions came from small-town orchestras, the ones that had survived.

Miriam, never married, had supported herself with her singing, while Shirley knew she would have been lucky to find a job as a librarian or an elementary school teacher—and even that would have required a degree—if Brian had ditched her, as he had sometimes threatened to do in the old, hot days.

Miriam said, "It was a pretty good harvest, for this kind of farm," and Shirley realized she had known all about it and had only asked when the harvest had happened out of politeness. "The crops were never rotated and Johnny used chemical fertilizer."

"Well, that's what Daddy told him to do." Shirley stopped the car in sight of the farmhouse and Miriam unfastened her seat belt and climbed out, deft and slender as she had always been (except, Shirley reminded herself, for one terrible summer when she was ten and Miriam, to everyone's amazement, had turned fat and sour at thirteen. But the episode had been brief; their mother had seen to that.)

She scrambled out of the car, following her sister who was climbing the farmhouse fence. "We can drive around to the gate," she called, but Miriam was already hoisting her leg over the top railing. She dropped to the other side, wincing on contact with the hard ridged dirt.

"Did you hurt yourself?" Shirley asked, hurrying after her.

"Just turned my ankle." Miriam leaned on the fence, massaging her right ankle; she was wearing bright-red shoes with heels.

Shirley was glad Miriam was too occupied to notice the way she hauled herself over the fence. It had been a long time since she'd faced such an obstacle, and she'd gained some weight although she kept herself in pretty good shape with weekly visits to the gym where the trainer sometimes complimented her on her strength and flexibility—but that was part of the trainer's job, to keep her clients happy. Now, Shirley was glad for every pair of weights she'd lifted—baby-blue five pounders; she was able to haul herself up the fence with only a few gasps at the top. She did not drop to the ground on the other side but lowered herself cautiously.

Miriam was trying her weight on her ankle. Nothing seemed to be wrong, and she struck off across the field.

The farmhouse, empty but still intact, was half-hidden by a mock orange hedge, its second-story windows lighted by the setting sun. Beyond it, a snaking line of walnut trees followed a wire fence. Through the trunks, Shirley saw the concrete flash of new foundations.

"They've started," she said.

Miriam didn't answer. Stooping down, separating weeds, she clawed up a handful of dirt. "Look, all clay, hard as concrete. Ruined even for corn after all these years."

Shirley reached a finger to touch the dirt. She noticed that her sister's hand was trembling.

"It could be turned around with the right techniques," she said.

"Do you have any idea what that would cost?"

Shirley studied her sister. How hard it had always been to accept Miriam's authority, shining now from her pale blue eyes. Her face was remarkably unlined and from a little distance she would still look like a tall athletic girl.

"I have no idea," she said.

"Believe me, I looked into it," Miriam told her. "The soil could have been reconstituted, you're right, but even aside from the astronomical cost, it would all have to be planted in soybeans, the only crop that's profitable now, and this farm is too small to—"

"Five hundred acres?"

"The only farms that are making money are thousands," Miriam said. "Everything's changed, Shirley. The government subsidies, the climate. Nobody grows corn and wheat anymore, unless they're just hobby farming."

"What about organic vegetables? I read restaurants pay good money for tiny peas."

Miriam sighed. "Too labor intensive. The only crop this land is good for now is houses." She waved at the foundations gleaming through the trees.

"Row after row after row," Shirley said.

"Actually not. This is the newest design, a real innovation. Laid out like a village, sidewalks, trees—"

Shirley had seen the plans, published a few weeks back in the local newspaper under an admiring headline. "Houses so jammed together they don't even have yards."

"Yards don't make ecological sense," Miriam reminded her. "The green belt we're planning—"

"A border. How wide?"

"We've laid aside twenty acres."

"Twenty acres in the gully, too steep for building."

"Doesn't that make sense?"

"Not my kind of sense," Shirley said. With the field under her feet, she felt the desperation she'd felt as a child when a beloved patch of earth fell to the bulldozers. She'd thought then she would willingly kiss each inch of the plain, scrubby fields that had been her kingdom, kiss every inch of the ten miles that divided the farm from town. Even now she would have crouched down on the torn ground and kissed it if she'd dared to risk her sister's laughter.

"I hate it," she said softly.

"What?" Miriam scrutinized the distance.

"What you decided to do. It's not fair."

Miriam looked at her. "I think Mama and Daddy divided their estate as fairly as they could. You get the farmhouse and five acres and I get the rest."

"The house will be surrounded by that." Shirley pointed at the foundations. "Row after row —"

"Not rows." Miriam raised her voice a little. "All the streets will be curved, and we're going to plant trees, to shield you."

"Three foot saplings. I'll be dead by the time they're big enough to provide a screen."

Miriam sighed. "What can I say? At this point I can't afford to run a farm. This is my only asset, this four hundred and ninety-five acres, to provide for me in a few years when I have to retire."

"Are you really going to retire? It seems so . . . unlikely."

"Oh yes. I do everything I can with makeup, but it's not only my voice they want. No one enjoys watching an old woman sing. And so, you see. . . ." She trailed off, shading her eyes to look at the house. "Shall we look inside? You must have the key."

"We really don't have time before your flight." If she saw the house again, Shirley thought, Miriam might find some way to possess it.

Miriam seemed to understand. She turned toward the car. "If there'd been any way. . . ."

"You could leave New York. That would cut your expenses."

Miriam stopped. "I will never leave New York. My whole life is in New York. Friends, professional contacts, music — everything." Her voice had sharpened.

"Well, I've lived here all my life. I've looked at this land since I first opened my eyes."

"I looked at it, too, until I decided to leave, but it never meant to me what it meant to you." Miriam broke a milkweed pod off its stalk and began to pry it open.

"Of course not. How could it? You were almost never here."

"We both made our decisions a long time ago," Miriam said, slitting the pod with her fingernail.

"And now we have the consequences. Don't scatter those," she added. Miriam was throwing a handful of white parachutes into the air. "Those seeds will spring up all over." Shirley knew her reprimand was ridiculous; the bulldozers would make short work of a field full of milkweed.

Miriam smiled. "I used to love letting them go." The parachutes floated down around their feet.

For the first time, something usable stretched between them.

"So you do remember," Shirley murmured.

"Every bit of it." Miriam folded herself down on the ground, risking the ruin of her good slacks. She patted the dirt beside her. "Sit down, Shirley. Let's talk."

Shirley lowered herself as best she could, wondering how she would get up and what damage she was inflicting on the gray skirt she'd chosen with such care. As she spread her hand on the dirt, supporting herself, she saw her sister's, long-fingered, deeply mottled, so like her hand she could only tell them apart by her wedding ring.

"I want you to understand," Miriam said, looking off toward the line of walnuts and the foundations beyond them.

"You've explained it before. I guess I understand it as well as I can. You need the money."

"I tried to find an alternative but nothing makes sense, financially."

"Did you really look into keeping it?" Shirley asked. How impulsive Miriam had always been, how quickly she had made the sale.

"Yes, indeed. I had quite a lot of correspondence with the state Ag Department—"

"They don't know anything about the new methods."

"You'd be surprised. They were quite well informed about crop rotation, natural weed suppression, that kind of thing. And of course I talked to other experts as well. I wanted to keep the farm."

"I never heard you say that before." Shirley smiled with relief. "But I still think you could have found a way."

"Not to farm it and make even a tenth of the profit I made off selling it. This is prime real estate now, almost flat, half a mile from the interstate. Twenty minutes into town, even at rush hour. People kill for houses with that kind of commute."

"Real estate—that's what land becomes when it goes on the market. An estate, and a real one. Nothing else counts, not the birds, or the deer, or the wild turkeys." When Miriam didn't respond, Shirley said, "What did you make off it." She had wanted to ask ever since Miriam sold the land; now shame prevented her from turning it into a question.

"I hate to disappoint you," Miriam said, "but not nearly as much as you imagine, after I paid off the back taxes."

"Back taxes?"

"Five years, I guess ever since Daddy got sick. Mama never kept up with that kind of thing, she just let it all go. I found a whole drawer stuffed with overdue bills."

"But we went over the house together." Shirley remembered the chill of the house after the funeral, the thermostats turned down and the curtains drawn.

"After you left," Miriam said with a gleam of foxy humor. "To go home to dear old Brian, waiting with dinner."

Shirley might have told her that Brian had never learned to cook; they'd had takeout that night, after a nasty argument over which one of them was going to get it.

"So that's when you did your snooping," she said.

Miriam laughed. "Oh, I was shameless. I even went through Mama's lingerie."

"Underwear."

"She used to rail against 'panties'—said the word was obscene."

"Panties—obscene!"

They leaned back, laughing.

"She was a stitch, a card!" Miriam said.

Shirley sat up. "She was a handful, these last years. Gave me a run for my money."

Miriam sat up as well. "I envy you that."

Shirley stared at her. "Three years of drudgery?"

"You got to spend time with her. I never spent more than an hour after I left home. She felt I'd defected."

"She accepted daughters leaving to get married, but not for anything else."

"Saw no reason why I couldn't pursue my career with the local chamber music society. And Daddy just wouldn't enter the conversation."

"It was pretty loud, for a conversation." Shirley, crouching on the stairs, had listened to the shouting.

"She never held it against you when you left," Miriam said.

"We settled half a mile away, and she always thought there'd be babies."

"But not." Silence intervened. Miriam picked a dry stalk and broke it into small pieces. "Why was that?"

"You're still snooping."

"Is it snooping, after all these years?"

"I tell you what," Shirley said, turning toward her sister. "I'll tell you why if you'll tell me how much you got for our land."

"Our land! Do you still really think—"

"Not think. Feel. I've walked here every day for the past three years."

"To get away from Mama?"

"That, and to feel something solid under my feet. Something I thought was solid, anyway. I saw a bunch of wild turkeys last fall, feeding under those trees." She waved at the line along the fence. "A gobbler and six hens. They used to be almost extinct." Marion wasn't paying attention. "So, do we have an agreement?"

"Mama took care of Daddy when he was dying," Miriam murmured, "so I guess it was our turn when her time came."

"Our turn."

"I was in Berlin," Miriam reminded her. "Probably my last important engagement. I won't be on the road much anymore, I'll need to find a small apartment to buy, in New York. Park Avenue, I think. Renting doesn't make any sense, long term."

"Park Avenue!"

"I'll have to devise a new life. Opera tickets, more friends. I don't intend to become an old lady nobody knows but the super."

"Park Avenue's terribly expensive."

"Not so much these days. The bottom's fallen out there, too." From her tone, Shirley knew her sister did not expect much of an argument.

"So that's what this farm will become—two windows looking out on a street."

"More windows than that, and maybe a cottage on the Cape."

"You're not even ashamed," Shirley said.

"Why should I be ashamed? You made your choice, I made mine. You never worked," Miriam added dryly.

"Never worked!" She heard her voice squeak and knew it was a hopeless argument. "It still isn't fair," she rasped. Her voice felt as though it were cracking open, letting something hidden escape. "Why did they do that, Miriam, when they knew I loved this place?"

"They had to divide it up some way, probably thought you and Brian would rather have the house. They knew I'd never live in it, while you two—"

"Oh stop," Shirley pleaded. "Please stop! I'm not talking about fairness now. This isn't a court of law! I'm talking about how much I love this piece of land."

"Then sell the house and buy land someplace else."

"The house won't be worth anything, surrounded by your subdivision."

"Not a subdivision," Miriam said wearily, "a village."

"You can't build a village from scratch. Villages take time. Houses have to come and go, fall down, be replaced, people have to move in and out, leaving their scents, their traces, shops disappear, new ones open—it takes time, lots of time, to make a village, and here you go and try to plop one down, ready-made. It's crazy," she said heatedly, "and all those people who want backyards for their barbecues are going to take one look at your houses all squinched up together and go elsewhere."

"My, what a sermon. I didn't know you felt so strongly."

Shirley yelped. "You didn't know?"

"I mean, I thought it was all about the land. You despise my plan, as well."

"I'd despise anything that takes my land away," Shirley admitted.

"By what right of ownership—"

"The ownership of walking on it! Looking at it! Smelling it! You talk about how you have to live in New York, your life is there. My life is in every broken cornstalk and milkweed pod on this place, every wild turkey footprint, every mock orange and walnut, and here you come and just sell it like some kind of old . . . remnant!"

"To me, it is a remnant," Miriam said reasonably, "of a life I never wanted to live, and I still don't understand why you want it, after all these years, particularly with no babies."

"So we're back to that again."

They stopped, staring at teach other.

"Well, babies—children—would have given this place a meaning."

"I give this place a meaning," Shirley said.

"Well, yes, of course, but if you'd had children—"

"Another meaning, but mine is just as valid!"

Miriam stood up suddenly, discarding her patience as she used to discard her clothes, strewing them around her room and tramping over them to the bathroom door. "I want to take you out to dinner before I have to catch my plane. Where should we go?"

Stunned, Shirley stared at her. It seemed they'd barely begun to talk.

"We can go on arguing in the car," Miriam said resignedly.

Shirley got up the way the trainer had taught her, hands and knees first and then a wobbling ascent to upright. Too late, Miriam slid a hand under her elbow. "I don't need help," Shirley croaked, shaking her off, but she was gasping.

Miriam withheld a comment, visibly. They walked single file back across the ruts to the car.

"Don't you see, it's the end of the world," Shirley said after they had climbed into her car and she had started the engine.

"It's certainly the end of our world," Miriam agreed. "We're the last, and with no heirs, the name will die out."

"There's cousin Harold, somewhere in Africa."

"Yes, but I doubt if he'll ever have children." They let that rest without comment. "How different it would have been if that last baby had survived," Miriam went on thoughtfully.

"Whose last baby?"

"Mama's. It was a boy, but he died right away. They didn't want you to know—they thought you were too young. Didn't want you to be upset, the way you were when Johnny drowned the kittens. You were always so sensitive," Miriam said.

"You never told me till now!"

"It wasn't my secret. After Mama died, I knew I could tell you. Should tell you," Miriam admitted, "but I didn't want to at her funeral, or over the phone. The reason Mama regretted, so bitterly, you never had sons. She cherished that name— Papa's name—way more than her own."

Shirley was speechless. She was driving so slowly another car, behind them, began to push in close to her bumper, and she pulled over on the shoulder so it could pass. "It makes the whole past look different," she said finally, "as though it's changed colors. I never knew that baby existed—"

"Well, it didn't really exist—"

"—And I never knew Mama regretted I didn't have sons. Or daughters," she added, her eyes fixed on the road. Ahead, the throughway appeared between the trees, car roofs flashing.

"Daughters wouldn't have counted," Miriam said. She was staring at the road as though she might need to grab the wheel to correct her sister's wavering.

"I never knew," Shirley said, "and Mama and I were so close those last three years. At least I thought we were close."

"Mama knew what a hard time you were having, taking care of her, and she didn't want to add to that," Miriam told her.

"Hard time! She told you that?"

"Said you were exhausted, as of course anyone would be," Miriam said kindly.

"But it was my last time with her—I valued that!"

"She knew that," Miriam said. "Maybe you should pull over a minute, before we get to the throughway." She reached for the wheel.

Shirley tightened her grasp. Traffic rushed by them like water released from a dam and she realized she'd been holding up the whole late-afternoon procession. "I'm sorry," she said. "I didn't know I was going so slow."

"Doesn't matter. Cut the motor, I want to get out of this belt." Released, Miriam stretched as though she'd been clamped in for hours.

"What else don't I know?" Shirley asked, staring at the passing cars.

"There're probably some other things—little things," Miriam said, "but I can't remember right now."

"Will you tell me when you remember?"

Miriam smiled. "I'll tell you if you'll let up about the farm. Deal?" she asked hopefully. "I don't want to go on arguing with you, Shirl. And it's done. There's no way back. We need to protect our relationship," she added. "We're all we have left."

"So I get the past, with those pieces you know about, maybe, and you get the future," Shirley said as though she was counting out cards on a table. "Is that fair?"

"I don't know about fair, but it makes sense," Miriam said, reaching to pat her arm.

"Sense?"

"Well—consequences," Miriam said.

"But the consequences are for all of us," Shirley said.

Miriam didn't need to ask her what she meant.

HEAVEN

No one cared any longer, and after a while Marion Crawford understood that no one had ever cared, really, and felt instead of a pang of disappointment a relief she couldn't describe, as if she'd stepped off a cliff into thin air but rather than falling, floated.

All those husbands, she thought, although in fact there'd only been two, but in memory they blossomed into a division. All those lovers! Not so many of them, either, but her thoughts about them and plans for them had taken up great swatches of time and space. Her life had been built, she thought now, on the sand of her expectations, shifting under the weight of each disappointment (those sleepless nights!). A house, or many houses, built on sand.

The truth was no one cared, really, for anyone but the shelled self—she included herself—and she was free, for the rest of her life, from trying to revise that truth. It was not cynicism. It was the fresh air of faithlessness, where any idea could drift and blow.

But in that clear air, something came to her. After a while she admitted to herself that she was still freighted with one old ridiculous belief: she believed in Heaven.

Heaven came to her in a dream one cold night when she had just turned seventy. The green pastures spread out before her as she stepped out of a door, which closed resolutely behind her. Far off, apple orchards were blooming, their bridal finery set against the pasture's green; there were sheep over there, gently grazing—the scene was out of a hymn she'd learned in childhood. Yet it was real, and it was for her, in spite of her experience.

Nothing in her substantial education had prepared her for this revelation.

She attended church now and then, a clean, friendly little Episcopal church in her neighborhood, as attractive at the houses around it. Heaven was never discussed there; in bringing in light, they'd dispelled darkness, for Heaven couldn't be discussed without Death. She couldn't remember a single gospel lesson or a sermon, all the cold winter, which mentioned either word. They seemed to have been discarded along with so much else—the incense and the robes. Yet her vision remained, even though nothing in her life—her advanced degrees, her long years as a corporate lawyer, her community work leading tours in the art museum—supported it, and none of her friends (who over the years had replaced, fruitfully, the husbands and lovers) would have even considered discussing the notion.

Her children, those two remarkable adults, would have been concerned for her sanity had she raised such a possibility: that there was a place, Heaven, green pastures, streams of living water. And that she intended to go there.

She didn't need anyone's affirmation of her belief, if it was a belief; it seemed to sustain itself—a feeling, even a passion, but silent by necessity, like all passions. The couples and single souls who sat next to her in the pews at church did not discuss the afterlife, as they might have called it; it would have been unseemly, like a raw debate about sex (that belonged to the days of liberation, long passed). Her minister, a devout-seeming, sparrowish woman, would, she believed, have been shocked by such a primitive belief, as though Marion Crawford had come to church dressed in sackcloth and ashes.

No one in Marion's circle had died recently, and so she couldn't be sure that Heaven was left out of the funeral service, but she felt unable, at first, to look for it in the little worn black prayer book her mother had given her at her confirmation.

A week later, her scrupulousness made her go to the ceiling-high bookcases in her living room and search for the prayer book, crammed in between more substantial volumes.

The yellowed front page hardly held her mother's dim handwriting; it seemed about to slide off the paper. "For my daughter Marion," she read, "on the day of her confirmation," and a date so far in the past she couldn't compute it.

For the first time in her life, Marion wondered what her mother had meant by giving her the prayer book; it was unusable now, written in the old language. She realized she had no idea whether her mother had believed in anything beyond the importance of a good healthy breakfast. Certainly, even on her deathbed, which had been small in both time and space, she had never mentioned Heaven, preoccupied instead with the jewelry she'd planned to parcel out to each of her many descendants. Her list, she'd felt sure in those last moments before she slid into unconsciousness, was out of date. She'd forgotten to add the latest granddaughter.

From these unprofitable memories, Miriam turned to the prayer book. It was musty, unused. Even in the days before revision, she'd never carried it to church, associating that with lace-edged handkerchiefs and crushed sprigs of artificial violets pinned to lapels.

She did not read much of the service for the dead. The gravity of the words alarmed her. They were too weighty for the life she knew. She skipped quickly to "dust to dust, ashes to ashes" because it was familiar, and so lighter. She felt as though those six words released her into her own vision, restored her Heaven to her, and wondered if the fires of cremation—now that everyone was cremated—might have the same effect, lifting the mourner along with the carrion flesh and carrying them both away.

Then she remembered that her sister had watched the plume from the highway-side crematorium on the day after their last brother's funeral—her sister had been driving to the supermarket—and thought it might be their brother turning to ashes and felt no sort of lightening at all. In fact Susan had horrified Marion by telling her, over the telephone—Marion had fled the day after the funeral—that she believed the smoke was all that was left of that cranky, imperious, unhappy man, vanishing into the polluted sky of a dim autumn day.

Yet it was not long after that call, and after the funeral, which had left her unmoved, that Marion had her insight, if she could call it that—her vision (the word was not usual, for her) of Heaven.

She remembered stories from her childhood of the dead calling to the living, appearing after they were supposed to have disappeared, in some shadowy corner of their old living place. The stories had made her shudder. She had a horror of things that refused to die, snakes run over in the road that tried to creep away, old crippled dogs dragging themselves across the floor. It was indecent, at some point, to insist on continuing to live. Perhaps that obscenity was why no one else seemed to believe in Heaven; the living deserved to be freed, eternally, from the dead.

But she did not think she was the only one who believed. Yet who were the others?

Her friends from childhood—the beautiful, cloudlike actress who still appeared, imposingly, in shawls and scarves; the sufferer of many diseases who held her fixed with her sharp fox eyes—neither of them, or any of the many others (she was barricaded with friends) would understand. They were all too well educated, too well-off, too sly. The appearance of some uncouth belief out of an ancient, unprivileged time would have seemed as unattractive as a dangling hem or a suspicion of body odor.

(Later, she wondered why she hadn't thought of the civilized old men with their clean ears and high foreheads she'd known most of her life, but she had never felt any bond with them other than the long-ago bond of attraction, had never attempted to find a way to another sort of intimacy, and now it might really be too late.)

However, there was one woman of her acquaintance who might legitimately be expected to believe in Heaven, and that was Mother Martha, her own rector, the young woman who presided at the altar as, Marion thought, she herself presided at her dinner table, dispensing hospitality. She remembered Mother Martha's small pale hands on the silver cup, the plate of wafers—serving, as she herself had served, for so many years. Surely there was a link, there, in such ordinariness, to belief.

She called to make an appointment. Mother Martha was on the road, as she often was, going to a convention, and so it was a week or so before she could see Marion. During that week, the point of her question sharpened. It began to wake her up at night, like a stone hidden in the mattress of her soft bed.

Finally, Marion went back again to the funeral service in her old prayer book. It came immediately after "Communion of the Sick"—as though there was never any recovery—and was called "Burial of the Dead," to be read at the raw edge of an open grave rather than in the sanctuary of a church. How brutal the past must have been, with its endless early deaths and farmyard burials. Then it occurred to her that her vision was somehow connected to muddy boots and the smell of upturned clods.

This time she read the whole service, halting at "Now this I say, brethren, that flesh and blood cannot inherit the kingdom of God . . . for the trumpet shall sound, and the dead shall be raised incorruptible, and we shall be changed." But into what? Her imagination balked at the idea of pure souls.

On the day of her appointment, she dressed with care— her belief was eccentric and so she wouldn't strike that note—and dug the prayer book into the bottom of her purse, hiding it like a grenade.

The wind was blowing when she drove up to the pretty little church, so like its neighbors, with their neatly-painted exteriors and trim yards. All Sunbelt communities, Marion thought, probably shared this neatness, these pastels. She'd thought, years ago, when she moved from the East, that her new home might provide her with a link to indigenous life; she'd read extensively about the local tribes and their spiritual practices—dances, sweat lodges, all that—but her attempts to attend their ceremonies and learn something from their closed faces had faltered. There was no nourishment, for her, there. Instead, the church of her childhood, long discarded, even scorned, had returned to her like a forgotten habit, harmless, even benign.

She parked her hybrid and walked in a gale of desert wind to the front door of the church, wide and white, like the entrance of a small hotel. The wind held the door closed and she wrenched at it fiercely, feeling, again, the sharp point that had been waking her in the night. Opened, the door flew out of her hand and crashed against the outside wall, and she was swept in on a torrent of chilly air.

When she was finally able to close the door, the stillness of the hall that connected the church and the parish house confounded her. She realized she'd never been in the building on a weekday and might have imagined that it ceased to exist after the service on Sunday. The busy life of the community had never interested her, although she heard the announcements about prayer shawl ministries and food for the homeless; the news, if it was news, slid off while she waited for the next hymn—she loved to sing, loved if she had dared to admit it the sound of her high soprano, embroidering the more earthbound tones of the people around her.

Now, in the quiet corridor, with the notices of all those meetings fluttering on the bulletin board, she felt the life of the church swarming around her, crowding uncomfortably close, and wondered for the first time if she had failed in her duty, somehow, in applying to the Sunday service for succor but offering nothing in return. Well, she did contribute financially, and her checks were generous, but perhaps in the end that was not enough.

But then there was, she reminded herself, her sharply-pointed belief in Heaven, which was a sort of tribute, at least, and perhaps as valuable as the shopping bags of canned food people brought to the altar on the first Sunday of the month, for the homeless—perhaps even more valuable, since no one asked the homeless what they wanted to eat, and she suspected that the bags were full of canned beans members of the congregation no longer wanted.

And did the homeless have can openers, or stoves, or pots? She wondered, to amuse herself, or was the definition of "homeless" the absolute absence of domestic necessities?

Marion did not mind—had never minded—making a fool of herself with this sort of speculation. She was amused by her own mind, its strange quirks and avoidances. It seemed to dance, at times, to music she couldn't hear, perhaps the old tunes from the musicals of the 1940s, the tunes she hummed while she ground her coffee in the mornings.

Mother Martha's office was a small, undistinguished room off the silent corridor. The door stood half open. Marion peered in, feeling shy. The minister, wearing a pair of blue jeans, a long-sleeved shirt and cardigan, was talking on the telephone; she turned in her squeaking chair and beckoned to Marion. At least Mother Martha was wearing her turned-around collar.

Marion could not help feeling a little disappointed by her casualness. Succor should come, or might come, at least, from someone dressed in wisdom clothes—whatever they might be—rather than looking as though she was about to go outside and pull weeds.

I'm getting old, Marion thought suddenly. My expectations have hardened.

Mother Martha cradled the phone and smiled. "Please make yourself comfortable. Would you like some water?"

One of the few distinctive features of the Southwest, Marion had found, was that she was always being offered water. Not coffee, or tea, or a soft drink or (God forbid) a martini, but water, plain, in a paper cup. This was what Mother Martha was handing her, although Marion didn't remember asking for it.

She sipped. The lukewarm water tasted waxy although Marion knew waxed-paper cups were a thing of the past. She wondered if her belief had also disappeared from modern life, as silently, as unremarked, as waxed-paper cups.

"So glad you could make time to come in and see me," Mother Martha said into the looming silence, and Marion knew she had to begin.

"I have a question." She heard herself gasp and felt gripped by panic.

"Yes?" Mother Martha asked encouragingly.

Marion looked at the rector's small, pale hands, the nails close-clipped, uncolored, and remembered them on the stem of the silver communion cup, tipping it so Marion could drink.

"I'm afraid I believe in Heaven," Marion said, deeply embarrassed. She began to dig in her purse for a tissue. Next it would be loud, tearing sobs.

"Is this a problem for you?" Mother Martha asked gently, pushing a box of tissues toward her.

Marion waved it away. "I'm afraid it is," she said, and now her voice was within her grasp again. It fluttered a little, in her throat, but she was able to catch it. "You see, it doesn't fit with anything else I believe, or the way I've lived my life. I mean, it's not rational," she said.

Mother Martha did not smile, as Marion had feared she would. Once, years earlier, she'd tried to talk to a young priest about Original Sin—the concept had dogged her, during her years of marrying, divorcing, and taking lovers—and he had smiled at her, shaking his head. That had been the end of the conversation.

"Have you always believed in heaven?" the minister asked. Marion felt sure she was not giving the word its capital letter.

"Never. I would have scorned the mere idea," she said, remembering living rooms in big cities, cocktail parties, silent people who'd been her seat companions on airplanes crossing oceans. None of those people—friends, acquaintances, or strangers—would have accepted that the woman next to them believed in Heaven.

"What brought you to it?" Mother Martha asked, across the current of Marion's memories. "I mean, was it something in particular? A moment," she added cautiously, "of grace?"

"Nothing like that," Marion said quickly. Moments of

grace were a far more distant concept. "It just came to me, a few weeks ago. I don't remember exactly when—maybe it woke me up in the middle of the night," she added, remembering the sharp point in her bed.

"Is it a problem for you?" the minister asked again. "This belief?"

"It doesn't fit," Marion said, and her voice began to flutter again. "It cuts me out." She didn't want to explain. It seemed unworthy of the size of her belief. But it would, if anyone knew, cut her out of all human exchange, except with priests and fanatics—people she had never in her life wanted to know.

"Cuts you out?" the minister asked.

"I can't explain." That would have entailed admitting that she was in the presence of one of the few people from whom she would not be separated, and that she definitely did not want to be joined to this woman in any way.

"Would you like to pray with me?" the minister asked, more softly. From long experience, she must have recognized the note of desperation in Marion's fluttering voice.

Marion did not want to pray with her, or with anyone else, or even alone. It was a habit she'd never developed. But in that setting—a church office—it would have been rude to refuse.

"Can we pray something from the funeral service?" she asked, digging the old black prayer book out of the bottom of her purse.

"I don't think we can pray it, exactly," the minister said.

"Then would you read something to me?" Marion asked, handing her the prayer book. "I'm afraid it's the old version."

Water in the desert, Marion thought as Mother Martha checked the index and opened to the page.

"We don't use all this anymore," the minister said, going through the text.

"Just one passage," Marion said.

"Do you have any favorites?"

Marion smiled, for the first time. It was as though Mother Martha was asking her to choose between flavors of ice cream.

"I don't have any favorites," she admitted, "but there is a passage I'd like you to read," and she reached for her prayer book. The tissue-thin pages were hard to separate but she found the place at last and handed the book back. "Middle of the Burial Service, Rite 11: 'O God, whose mercies cannot be numbered. . . .'"

Mother Martha took up the reading, not in what Marion thought of as a church voice but in the same voice she had used all along: "Grant him an entrance into the land of light and joy." She looked at Marion significantly, having added the emphasis.

But that was not it at all. Marion protested, "That's the closest it comes to describing Heaven—it sounds like some kind of camp!"

"How do you see it?" the priest asked, closing the prayer book.

"I don't see it," Marion admitted, "except once, in a sort of flash."

"And was it so different?"

"No," she admitted. The priest lifted her hand, as though to close the interview, but Marion did not intend to be sent away with a mundane matching of her vision to the hackneyed words in the prayer book. "There's another problem," she said. "If I go on believing in Heaven, I'll have to believe I'll see everybody I know there too." She snatched her prayer book back and paged rapidly. "There it is—'the corruptible bodies of those that sleep in him. . . .'"

The minister took it up: "'shall be changed and made like unto his own glorious body—'"

"That's what caused it," Marion exclaimed with a sort of triumph. "That's what started the problem. If I have to believe in Heaven, I want to know that more than their bodies will be changed. Their bodies were not the trouble," she added, "or at least they weren't the cause of the trouble."

Mother Martha looked puzzled. "Would you explain?"

Marion launched in, with appetite now, and energy. "You see, if we're all going to be changed after we die, that resolves my problem with Heaven—if I can believe that," she added more quietly. When she saw that the minister still didn't understand, she went on, "I'm disturbed by the thought of going to Heaven and finding people there I got rid of on earth."

Mother Martha looked startled. "I don't mean I murdered them," Marion said, "but I did get rid of them—tossed them out of my life. And for good reason."

"Who were they?"

Marion hesitated. It was an old story, self-serving. Finally she admitted, "My last brother, and my last husband," then was grateful the minister didn't ask her how many brothers and husbands there'd been.

In the silence, she knew she'd have to go on. "My brother was violent," she said, and the vision of his face rose up, the broad, glowering forehead, eyes yellow as a goat's, the beautiful, red, sneering mouth. It was a vision she'd fought hard to subdue. "And my last husband was an alcoholic." A relief to seize on the correct term.

"They harmed you," Mother Martha said.

"Yes. I don't mean anything dramatic. Pinching, pushing, in my brother's case, and my husband couldn't control his temper." Then she realized she'd damped the whole thing down. "It went further than that," she admitted.

"Do you want to tell me?"

"No." She laughed, admiring her honesty. "But I have to, if I'm going to see them in Heaven. Unless," she added, but it was a small hope, "they'll be entirely changed."

"From what to what?" Mother Martha asked reasonably, and so Marion had to tell her.

It came in pieces, chokingly.

"I was fourteen. He — my big brother — chased me around my bedroom. I just had time to run in the bathroom — there was a lock on that door. He wedged his foot in but some strength came to me and I slammed the door and squeezed his toes out." She could still see the toes, pulling back. He'd cursed, crashing his fist into the door so the mirror on her side shattered, but it hadn't mattered. She'd stood among the gleaming shards, laughing. It was the end of years of torment. "I never saw him again till I saw him in his coffin," she finished. "And then I was glad." With horror she remembered how she'd glared triumphantly at his white face. "He was dead, and I was alive, and I was glad." Marion glanced at Mother Martha apprehensively. "I've never told anyone that."

The priest was silent. It was her silence that, suddenly, penetrated Marion's restraint. There would be no drama, no theatrics, and she realized that her little tale was nothing compared to the horrors the priest heard about every day.

"What about your last husband?" Mother Martha asked, as though she didn't need to hear anything more about the brother, or Marion's outrageous triumph at his funeral.

"Don't I need some sort of forgiveness for that?" Marion asked, taking a sip from her paper cup.

"For what? Closing the door on his foot?"

"No — nearly laughing at his funeral."

"You're living with guilt. Isn't that enough?"

"I'm not really sure I feel guilt. It's something . . . sharper."

The priest looked at her speculatively, and Marion noticed her coffee-colored, small eyes, set in pale lashes. "Do you want me to absolve you?"

It seemed possible, shockingly, that absolution was what she had come for, even though she'd never uttered that word in her life and did not know what context would make it appropriate. "Let me tell you about my husband first," she said.

But the priest was beckoning her, actually beckoning, with one small, shapely hand. "How did you come to this . . . career?" Marion asked suddenly.

Mother Martha smiled. "I was drawn to service."

"Wasn't Martha the sister who served in the kitchen while the other one, I've forgotten her name, sat at Christ's feet?"

"Mary," the priest told her. "Yes."

"Is that part of what you do?" Marion remembered the kitchen she'd seen once when she was reluctantly participating in the after-service social hour; going to look for milk, she'd seen a mess of pots and pans, unwashed, maybe for days, piled in the sink and on the counters. Perhaps Martha washed all that—could it be one of her priestly duties?

"We'll talk about what I do later, if you want," Martha said. "Right now I want to hear about your last husband."

"There were only two," Marion murmured, abashed.

"And?"

The term she'd been using for years to sum him up and dismiss him would not come to her; it no longer fit in her mouth. "He had his problems," she said neutrally, unable to think of anything more definite. "He used to get mad." That sounded childish, and she glanced at Martha apprehensively. "Really mad, sometimes," she added, but still it had no weight and she wished she could again use the term that had summed him up for so long.

"Did he strike you?"

"You mean abuse?" There was a term that did it all.

"Anything like that?" Martha asked neutrally, and again Marion understood that this was nothing in the lexicon of grief.

"He threw a skillet at me once, an iron skillet, but it missed me." She saw rather than heard the skillet hitting the wall above her head, the long crack in the plaster she'd refused to have repaired. "I told him I'd leave him if he ever tried anything like that again," she said proudly, then realized she'd reverted to the old script. "I was always afraid, when I was living with him," she added in a lower voice, looking at her lap.

"So you had to get out." In the priest's mouth, it seemed the only possible outcome for the story.

"But he went downhill after that. Friends told me his heart was broken. He died," she added, wondering how that volcanic fury could have come, so quickly, to the earth.

"And you blame yourself."

"No!" She was startled by her own vehemence. She'd spent years fighting off that simple, bald observation; she would not wedge herself, now or ever, into it. "I just don't want to meet him in Heaven." It was so outrageous she had to laugh.

The priest didn't laugh, or smile; Marion observed her carefully.

"I'd be afraid again," Marion went on when Martha said nothing. "Afraid in Heaven, for the rest of time, of those two men. Afraid of them even though I got rid of them. I never think about them," she added. "It's only now when this ridiculous idea. . . ."

Martha stood up, and Marion thought she was leaving, perhaps shocked, or bored beyond patience. She saw the priest's long, thin legs inside her worn blue jeans, saw the backs of her hands, mottled with age spots. They were about the same age, she realized, although she'd assumed the priest was younger. They belonged to the same time and space.

Martha was not leaving. She was searching among the disorderly pile of papers and books on her desk, fishing out, at last, an old black prayer book that looked almost as shabby as the one Marion was still holding on her knee.

"Do you remember the Exhortations?" Martha asked, paging rapidly.

"The passage they used to read sometimes before Communion?" Quickly, she added, "Yes—I remember that. They cut it out a long time ago, didn't they?"

"Yes," Martha said, finding her place. "Would you like to hear it again?"

"After all this time?"

"It may have another meaning for you now." Without waiting, Martha began to read in her quiet, steady, ordinary voice.

The first sentences ran on smoothly; Marion hardly heard them, focusing instead on the priest's face. What had caused the pucker between her colorless eyebrows? Why were her ears exposed, her long, dark hair tucked carelessly back? What had made this woman who she was—a question Marion thought was hardly a question, but a statement of unknowingness, of ignorance so dense it seemed eternal. I've never wanted to know anything about her, she thought, as the words of the prayer book streamed on, meaninglessly. I've never really wanted to know anything about anyone, unless it wouldn't upset me.

Suddenly, she held her own prayer book up like a shield.

"'So is the danger great,'" the priest was reading.

"Stop there," Marion gasped. "I don't need to hear any more."

The priest glanced at her curiously. "You remember the rest?"

"I remember it too much."

Martha closed her prayer book. "What does the rest of that sentence mean, to you?"

She was using that voice, the voice of the professional counselor, and Marion stared at her with dismay.

"It means you're damned if you don't repent before you drink of the cup. But what about forgiveness? Where is forgiveness in all that?" She began, again, to dig furiously in her purse for a tissue.

This time the priest didn't push the box toward her. "Is that your problem with Heaven?" she asked, and Marion felt sure she'd given it its capital.

"Either everything is forgiven, and they are there, or they are not there, and then neither am I," Marion said.

"No one is 'there' unchanged," Martha said.

"But how can they change? How can anyone change? You didn't know them," she added recklessly. "They were fixed in themselves."

"Haven't you changed?" Martha asked, leaning toward her. "All these years—suffering like this?"

"Suffering?" She spat the word. "What in the world do you mean?"

"This pain, this fear, this guilt."

"It isn't that," Marion exclaimed, and then she remembered the sharp point in her soft bed. "Is that what it is?" she asked. "Is that what's been bothering me?"

"Can't you forgive yourself?" the priest asked.

"I didn't come here for this," Marion said, cringing back in her chair. She felt the hard, coarse wood against her spine. "I came here to ask you about Heaven."

"I think you have your own definition," the priest said.

Martha stood up. They were the same height. Marion turned toward the door, sliding past the priest, who did not attempt to stop her.

She rushed out into the bright, chill air and stood blinking. Behind her, the big church doors swung closed and snapped. She wondered if Martha had hurried behind her and locked them, wondered how often the priest ministered to unclean spirits before the spirits went squealing and charging over the nearest cliff.

Then she began to look for her car. As soon as she found it, unlocked it and climbed inside, she would be back in the interior of her own life, her calm, beautiful life alone, where there were occasional moments of distress (she knew that, of course; it did not alarm her) but not the horror she had just felt, the horror of being explained.

Of course there is no Heaven, she thought, as amazed by

the idea that she might once have believed as she would have been by any other childish form of irrationality. Of course those two men are gone, for good. They lived, they died, they burned to ashes, and their ashes are dispersed.

There's a harmless sort of kinship in that, she thought as she started her car, for all ashes are the same, and even her own, she knew, would have no particular color, or smell, or taste, and would disperse, as quickly, into the endless sky.

ANYWHERE YOU SEND ME

THEY CAME BEFORE I WAS READY, but how could I ever have been ready?

Seven people: the old couple, their daughter, her four-year-old son, the drifter (as I called him right away), the crone and her hanger-on. When I first saw them, they were sitting in the van I'd hired to bring them from the airport, staring straight ahead while Sid unloaded their luggage: a crate tied with twine, a bunch of lopsided shopping bags, three bursting green plastic garbage bags and one of those cardboard suitcases I didn't think existed anymore, tied up with twine.

When I went to greet them, not a single head turned. Eggs in a carton, I thought, black eggs, then corrected myself. Of course they'd been traumatized.

Sid slid back the left passenger door and a smell I won't describe rushed out. I remembered pictures of tent cities, gutters running with refuse, latrines clogged and overflowing. That smell had traveled with them.

Sid stepped back. He's my handyman as well as my neighbor, and he's learned when not to comment.

"It took you a while," I said, to say something.

"Tie-up on the expressway outside the airport," he told me.

"Welcome," I said into the van.

Sid reached in to help the nearest one, the crone, but she batted his hand away and turned to the stick figure beside her who grabbed her elbow and began to fulcrum her down.

I stepped aside as her feet, in battered pink bedroom slippers, scuffed at the gravel.

Then she was down, leaning on the stick's arm. He was tilting against her shoulder and so they somehow tottered toward the porch steps.

The others began to come out: the teenaged boy with his head scarf and damaged shorts jumping across the van step as though he scorned it; the old couple, livelier than I'd expected, nodding at me with a sort of grandeur as they descended, the woman holding the hand of her grandson; and then the pièce de résistance, a glittering young woman, wrapped in a sort of ceremonial robe, feet stepping smartly in gold sandals, toenails an unblushing vermilion, dreadlocks arranged in a single waterfall, and obviously, alarmingly pregnant.

I held out my hand as they formed a line, schooled, I realized, in dealing with authority. As I shook each hand, wire-coarse or fragile as a leaf, each one announced a name, and it was an announcement made by voices used to procedures.

I understood how, with the help of Nancy, the young Mercy Corps volunteer, they had worked their way through passport lines, visa applications, airplane reservations. I'd only supplied the money, in a cashier's check which Nancy deposited at the one bank still standing and functioning in Port-au-Prince.

Cordelia: the crone.

Captain: her helper.

Dulce and Martin: the old couple, my age-mates.

Philippe: pronounced in the French way, the teenager, who seemed to have no attachment to anyone.

The little boy, Claude, Dulce and Martin's grandson, already down in the gravel poking at an anthill with a stick.

And his mother, glorious Bathsheba, queen of all the rest.

Sid was gathering up their belongings. "Please help," I told Philippe, conscious of the need to exert my authority, and they all turned to pick up some of their bundles.

The house waited behind them, not the house I live in, that's across the field, but the frame cottage that had held four or five generations of tenants when my farm was a working enterprise.

The two steps to the screened porch were crumbled cement, and I watched as Cordelia tested one with the toe of her pink bedroom slipper. Reassured, she mounted steadily to the porch as Captain pushed companionably on her hip, more for his support than for hers. On the porch, they stopped and looked around. I wondered if they were noticing the sagging screens, a thought I wouldn't have encountered a few minutes earlier, although of course I knew their history, Toussaint dying in the French mountains, the island declared the first Negro republic. They would have expectations.

As the others followed, I realized they'd established some sort of rank, or precedent, with Cordelia and Captain always in the lead and the others in order behind them.

Dulce and Martin, my middle-agers, stopped as the other

two had done and surveyed the porch: damp cretonne cushions on rusted outdoor chairs, a sagging sofa, and a caved-in floor plank near the front door. It had been raining in a warm, irresolute way for days, and I sniffed a sour smell, probably from those old cushions. Rain suddenly began to pour again as though from an overturned tub, pounding on the tin roof, but the others did not hurry their procession. Only Philippe raised his hood over his head to protect his elaborate coiffure.

When they were all on the porch, they looked at me, waiting, and I realized with panic that, other than announcing their names, no one had said a word.

"Soyez bienvenus," I said in my schoolgirl French, although I'd been told they all spoke English, or a version thereof, another truth that would soon be open to question. There was no response; all eyes regarded me neutrally. Behind me, Sid heaved a sigh.

Then Philippe stepped forward and reached for my right hand, which he shook heartily. A long spiel of words uncurled from his mouth. I realized I could understand nothing.

I'd been warned. Their accents would not be familiar, in English, French, or Creole, but I hadn't expected the assurance with which Philippe spoke, as though he assumed I would understand.   .

Sid edged around me and opened the front door, holding it for them to pass through in their ordained order. With a gesture that might or might not have been authoritative, I consigned them to the three bedrooms as I'd planned.

How small those bedrooms became as soon as each one was filled with two of these strangers and their belongings; Philippe would sleep on the foldout couch in the living room. I'd taken pride in countrified charm, hanging pretty cotton curtains at the windows and making up the beds with new, if discounted sheets. Now I heard flies buzzing up near the ceiling in the first bedroom, where Cordelia and Captain would stay on two shrunken-looking twin beds. How thick the motionless August air, drenched with rain, felt in the second bedroom, which I assigned to the ancient couple, Dulce and her tottering Martin, who collapsed right away on the double bed. Philippe, not yet assigned, hung in the doorway with his unsettling smile; he was very black, and very handsome.

Bathsheba and her boy had the largest bedroom. She didn't seem dismayed by the lack of a crib or cot although I found myself apologizing. They had spent the last six months with her parents in a camp staked on a highway median, without water or electricity, the latrines requiring a dash across the busy road and once there, I'd read, danger of rapists and thieves. Under the weight of that thought, I looked at Bathsheba's belly, swelling out under her robes; was there even a question about the father, or Claude's father? The grandparents had taken over.

Philippe was, at least for now, my only source of information; I gestured, "When is she due?"

Bathsheba began to rake through her boy's hair while he squirmed and protested. I worried about lice.

By now my question had evaporated; Philippe was staring at me blankly. I tried a few words in French but I didn't know the operative verb, and my American accent must have made me unintelligible. Until then it had only served to infuriate waiters. Because my need to know was so urgent, I mimed my question, hunching, squatting and groaning.

Bathsheba continued to rake her son's scalp.

Philippe's laughter drew the others, who peered in the doorway and began to laugh as well at my display. They spoke rapidly to each other.

Now, Philippe understood. "September," he said in unaccented English.

Sid, behind the crowd, peered at me in dismay.

"My God, it's August twenty-second now. I didn't even know about this," I said before realizing the impotence of my confusion. Why should anyone have thought to mention

Bathsheba's advanced pregnancy in the messages that had flown back and forth? It seemed to me an abuse of my good will, yet since they were all still laughing, I could only grin my way out of my annoyance.

As though on cue, each couple now retreated to the room I'd designated, but as I passed along the hall to the living room, the three bedroom doors still stood open, and I looked in on tableaux of . . . exhaustion? Confusion? Relief?

Philippe was standing in the kitchen in front of the open refrigerator, surveying its contents with a critical eye. To start them on a healthy diet, I'd stocked fruit, soymilk, and vegetables as well as some sugarless drinks.

When I pointed out the sofa bed, he looked at me as though something entirely different was being transacted. I knew right away he would be not only my interpreter but also my problem.

Turning my back on him, I went out. Sid was waiting by his truck. He pulled his cap down low on his forehead, his way of warning me of combat.

We've known each other for a decade, ever since I bought the farm and hired him to work the few fields I wanted kept in cultivation, but his sour countryman's ways have never deserted him, and we have been more often antagonists than colleagues, especially since I have made him give up chemical pesticides and fertilizers. Without them, he's told me, the farm will rapidly collapse, assaulted by armies of nettles, wild roses, chickweed, poison ivy and spindly volunteer poplars. So far he has been proved about half right.

Now a different argument was looming. I tried to forestall him with courtesy. "So, what do you think of them?" I asked.

"Terrible," he said, his breath stinking of last night's beer. "You must be crazy."

"That's what my friends are all saying. Prejudice pure and simple."

"You done forgot where we live? What we have for neighbors?"

"The county sheriff and the big new Baptist church—half a mile away. Too far to see or hear anything."

"Not when the leaves come off the trees. Not when they come and go."

"They're not going to be doing much coming and going."

"You want to know what I think about it?" he asked.

"Not particularly. You going to make some kind of fuss at this late date?" I asked him. "I told you what I was going to do. I need you to cooperate." I realized the poison he'd suppressed when I laid out my plan was spewing now that he'd actually met them.

He glared at me, bristles on his jowls gleaming. "If I have to make a fuss, I sure as hell will."

"Who're you going to get to listen to you? They all think I'm crazy, anyway. This'll only be the latest proof." When he looked away, simmering down, I added, "Besides, after all these years. . . ." I didn't need to remind him of our history. "And don't forget, you work for me. There aren't many other jobs left for old farmers in strip-mall heaven."

"Won't stop me none if they commence to act up," he growled, glancing at the house. I saw Claude's face disappear from a window. "Ain't none of them ever worked land around here—"

"You have slave cabins behind your own house," I interrupted him. "And what about my graveyard? That archeologist went poking around, told me there might be slave graves outside the wall."

"That time is long gone," he said, but he was still simmering down. The connection I'd made with slavery seemed to relieve him. "They got to work, the ones that can. You told me that, yourself."

"It's in our agreement." I didn't plan to show Sid the

actual document. It was duly signed and notarized, lacking in particulars but dense with warnings. "Remember, I only committed to ninety days," I said, feeling my own unease.

"Then what? Turn them lose to beg at the gas station?"

"Their airfare back is guaranteed. We'll cross that bridge when we come to it." I turned toward his truck. "Ride me back to my house. We'll talk about their schedule on the way."

"That pregnant gal ain't going to work worth a dime," he grumbled.

I chose not to answer, sliding onto the busted bench seat in his truck. He turned on the ignition with a savage twist and wrenched at the gears. "You giving them money?"

"Pocket money, to tide them over. It's in our contract."

He tried to pry the amount out of me, but I wouldn't give.

"Enough to buy groceries the first few days," I conceded, "before they've earned enough to take care of themselves."

"You counting on me to tote them?"

"Not unless you clean up your attitude."

He snorted. "No bus out here, Missy. You want them to walk? Stand out on the county road and hitch? It's close to five miles to the A&P."

"We'll deal with that later. I already stocked the refrigerator." I didn't tell him about the healthy diet.

"Coal in the bathtub," he muttered.

"What?"

"When the government come through and give them mountain people inside fixtures, they went to keeping their stove coal in them brand new bathtubs. Never heard what they did with the toilets."

"Mountain people, Sid—a long time ago."

"Ignorant," he spat. "That's all I know."

I could have reminded him that he'd told me once after a few beers in my kitchen that he'd dropped out of school in the sixth grade to work on his daddy's farm; years later, it went into foreclosure and I bought it from the bank.

We were rattling over the dirt road that runs between my farm and his house, passing my other big field that I've given over to native grasses. They turned out to be mainly big purple thistles, their stalks as thick as my wrist, and dense, brambly wild roses.

"Field going to ruin," Sid said. "We used to get a good corn crop off that."

"Corn depletes the soil. My easement won't allow it. I'm required to let some of my land lie fallow, so it'll go back."

"Back to what? Weeds and thistles?"

We were in agreement about that. "You know how the easement saves on my taxes—the only way I can afford to keep this place."

He huffed. Sid persists in believing I have a hoard of secret funds, maybe hidden under my mattress.

My farmhouse appeared in an opening between two big, half-crippled paulownia trees, planted by some long-ago Dutch immigrant in memory of his queen.

"One thing you'll never worry about is foreclosure," Sid said, and I heard his old bitterness well up.

"At least I saved your old place from turning into a strip mall," I reminded him. He rattled off in a cloud of dirt and gravel.

I passed the rest of the long hot afternoon in the feeble breeze from my floor fan, which did nothing to dissipate the haze of anxiety that Nancy, the Mercy Corps volunteer, had warned me might develop into burnout. Several other well-intentioned efforts at resettlement had gone up in a blaze of guilt and resentment, and it was only after a meticulous review of my community involvement—years at Head Start when there was such a program, rape crisis counseling at all hours of the night, a lifelong if ineffectual commitment to easing poverty—that Nancy and her staff were persuaded I offered at least the possibility of a new start to these seven individuals.

Toward five o'clock when the sun scorched a path across my cornfield, I followed it on foot to my tenant house, arriving breathless, in a sweat. From a distance, I'd seen tendrils of smoke, and I thought they might already have fired up the barbecue to grill the buffalo burgers and chicken dogs I'd left in the freezer.

Instead I found five of them standing over a twig fire smoldering dangerously close to my corn.

"Hey!" I shouted. "Put that out!"

They turned to stare at me, impassive as cattle. Then Cordelia, detaching herself from Captain's clutch, came toward me. She reached out and patted my arm, nodding at me reasonably as though all necessary precautions had been taken. Behind her, Philippe added another twig to the fire.

"You'll burn up my corn!" I told Cordelia but she went on clucking, patting, and smiling. When I saw the food spread out, I realized I was too late to stop the picnic. The buffalo burgers and chicken dogs were lined up on a sheet of newspaper with the condiments alongside.

I turned to Philippe, walking toward him crabwise with Cordelia still attached to my arm. She was surprisingly heavy.

"I bought you a grill," I told him.

He nodded. "Wood fire better."

"At least bring the hose around and soak the edge of the corn." He went off reluctantly, returning with the hose draped over his shoulder.

I turned to the others. "Do be careful!"

Philippe answered for them, showing his teeth in what passed for a smile. "Surely, Madam."

"My name is Helen. Please call me that."

His lips parted a little further. "As you say. We cook our dinner now," pointing to the food.

I'd been warned not to expect them to eat ordinary American food, but it seemed that was another piece of misinformation. Martin was sharpening a bunch of sticks for the hot dogs with a knife that seemed larger than necessary for that purpose.

They received the sticks as he handed them out and began to thread on the hot dogs while Philippe balanced the buffalo burgers on the coals. Their eagerness touched me; I wondered how long it had been since any of them had eaten. "I should have bought marshmallows," I said.

Except for Bathsheba, they were all busying themselves to an unnecessary degree, shifting condiments around on the newspaper, fetching more sticks. They avoided looking at me. Philippe, alone, was not occupied, and I wondered if he was the group's favored son, spoiled and entitled even in the midst of destitution. It was not a welcome thought.

I sat down next to him a little gingerly, tucking in my legs. I have reached the age when ground-sitting is still possible but entails planning how to get up again.

Philippe handed me a stick with a dog already on it. I remarked crabbily to myself that I could have fetched my own dog.

I began to wonder what they had been told about me before they left their cursed island. Nancy would certainly have described me as a lady, a designation I've always abhorred as my mother before me—a beautiful New Orléanais—had abhorred being called a belle. Both labels were probably appropriate, and I had to admit that the tradition of benevolence, inevitably female and inevitably genteel, clung to me like a second skin. Only ladies have the necessary means to earn the dubious rewards.

Nancy would have explained that I had a big farm in the American South; the climate, at least in summer, would be somewhat familiar. Beyond that, I doubt Nancy found much to say, other than the implication that I could afford this saving act. These are desperate times and desperate circumstances, and her research would have been limited by her need to get at least one group out. They would know I had contracted for ninety days, after which they were to return home or launch out on their own, somehow. Defining precisely how that might be done might have capsized the whole enterprise.

I was devouring my hot dog, and they began to talk among themselves, softly, in that patois I was never to understand. Dulce laughed suddenly, glanced at me, and hid her mouth with her hand.

Now I saw that she was only middle-aged. Sitting on the ground, she'd thrust her feet out in front of her; her legs were still beautiful, and her toenails were painted a vicious green.

I turned to Martin, her companion or husband. He returned my look with a nod as though recognizing me for the first time, then threw back his head to drain a can of beer. I didn't know, couldn't imagine, where that beer had come from. It was a US brand.

Now Bathsheba heaved herself up and lumbered into the circle around the fire, Claude hanging from her hand. He was complaining shrilly about something, lip extended; his shirt was hiked up, showing his ribs. He had the belly of the nearly starved.

Bathsheba settled him with a smack, and I was relieved. I couldn't be expected to correct her. In terms of probable results, smacks or kisses were all the same, in my view. Claude didn't cry, his attention taken by the chips that were nearest to hand. He began to crush a handful into his mouth.

I felt for the first time a need to talk to this mother who had saved herself and her child.

"How old?" I asked.

Bathsheba looked at me fixedly, as though some syllable of sound had reached her.

Philippe translated, and she held up four long fingers, the nails painted a brilliant violet.

"The father?"

This she understood and replied with a rapid string of words Philippe translated simply as "Not here."

Now Cordelia beckoned me to sit beside her, and Philippe graciously hauled me up and lowered me onto the dirt. Captain offered another skewered hot dog on his expertly sharpened stick. As I held it over the fire—fed by more sticks and a broken porch chair—I noticed that sparks were spreading like a peacock's tail toward my corn, yet the sharp point of the threat was unaccountably dulled. My sitting with them had done that.

Now Dulce began to speak, and I realized that she was thanking me with birdlike nods and dips of her pointed chin. The others joined in, murmuring and nodding. I nodded back my gratitude.

Finishing my food, I managed to fulcrum myself up without help. The fan of sparks was dying into ash.

Philippe was at my side. "I drive you home, then take your truck."

I stared at him, astonished by his fluency and his command.

"That's not in my contract," I told him curtly.

"Go to Walmart," he explained with the same authority. "Get things they need." He gestured at the silent, watching group.

"Make me a list. I'll go tomorrow."

He stared at me as though he'd never been refused before. Then, with something that looked to me like an ironic bow, he stepped out of my way.

I turned to tell them goodnight. They replied with waves and smiles.

At home, I heaved my bed closer to the eastern window; propped up on two pillows, I could see the tenant house lights burning across the dark cornfield. I made a mental note to tell them to turn off the lights when they went to bed, then realized I would miss the sight. Those windows had been dark for years.

In the morning, before my coffee, Sid came rattling by in

his pickup. Usually I give him my "orders," so-called, around ten, but since the farm used to be a part of his, he had certain rights.

"You going to work them today?" he asked from the kitchen doorway.

"That's what my contract says, after 'one day rest and recovery.'"

"They just got here yesterday. Awful hot," he added.

"Not going to be any cooler tomorrow," I said, taking my moss rose coffee cup to the sink. I still hold to some of my lady ways, like Spode coffee cups and crystal wineglasses and a couple of designer outfits for the inevitable benefits. "I have a hunch they'll want to get going."

"You want me to round them up?"

"I'll go with you."

I rinsed my cup and followed him to his pickup. Climbing in, I asked, "How come you still hang on to those old baby shoes?" They were dangling from the rearview mirror. "Carl must be, what, twenty-one?"

"Twenty-two. You keep anything?"

It took me a minute and then I said firmly, "Not a scrap. I don't need reminders."

We were close enough to the tenant house to see smoke spiraling out of the chimney. "My God, a fire, in this heat!"

"Got pretty chilly before the sun come up."

I glanced at him. He'd tried to argue me out of "that fool idea" and now in less than twenty-four hours, he'd become their advocate.

Parking in the shade of the old hickory, he asked, "You still planning to take them up the hill?"

"That's the most overgrown spot on the entire farm." Getting out, I checked the truck bed. He'd loaded up with all the tools we'd need.

When I turned around, they were coming down the steps from the porch, single file, like some kind of sad parade.

Cordelia was wearing the same old print dress—I guessed she'd slept in it—with a big canvas apron tied on top. She had a kerchief tied over her head. Captain had on his overalls, no shirt, and a busted straw hat. The others wore various combinations meant to look like work clothes. They'd been farmers on their island, had chopped cane, raised chickens, still knew how to milk a cow. That had been my only stipulation; I couldn't use city people.

They began to climb into the truck bed among the tools, the younger ones hoisting up their elders. When Bathsheba came rolling along in a sort of pinafore, Claude clutched in the crook of her arm, I said, "It's awfully hot. You ought to keep him home."

She stared at me with a fierceness that made me step back, then said something short that required no translation.

"Dulce's going to sit up front with me," I said as I unfastened Captain's claw from her arm.

I moved to the middle, straddling the shift. Sid's thigh was as solid as a ham hock next to me. Dulce's feet, in big, unlaced sneakers, didn't quite reach the floor, and I felt a clutch of panic. How could she work? How could Captain, or Cordelia, or Bathsheba? I hadn't counted on getting much out of any of them, but the idea of their idleness frightened me. What would they do?

Sid ground the truck uphill in low gear. At the top three scraggly pines guarded the plot, and I wondered why those old settlers always chose measly southern pines for their graveyards. Green all year around, like remembrance? But after many summers of drought, those pines were brown.

The hand-built unmortared stone wall was tumbling. Built to keep out cattle, it had long lost its function. Sid parked by the little wooden gate hanging off one hinge and we all tumbled out. They took shovels, hoes, and shears out of the truck bed without being told and followed me through.

Inside, one upright stone rose above a sea of parched-looking green. The other stones were submerged; I only knew they were there, seven of them, from winter visits. Bull thistle, Queen Anne's lace and yellowed leaves from the spring's daffodils hid them now.

I picked up a hoe and began to hack at the root of a bull thistle, its big purple flower waving over my head. As it began to topple, I smelled ruptured green and musty upturned soil. The others had spread out around me, beginning to hack and dig, even Cordelia and Dulce moving quickly, with a kind of fury. The stack of weeds outside the wall began to grow, and the sharp smell of broken stems mixed with the torn-up clay.

After an hour I was streaming sweat, my shirt soaked to my skin. They seemed ready to work on steadily, but I told Philippe to announce a break. Sid brought the cooler of water out of the truck and they sat on the ground outside the gate, as though to drink inside would have dishonored the nameless dead. No one seemed half as thirsty as me. They'd been through a severe water shortage on their island, and I wondered if they had somehow adapted.

Philippe got up and wandered along the wall. He kicked something with his foot, leaned down, and separated the weeds.

"What'd you find?" I called.

He bent the weeds back and I saw it was one of the mounds outside the wall.

"How come out here?"

In the silence, I heard the afternoon cicadas begin their sawing. Sid was watching me.

"A long time ago, they buried their black people there," I said.

"Who all?" Philippe asked, hands on hips.

"You heard me. Black people. African Americans," I added with an effort.

"Outside the wall," he said and turned to the others. "Les esclaves," he told them.

Sid muttered, "You had no business bringing them up here."

There was a murmur, or a rustle, the sound of seven bodies turning toward one another. Then all stood and were back in the truck before I could say a word. Even Dulce climbed in back.

I followed them. "We're trying to show respect," I explained, "by cleaning up the whole area."

Sid climbed into the cab and started the motor. They were about to drive off without me. Suddenly, I couldn't see, but it wasn't sweat stinging my eyes; it was rage.

I jumped into the front seat as Sid took off.

"They all come from slaves," Sid said, eyes fixed on the road.

"I know that!"

"They made a war, killed all the whites, set up the first—"

"Black Republic, they called it. You think I don't know that, too?"

Sid was silent.

"They had their tyrants, too." My eyes were beginning to clear. I looked through the cab's back window. Claude's little face was pasted to the glass; we were staring eye to eye when I said, "Well, I know one thing, they owe me a day's work. We'll go to the other graveyard."

"You sure?"

Bathsheba pulled Claude away from the window.

"Of course I'm sure. Plenty of weeds there, too, enough to keep us all busy. Back up and take the turn."

The truck clunked into reverse.

Sid took the turn at high speed, gravel dinging the sides of the cab; they must have been holding on hard, in back. Work had to be found, especially now in the face of their rebellion.

We rattled down into the valley, past the old gristmill lying in ruins, then descended into deep shade on a high-crowned dirt track. I began to cool. I'd chosen the first graveyard to keep them out of the sun, to begin with an easy task, and perhaps even to connect them to the farm's history; it hadn't occurred to me that they would find those mounds outside the wall. Well, it happened, and we would all survive the breach.

The iron gates were in front of us, with their dilapidated cement angels. Sid braked out of respect and drove through. In deep shade under tall poplars, the monument shone.

They were already out of the back and picking up their tools.

I led the way. At my feet, the yellowed leaves of the iris I'd planted three years ago needed cutting; I pointed this out to Captain, who had the shears, and he fell to work with a will. Dulce would rake the path, and Philippe could move some rocks that had tumbled down the hillside. Cordelia took her rag to the monument itself. A spider had crowned it with a web, and leaf debris was stacked at the foot. Martin began to rake those into a pile. I gestured to Bathsheba to take Claude and sit down on the hardware store bench I'd once occupied for hours. She obeyed.

Sid stood back, observing. Once in those first months he'd come to join me on the bench, but I would have none of it.

A few minutes passed in what seemed almost companionable silence. I picked up the broom and began to sweep the area, fighting off the visions that always attacked me at that spot and that time didn't temper. They came at night as well, but bright lights and a bourbon toddy usually dispelled them.

Cordelia turned to me, rag in one hand, while with her forefinger she traced the name, her eyes questioning.

"Elizabeth Mackay Robinson," I told her. "My daughter."

I expected them to stop what they were doing but they went on, glancing at me from time to time.

I dropped my broom and went to the stone. I read out loud:

"June 16, 1992

October 3, 2008

Rest in Peace"

Philippe stopped with a stone in his arms, calculating. "Sixteen?"

I nodded. "Murdered."

At my elbow, Sid said, "I can take you back to the house and pick them up later."

"That won't be necessary." I picked up the broom and went on sweeping, little mounds of leaves and gravel stirring and reassembling, and for a long time there was only the sound that tools make.

By the time we drove them back to their house for lunch, I'd entered that numb shade where I'd lived for two years.

On the way back to my house, Sid said, "Better start showing them they can't push you around like that."

I said nothing.

"They're taking advantage. Better stop them now."

I summoned the energy to ask him how that might be done.

"They don't do a full day's work, you cut back on the food deliveries."

"Starve them?"

"Cut back."

"They have to live."

"They have their ways. Where'd that boy get his beer?"

"Probably in the airport."

"That was nothing but stubbornness, that business about the graves. Anything to get out of work." In the course of the day, he'd reverted.

"I'm not going to cut back on their food," I said, getting out of the truck under the shade of my paulownia. Sid roared off in a cloud.

In my kitchen, I cut up lettuce and tomatoes from my garden, finding solace in the task. I've learned how to take care of myself, which is worth a lot, even if it's the only thing I know. Listening to condolences taught me that. Now, eating those warm tomatoes with their smell of heaven and earth, I thought of the slave graves and of my daughter's monument.

We soldiered on. A strange calm persisted for several days. During their work hours, they hardly spoke or looked at me, like children who know they have offended but don't want to make things right. At night I lay in my bed and watched their lighted windows and felt, in spite of everything, a sort of neighborliness. That state of affairs might have gone on for the rest of their time.

About two weeks later, at some late hour, I woke up halfway, hearing a dog howling and wondered which of my distant neighbors had picked up a pound puppy, then left it outside to howl all night alone. Air conditioning makes such abominations possible.

Coming to the surface, I realized it was a human howl.

I sat up.

Crawling out of bed, I pulled on jeans and shirt and ran downstairs. As I started my car and raced down the dirt track, I thought how far away help of any kind was, Sid in his cabin on the other side of the farm, police five miles away. I regretted my decision not to put a telephone in my tenant house, for fear they would use it too much.

The front door stood open. I went in, hesitating for the first time; it had become their house. Stuff was stacked and strewn everywhere, as though a hurricane wind had swept through. Through the open bathroom door, I saw their backs. As I approached, they separated as though they were expecting me.

Bathsheba was on her back in the tub, supported by a mound of bloody towels. Her enormous thighs were spread, her vulva straining open. As I stared, a spasm passed across her belly, and she howled. Dulce, kneeling at the foot of the tub, inserted both her hands into the birth canal.

"Turning it. It's laid wrong," Philippe said from somewhere in back of me.

Twisting, straining, a scowl knotting her face, Dulce finally wrenched her hands out and a fresh gush of blood soaked her arms to the elbows.

Then she reached in again. Cordelia leaned over the tub to wipe Bathsheba's face with a wet towel.

Another shudder rode down Bathsheba's belly, and I saw her bear down. In the moment of silence, I heard Claude crying in the next room and Martin muttering something that sounded like a prayer.

The infant shot into Dulce's hands, covered with streaks of something white and blood.

Dulce dangled the whole mess upside down, and the infant began to wail. It was a boy.

With a jerk of her shoulders, Cordelia signaled me to go to Claude while she began to clean the infant. Bathsheba was sunk at the bottom of the tub, silent.

I went, passing through the living room where Captain sat on the sofa, smoking. Philippe was turning the blades of shears in a candle flame.

Claude's little room reeked of urine; he was standing on the bed, furious. I went to him and pulled down his soaked diapers. He screamed louder.

I picked up his wet naked wriggling black body and carried him to the window. Outside, the cornfield was blanketed with fireflies.

Soon, he went limp, staring, tears streaking his cheeks. The fireflies rose and fell, blinking on and off.

I held him there for a while, and when he began to twist and whimper again, I patted his scrawny shoulder and sang the only lullaby I remember from my scrubbed-out past: "Faites do-do, mon cher petit frère, faites do-do, tu aura du lo-lo."

I sang these few lines over and over; I'd forgotten the rest. He quieted and after a while sagged against me, half asleep. I sat down and held him in my arms.

Next door there were murmurs and stirrings. I heard them, but I had no place there. Strange thoughts came to me in my detachment:

Why are they born?

Why do they die?

The Touching Hand

WINTER TERM

IT WAS INCONVENIENT. AND WORSE: Hal watched the woman behind the desk ruffle through filing cards and wondered if she had noticed that he came to the library every evening. She must have noticed, for during the past month he had looked at her so often that he had begun to recognize her dresses and the two ways she fixed her hair. He often felt that she was watching him and Ellie and feeling surprised that they came every night. During the day Hal sometimes planned a new kind of evening, in the library still, for the dancing-and-movie Saturday nights he spent with Ellie were even more stereotyped. Sometimes he imagined that Eleanor would be there when he came, or that she would not be wearing lipstick, as when he had first seen her. He knew that the small change in details could not alter the whole evening. And so in the past week he had begun to imagine the only possible change: that Eleanor would not come at all. Hal planned to wait at the library until a quarter past seven, and then if she had not come he would leave, not pausing to button his coat and turning at once onto the street.

"Why don't you take off your coat?" the librarian asked him. He had never heard her voice before. It was pleasantly colorless, and he was surprised that with such a voice she had spoken to him at all.

"Oh, that's all right," he said vaguely. "I may have to leave in a few minutes." She pulled out another drawer of filing cards and began to go through them from the back. As he watched her, Hal became more and more surprised that she had spoken to him. It reminded him that he was still an intruder, even after a month; there were usually only one or two other boys in the library, so few that the girls stared openly. He walked over to the reading room door and looked in; the red-haired boy whom he had begun to speak to on the street was studying with his girl. Eleanor said they were engaged, although Hal pointed out that the girl was not wearing a ring. Eleanor said that it did not really matter: they never went out except with each other, and on Saturdays and Sundays she had seen them having breakfast together in the Waldorf. Hal remembered asking her what they had been eating; it was a new way he had of testing Ellie, to see how long it would be before she laughed; he knew that if he teased her for a certain amount of time she would more probably cry. "French toast," she had answered promptly, "three orders, with maple syrup," and then she had asked him why he had laughed, and when he shook his head and went on laughing her mouth had begun to quiver in the way that made him tighten, and she had asked: "Why do you always laugh at me?" They had had a bad evening. The tightening had started it, Hal knew; he granted that to her in the careless objectivity of his remembering. He wondered if he would ever be able to prevent himself from feeling like that when she didn't laugh with him, or when she was inexplicably depressed, or when she asked him: "What are you thinking?"

He looked at the clock. She was already seven minutes late. It happened every night; he imagined her dawdling over combing her hair, watching the clock and planning not to leave in time. She often warned him against taking her for granted. Surprised by his own bitterness, he thought, Oh, God, why do I always have to be so hard on her; lately she can't do anything right. He remembered the way he used to feel when she came toward him, running because she was late, or to get in out of the rain; she would shake the rain out of her hair (too vain to wear a scarf), and her face would be flecked with drops. Then her coming had canceled irritation.

Eleanor came in the door before he could decide when the change had begun. She started toward him, red-faced from the wind she had fought for four blocks. "Hello!" she said, and he knew that if he had looked permissive she would have kissed him, in spite of the librarian. It was one of the things that he first liked about her: she was willing to kiss him even on the Saturday night subway, when the whole row of people on the other side of the car was watching them. Hal remembered how surprised he had been when they first danced together and she had pulled close; the action did not suit the mild, high-necked dress she was wearing, or even the coolness of her cheek.

She was peeling off her coat and sweater, and he noticed how limberly she bent to unfasten her boots because he was watching. Her figure had improved since she gave up sweets. He remembered proudly that she had started to diet because he had told her once that a dress was too tight; he never had to tell her again. Now her hips were straight under her skirt, and he knew from looking at them how they would feel, very firm as she clenched the big muscles and smooth through her slippery underpants.

They went into the reading room. Hal had grown accustomed to the people who looked up as they walked down the corridor between the tables, but he knew from the way Ellie was smiling they still made her uncomfortable. When they sat down she whispered to him fiercely, "You'd think they'd learn not to stare every night!" and he whispered back, leaning so close her hair touched his mouth, "It's just because you're beautiful."

"You've said that before," she told him, mocking and pleased, but he had already realized it; it did not matter how often he repeated the compliment, for each time the situation was the same, until the lie had become as familiar as the library room. He did not think he would tell Ellie that she was beautiful if they were in a new place, a city or a green park. He looked at the clock.

"Bored?" she asked quickly.

"No." He tried not to frown. She made a little face at him and bent over her notebook.

Hal wished that he had not learned to translate her expressions; when he first met her he had been charmed by her good-humored pout or her wide-eyed expression after they kissed. But now he knew that the pout was made to conceal the quiver in her mouth, and if he watched her he would see that she was not reading; she was staring at the page and trying not to look at him. And as for her expression after they kissed—it always seemed to Hal that he was watching her rise through deep water—he did not know what it meant, but it irritated him. It reminded him of the way she acted after they made love. She went into it as exuberantly as she jumped up to dance, she left it to him to make sure that his roommates were out and that the shades were down. By the time he had checked she would have pulled her dress over her head, rumpling her hair in bangs like a little boy's. He began to undress, folding his clothes on the chair — "Ellie, won't you hang up your dress?" — but when he turned around and saw her waiting, naked under her slip, he went to her and forgot what he had been about to say.

But afterward, if she did not cry, she would not let him go. She clenched him in her arms when he tried to get up, and he had to hurt her in order to break away. When she clung to him with her fingernails pricking his back he tried to force himself out of his sleepiness, to smooth her hair and kiss her. But her mouth tasted stale when he was so tired, and he was afraid she might think he wanted to do it again.

"I'm sorry I was late," she said, not looking up from her book, and he realized that for the last five minutes she had been trying to decide why he seemed irritated.

"I thought we said we wouldn't apologize anymore." He wanted to sound gay, but he noticed at once that he was still raw to the subject; she said softly: "I wish you could forget that." She was bending down the corner of a page and he wanted to tell her to stop; the little mechanical action irritated him out of all proportion, and he wondered if he was so tense because they hadn't made love for four days. How did she feel about tonight? He knew that his roommates were out. He looked at her, but he could tell from the way she was hunched over her book that she was not thinking about making love but about the evening a week before when they had quarreled and then made a list of resolutions over coffee in The Grill. One of them had been not to apologize to each other anymore, for they had agreed it was hypocritical: apologies were only dog-in-the-manger ways of saying, I was right all along but I'll give in for the sake of peace. It had been a terrible evening and he wished that they had not gone to The Grill, for before they had both associated it with one of their first evenings together, when he had held her hand between the salt and pepper.

"Oh, I forgot to ask you about the exam." She had not whispered, and the girl at the next table glanced up, frowning. "How was it?"

"Terrible!" The word did not relieve him; he had come back in the winter darkness, coffee-nerved, fingering the three pencils in his pocket whose points were worn flat. He remembered cursing himself for not reviewing more, and he wondered if he could have written at the end of the thin, scratched-out bluebook, "Circumstances beyond my control . . ."

"But I thought you were so well prepared; you've been reviewing for practically a week."

He tried not to say it, but the words promised too much relief: "Yes, but I can't really study here." He knew before he looked at her that she was hurt. As soon as he saw her mouth he felt the tightening; he wanted to laugh out loud and throw his head back and yell with laughter, and at the same time he wanted to pull her into his arms and fold her so tightly that her breath came in gasps and she groaned, Hal, Hal, you're hurting me . . .

"You never told me you couldn't study here," she said, and he knew how carefully she had weeded the hurt out of her voice.

"Well, I mean, what do you expect? How can I concentrate with you around?" He had meant it to be a compliment—he wanted to see her smile, flushing a little and looking up at him—but it sound like an accusation. As she turned her face sharply away he thought, Oh, God, not another scene! And then he noticed abruptly how thin she had grown; he could see the point of her collarbone through her sweater, and her little breasts stood out almost too sharply.

Ellie had bent down the corner of the page so often that it broke off in her hand. She turned to Hal, smiling brightly. "You should have seen the dormitory tonight." In spite of the new-paint smile, Hal wanted to kiss her for changing the subject. He thought that afterward he would buy her an ice cream cone at the drugstore on the way back to her dormitory. She loved sweets, and she hadn't had any for at least two weeks; he remembered her inexpensive salad dinners, even on Saturdays. And she was really almost too thin.

"You know Wednesday night's usually bad anyway," she was saying. The girl at the next table looked up again, annoyed, and Ellie put her hand to her mouth. She would not have gone on if Hal had not asked, "Well, what happened?" And then she turned to him and whispered so softly, hesitantly, that he could hardly hear. "You know Wednesday night is boy night, and they have candles and ice cream for dessert. Just because we eat at a quarter past six instead of six! Tonight I sat at a table with three other girls and their dates and I literally didn't say a word!" Hal had heard it often before; he looked around the room, trying to distract his attention from his own irritation. Why was she proud of not talking for a whole meal? He noticed the pretty girl who was in his humanities class; she was winding a shank of hair around her finger as she studied. Pretty hair. But she looked even more tense than the rest of them. During exam period you could cut the atmosphere in the reading room with a knife. Most of the girls looked overtired and ugly, and they had not bothered to comb their hair. Hal remembered that the library was the one place they had not expected to see any boys. But Eleanor hated the men's library. She said she felt too stared-at when there were so few girls. Hal had seen some of the looks boys gave her when they walked down the corridor, and he agreed. She had such a damn good figure.

"You're not listening," she said. "I know—don't apologize; I shouldn't be bothering you." As though her rigidly calm tone really expressed her feelings, Eleanor neatly wrote the date at the top of a notebook page and began to read.

"I am interested!" he lied, feeding her hurt. "It's just that I'm interested in this place too." She did not answer, and he slammed his book open and turned the pages roughly, looking

for his place. They sat for ten minutes in silence. Hal tried to
read but he was too conscious of the tip of her elbow, almost
touching his; it looked a little chapped, and he remembered
how hard the winter weather was on her blond skin. Then
he wondered how he had known that—he had been through
no other winter with her, or even a spring or summer—and
inconsequentially he wondered what she looked like in a
bathing suit. He hunched his shoulders and bent closer to
the book, trying to force the words into his attention. There
were long, ruler-straight lines under some of the sentences,
and minute notes were printed in the margins. He had written them in October, when for a week he had devoted himself
to Schopenhauer, reading each page passionately, proud of
the learned comments he wrote in the margins. He had even
found time to go into town to visit the museum, where there
was a portrait of the philosopher, and he remembered how his
head had pounded as he climbed the long steps and hurried
down the corridor to the door of the room where the portrait
hung. It had been a disappointment: an old, placid gentleman
in conventional black. Did pessimism embodied look like
that, he remembered wondering, like your own grandfather?
But he had come back with a feeling of accomplishment.

Now he could not read his own notes. When Ellie was
hurt the consciousness of it ticked like a clock at the back
of his mind and he could not concentrate on anything. He
gave up trying to ignore the point of her elbow. He wondered
if she would move first, as she often did, slipping her hand
into his or turning into his arms as soon as they were alone.
He noticed how rigidly she was sitting; why did they both
keep on pretending to study? He looked at the clock. Already
half an hour wasted. God, I wish we'd had a chance to so
I wouldn't feel like I'm going crazy! Exams—we couldn't
afford the time. He remembered how self-righteously they
had avoided his room, knowing that once they were there,
where they had first told each other that they were in love,

their resolution would dissolve in a panic of desire. Their coming together was always too violent, he thought, like the too-big lunch you ate after missing breakfast, snatching and tearing at the food if no one was watching. But I bet she needs it now, he thought, that's why she's so quivery, close to tears, and maybe that's why I loused up that exam. He knew it was not an excuse, and he felt his resentment heating as he wondered why he had not really reviewed. But she's right: I spent all last week on it, he thought, and then he added, enjoying his own bitterness, Yes, but you know what studying here means, jockeying for position for three hours with our knees about to touch or our hands, and she's always looking up or else I'm looking at her until finally we give up and hold hands though that means I can't write or else she can't. Why didn't I have sense enough to tell her I had to study, two evenings would have done it . . . but I knew she'd cry. Not over the phone but in the booth after I hung up, so she couldn't go back to her room without the other girls see-ing she'd been crying. He wanted to turn to her and break the thin, unreal wall of her concentration by asking, Why does everything hurt you too much? And why do I always have to know? Although he knew the last, at least, was not her fault.

He heard eight strike in silver, feminine notes from the clock over the girl's gym. That clock would never let him for-get the amount of time he was wasting; all evening he would have to listen to its reproachful chiming. The thought drove him to the peak of his irritation and he slammed his books closed and began to stack them together. Eleanor looked up and he saw the terror in her eyes that he had seen once before when he told her that he would have to go home for the week-end. She had said: "You know that means three days without talking to anyone." And he had answered, trying to laugh: "But there must be someone—all those girls."

"I'm not a girl's girl; I don't really know how to talk to them. And anyway I haven't been spending my extra time in the smoker, so they hardly even know my name." He had understood what she had been unwilling to say, that he had taken up the evenings she might have spent padding herself with her girl acquaintances against the time when she would be alone. In the end he had left without telling her goodbye and the weekend had been spoiled because he had known how she was feeling.

He stood up, although he had not decided what he was going to do; only, no more waste. "You want me to leave?" she asked, hurriedly gathering up her books, and Hal knew that she thought he was going to walk out without her. If she began to cry he would be more than ashamed; he would feel that his hands were as clumsy as trays as he tried to soothe her, and when he struggled to think of something gentle to say he would begin to go mad with irritation. He started toward the reading room door before she was ready, and he heard the almost hysterical ruffling of pages as she closed her books. He waited for her on the other side of the door, and when she came, almost running, he saw her face become young again as she smiled with relief.

"I agree with you; let's get out of this dreary place," she said, and Hal wished that she had been angry.

"Look, I'm going to walk you back now," he said as they went out into the sudden coldness. She began to fumble awkwardly with her scarf, adjusting it inside her coat collar.

"Right now?" Her voice was carefully casual.

"Look, Eleanor, I've got to get something done tonight. Friday's the Phil 101 exam."

"Oh, I understand." They began to walk, conscious of not holding hands. The quadrangle was dark except for the library windows and the illumined clock over the gym. It was always five minutes fast, on purpose, Hal knew, so that the girls who were late starting would still get to class on time. In spite of the clock Ellie was always coming in late; she would drop into the seat beside him, panting, and snatch off her gloves.

"You taking our history class next term?" Ellie asked.

He wished that she would not keep her voice cheerful.

"I guess so. You can't divide it." He was ashamed of his grudging tone, although it was easy to justify it; even if he broke with her now (it was incredible, the idea of pushing off her hands and running without hearing her calling), he would still have to see her every Monday, Wednesday and Friday at ten in the history class where they tried not to look at each other.

Her dormitory was full of lights. "At last they've taken down the wreath!" he said.

"And high time!"

Her voice had revived with his cheerfulness—real, this time, although he knew it was ridiculous that the tarnished wreath should have depressed him. It had been a soiled reminder of the Christmas vacation they had spent straining to be together, through long-distance calls, which they spent saying goodbye, and too many letters.

They stood under the porch light and she held out her hands. He took them and slipped his fingers inside her gloves. Her palms were soft and lined.

"Look at the bikes," he said, "you'd think they'd give up in this bad weather," and they both looked out at the heaped, stone snow. He remembered that he had a long walk back, but as he bent hurriedly to kiss her she slipped her arms around him and he had to pull back hard in order to get away. She let go at last and, no longer smiling, she whispered: "Hal, don't go." He hesitated. "Please. Don't go. Please." She was rigidly controlling her voice, but he knew the limit of her endurance and he wanted to be away before she began to cry, for then he would never be able to leave. He would have to stay until she was calm, rocking her in his arms and kissing her hair. Afterward when he walked back to his dormitory he would avoid looking at clocks. But when he was in his room he would see the tin alarm clock that was already set for the morning and then he would throw his books violently into a chair. He would go out and buy coffee so that with luck he could study until three. By that time nearly all the lights across the courtyard would have gone out and often it would have begun to snow.

Eleanor was watching him. "About tomorrow," she said lightly, wiping a fleck off one of her books, "I know we both have a lot of work. I'll call you up in the morning and we can decide then. Maybe we ought to study by ourselves tomorrow night." Her voice was so matter-of-fact that if he had not known the pattern Hal would not have believed that next day, when they came to the deciding, she would plead with him to study with her—"Really, I promise, we'll get something done"—and offer to sign a pledge that she would not speak to him for three hours. Now she was looking down and running her fingers along the edges of her books. "Hal," she said, "I'm sorry about tonight. You know how I get sometimes." He put his arms around her, trying not to tell her how sorry he was, trying to choke back his softness. "Oh, God, Ellie," he said, and he heard the almost-tears in his own voice, the rawness that was both tenderness and irritation. She strained up to kiss him and when she opened her mouth he felt tricked, for if he put his tongue between her lips he would not be able to leave. He kissed her, beginning half-consciously to forget that he should go. She dropped her books and they tumbled over their feet. He was only vaguely conscious of the porch and the staring light as he pulled her against him, hearing her moan with pain and excitement. Then he drew back and said, his voice already labored, "Isn't there anywhere we can go?" Her face was flushed, reminding him in a twisted way of a child waking up, damp and fresh. She was trying to think of somewhere to go and holding his hands tightly as though she could brace his desire.

"It's too late to have you in the dormitory," she said, and they silently checked their short list of private places. It was too cold for the park — they had been nervous there, on the bench behind the thin screen of shrubbery — and it was too late to go to his room. Parietal rules! He wondered how many people they had forced into marriage. They had talked now and then of renting a room but Hal knew they would never do it; they were still too aware of the connotations. And although they prided themselves on their indifference to surroundings, Ellie's face seemed to reflect the gray walls when they lay together on his bed.

"At least let's get out of this porch light," he said, and they went down on the steps and stood hesitating on the sidewalk. She was looking around eagerly and hopefully, and he wondered again how much of her desire was passion and how much grasping; girls used sex to get a hold on you, he knew — it was so easy for them to pretend to be excited.

They wandered down the sidewalk. As they passed the parking lot Eleanor hesitated. "Look, we could — " She did not go on, but Hal knew that she meant the cars, the college-girl cars with boxes of tissues and clean seat-covers that were parked in the lot behind the dormitories. "All right," he said, knowing that the whole time they would be afraid of someone coming, listening for steps. They walked around the lot, comparing cars, and Ellie was laughing so that he would not think it was sordid. Hal wondered why it had become so easy to accept the backseats of cars and student beds with broken springs. Finally she chose a station wagon, and he felt himself growing more excited as she climbed into the back. He followed her and she turned to him and they sank together down onto the seat. For a moment her willing softness seemed to cancel the whole tense evening. He began to unbutton her blouse, feeling her stiffen and gasp as he traced her breast. Across the quadrangle the gymnasium clock chimed. Nine o'clock. Suddenly violent, he tore her blouse open, and as she whimpered, terrified, and tried to push him off, he pulled at her slip. "Stop it, Eleanor, God, stop it," he said when she tried to hold his hands, and as he dragged the straps off her shoulders she began to cry.

THE BANKS OF THE OHIO

EVERY AFTERNOON THAT SUMMER, RAIN OR SHINE, the yellow taxi would turn into Pion Way at a little past six o'clock and stop in front of the house. Bay's mother would spot it from the window where she had spent the day, addressing envelopes for charity and watching the world go by. "Lamb Tail, I believe I see him," she would call. Given half a chance, she would add, "Bay, I'm not at all sure he should park there. It says No Parking and you know I try to be impartial."

"He's not parking," Bay would say, and then she would run down the stairs with the long day coiled like a spring behind her.

Outside, she could walk more slowly, under the weight of her mother's watching, across the strip of sunburned grass to the yellow taxi. Shriver had never been known to get out for her, but he would lean across to open the door.

Several times a week, Bay brought a picnic basket, packed with tuna-fish sandwiches and deviled eggs, the same meek food she and her mother took every April to see the wildflowers. For Shriver's sake, she would add a pickle jar of gin and ginger ale. The picnic was to be eaten in his rowboat, the *Dolly*.

The *Dolly* was the only thing Shriver owned. The taxi, of course, was borrowed — he was a college graduate and the taxi job was only for the time being — and the room he lived in on Third Street was rented by the week. Even the town where he worked, the town where Bay bought every stitch she wore and shared lunches with girls she had known in school, had no claims on Shriver. He had hitchhiked up from Florida, stopping in Louisville because the trucker he was riding with had a load to deliver there. Now, after two years, Shriver still did not know the names of the streets, and he often telephoned Bay for directions, breaking into her quiet morning with a question about a place she might have heard of but would surely never want to be. For some reason, most of Shriver's passengers wanted to go to the wrong end of town.

He would never have kept his job for so long if his boss, a man named Armstrong, had not had so much respect for education. Mr. Armstrong had never had a college graduate driving for him before, and he gave Shriver special favors, even letting him keep the taxi at night, after work. Bay sometimes thought of telling Mr. Armstrong that she knew every crack and seam in the taxi's brown plastic upholstery; but that was ancient history, before the first of July when Shriver bought the rowboat for twenty-five dollars and christened it with a bottle of beer.

One afternoon toward the end of August, they parked the taxi on the public pier and carried the picnic down to the *Dolly*. Bay got in first and settled herself in the stern. She was worried about her white piqué dress; the *Dolly's* seats were still not really clean, although she had scrubbed them with a brush. Shriver cast off from the iron ring and gave the shore a shove with his foot, and they drifted out into the oily river.

It was hot enough to raise the smell of the mud which the spring floods had left caked on the low-hanging trees. Under the trees, the banks were bare except for poison ivy, lovely in autumn; back farther, green corn nobody owned grew as high as a forest. The bare roots which humped along the banks were used by the houseboats for moorings. They drifted past one, the *Sugar Belle*; there were geraniums in her window-boxes, and deep inside, a radio was playing softly.

Shriver dropped the mooring rope in a wet knot on the bottom of the boat, and Bay said, "If this is my house, you ought to be more careful." She picked up the rope and began to coil it. Shriver said, "Watch out, now," and started for the rowing seat. He was a tall person, not heavy but large, and each time he put his foot down, the boat tipped to that side. Finally he sat down and put the oars in the oarlocks and pulled the *Dolly* around in a tight circle. "I don't know how I ended up with a girl afraid to dirty her skirt," he said, seeing the way Bay was holding off the wet rope.

"You haven't ended up with me yet. Look out for that boat." The river was crowded in the late afternoon, and most of the people on it didn't know what they were doing. The big motor cruisers were just excuses for lechery; they were always running aground on Seven Mile Island with an unmarried couple in every berth.

Shriver pulled the *Dolly* to the left just in time. He did not even look at the houseboat churning by. "Was your mother mad about you getting home late last night?" He sounded hopeful.

Bay did not answer until she had taken a good look at the houseboat, the *Doreen Ann*, and drawn her own conclusions from the beer bottles and the fat women sitting with their feet up. It was Shriver's river, not hers. The only river she knew was the stretch below the yacht club, where her father had sailed every Sunday until he died.

"She didn't say anything except she had gotten lonely," she answered Shriver finally, and when he snorted, she decided not to tell him how her mother had said, "Lambie, these nights go on and on." Her mother's sweet wistfulness, and the pink crêpe de Chine nightgown she was wearing had reminded Bay of the night just after her father's death, when they had been close and sorrowful as two birds in a nest. Shriver did not know anything about the sweetness of that bedroom, where the shades were always drawn. He said she couldn't eat her cake and have it, but her mother needed her, and for more reasons than one.

"It would be better if she did get angry," Shriver was droning on. "Then maybe something could be discussed." He failed to understand that nothing could be discussed with her mother except clothes or the weather, which covered a good deal of ground. "Eighty-nine at ten-forty-five; I heard it on the radio," her mother would remark, and if Bay replied, "I didn't suffer," it meant her evening with Shriver had been unremarkable. Twice her mother had almost lost her, when the humidity had risen as high as the heat and the only thing Bay could think of was to shed her clothes and lie back in cool passion, allowed if not admired.

"Duck," Shriver warned, and he leaned on the oars while they floated under a low limb. "The funny thing is, I like her," he said, beginning to thrash with the oars again, "and I believe she likes me. Remember that time I came to dinner? She kept saying, 'Thank you, Mr. Ellis, for giving my little girl some excitement.'"

"Excitement!" Bay laughed.

"That's all it's been, I guess."

"Oh, Shriver, we've been over and over that ground."

"Well, we're spared a lot," he said, going back to joking. He never would drive her to the wall. "Think if she took me seriously. Over the peach soufflé, she'd be asking me my intentions."

"It's not that I mind Shriver Ellis being poor and half-educated and having no future," Bay imitated what he must think her mother would say. "It's just that he's such a plain person."

"Does she mean my face or my soul?"

She looked at him. It hurt, to have to say. She knew his face so well she couldn't defend it, even from her own spite. He was tanned from the summer on the river, and his lashes and eyebrows were bleached white, so that he looked as though he was always startled or staring. Yet it was a plain face, one she would have had no trouble losing in a crowd. He had spotted brown eyes as meek as a cow's and his cuticles rose halfway up his nails and she could never think of his size with any comfort. Sometimes she thought it was his sheer bulk which prevented her from wanting to see him naked and not, as he was always hinting, the look she would find afterward in her mother's eyes. He would simply have too much flesh, once he was bare. And such solemn flesh! She had known from the first time she rode out from town in his taxi that he was different from the boys she had grown up with, who would roll all over you on the country club golf course and then go back to college and send you a card.

"Your soul, I guess she means," Bay said, and then hated herself because after three months of necking and straining she was still holding him to jokes. "Oh, Shrive," she said, "it looks like we never can be serious."

He dropped the oars and came for her, getting over the seat on all fours like a bear getting over a log. The boat dipped to one side and Bay held on with both hands. "Go back, Shriver, you'll sink us both." But he was already kissing her and leaning his whole weight on her shoulders until she thought she would cave in. "How about some supper," she said, reaching under his arm for the picnic basket.

He sat back then. "All right, church social. How much am I bid for this box?"

As she unwrapped the sandwiches, Bay pressed each piece of wax paper out flat and laid it back in the basket. "You should marry a poor man, with your ways," Shriver said.

"Don't get ugly with me. Shall we tie up to the shore?" She feared for her life, floating sideways in the middle of the river.

"If we tie up, I'll try to get you to go on the bank and you'll fight me about it for an hour."

Bay had no answer for that. I am just a girl, she would have liked to say; I wear garter belts with blue roses and cotton petticoats with eyelet embroidery and I have never been used to holding up much weight. But Shriver had shamed her out of those reasons. "All right, we'll just float wild in the river," she said, handing him a tuna sandwich to plug his mouth.

Watching him eat, she knew that was what she really wanted—to feed him, with homemade cupcakes and gummy pies, beef stew and jellied consommé, until he was full and could let her be. "You don't care anything about all the good times we've had," she said sadly. "All the good food we've eaten together, the picnics and the casseroles and the steak dinners. Nothing means anything to you, except getting me into bed."

"It's been pretty thin pickings, Bay."

"Not for me, it hasn't."

"Well, maybe not, but you have your house and your mother and pretty soon your job running the library or practically running it."

"I don't see why you don't have the same. You have your

job, your life—" She had to stop there. Hitchhiking up from Florida with his family dead or gone; he didn't even have a picture to show her of the place where he'd been born. Thin pickings indeed!

"You're right," he said as though he had heard her. "All my life, I've had the whole weight of myself on my hands. It's not a satisfaction."

"Have a deviled egg," she said. She refused, of all things, to pity him.

As she held out the egg bag, she heard the drumming of a big boat, coming down the river. She shaded her eyes to admire it, a blue motor cruiser, coming toward them slowly and trailing a wide wake. She read the gold letters on the bow: "L'Heure Bleu, Port of Lou." As the boat came closer, she saw three people lying in lounge chairs on the deck. One of them shouted something at the man who was steering, and they all laughed. The big horn honked twice.

"Blat, blat," Shriver said without looking around. He was concentrating on Bay. "You're bound to know I can't go on starving forever."

That made Bay angry; she wouldn't stand for threats. "You know what I wish?" she said. "I wish I was sitting on that big boat with a Tom Collins in my hand. Just for five minutes, so I could enjoy myself."

"All right, Miss Priss," Shriver said. "I thought it was something else holding you back, but I guess it's nothing but goddamned prissiness."

"Don't you curse at me!"

Blat, the horn went over their heads. Shriver grabbed an oar and began to thrash the water. Bay looked up and saw the big boat hanging over them.

She reached for the other oar. Shriver was pulling them around in a circle. She screamed at him but he gave one last desperate thrash and they turned in under the blue cruiser's bow. Bay reached up to fend it off and then she felt Shriver's hand in the small of her back and fell, scraping her leg on the side of the rowboat.

Coming up with a gasp in the warm water, she thought, Thank God, no more arguments.

A wave slapped her in the mouth and she drew in a long gasp of water. Choking, she spat out and began to breathe through her nose. It felt stripped. But she had been in the water all summer, and after a moment, it felt more comfortable than the air. Treading water, she began to work off her shoes.

The cruiser was already some distance away, but the loud thumping of the screw still vibrated in the water around her. Hearing that, Bay realized for the first time that she was in danger, and she slid onto her back and began to kick for the shore.

After two kicks, she thought of Shriver and came up in the water, pushing her wet hair out of her eyes.

He was floating ten yards downstream, hanging onto the *Dolly*, which had capsized. The blistered brown hull rose and fell gently in the water. "Swim for the shore," Shriver called when he saw her looking. "I'll hang on here." Then he turned his head as through he did not want to see her hesitating.

Bay hung, treading water. One day on the pier, she had asked Shriver if he knew how to swim, and he had answered, "Don't you know I was raised in a country club pool?" She turned on her back and began to swim toward him.

The river, so calm and oily on the surface, was fierce a few inches underneath with an offshore current. Each time Bay kicked, the current caught her foot and pulled it sideways. She turned over on her stomach to see how far she still had to go.

Shriver and the boat had floated farther away.

This time she did not hesitate. She turned over on her back and began to kick furiously, dragging her arms up over her head and down through the water, making time against the current. A long way downstream, the big motor cruiser was nosing along the bank, and for the first time, she thought, the bastards! They never even bothered to stop.

A little later she began to notice the soaked weight of her dress, and she let her feet drop and came upright in the water to work on the side fastening. She wrenched at the tiny hooks and finally eased the dress off one shoulder and then off the other, sinking at the same time below the surface. The dress was hanging around her waist when she realized that she was about to put her foot on the thick muddy bottom. She pumped hard and came back up. She rested for a moment, and then doubled over and worked the dress down over her knees. It fell away and hung in a white clot just off her feet. She leaned back on the water and swam on.

She grew tired quickly and turned over on her stomach to try the crawl, but her legs kept sinking deeply below the surface. At each breath, she checked the shore. After ten breaths, she knew she was not getting anywhere; the white sycamore which had been by her head when she started was now just off her knee. She lay and floated, giving herself up to the tug of the current, until she thought of Shriver drifting farther and farther away and started up again, hammering through the water. This time she had to stop almost immediately. Her legs had gone soft and the current was pulling her out to the middle of the river. Raising her arms once more, she thought, Here I am in the middle of the Ohio River, drowning, and nothing has ever happened to me.

Shriver caught her by the wrist and pulled her to the side of the rowboat. "Hang on," he gasped. "I can't hold you." He pressed her fingers over the narrow ridge of the keel and then he let go of her and hung from both hands for a moment before putting his left hand back over hers. She shook her head to tell him she could hang on by herself—she knew, from his face, how long he had been waiting—but he kept his hand clamped over hers. So for a while she lay resting with her legs streaming out behind her and her cheek on the scaly hull.

"I tried to push it toward you. I guess I did, a little," Shriver said.

At that, Bay raised her head. "We'd better get started." She looked around the end of the boat; the shore at the river bend seemed closer. She took a new grip on the keel and began to kick, and after a minute, Shriver started too and the boat lurched forward.

Their combined kicking seemed strong, and Bay turned her head to smile at Shriver. Then she wondered why he had to look so white when the shore was practically within reach. A minute later, he laid his head on the side of the boat and she heard his kicking falter and stop. "Too far," he gasped. "You swim. I'll wait."

"I'm not leaving the *Dolly*."

"She's served."

Bay was frightened; his voice sounded so peaceful. "Not yet, she hasn't," she said, trying to sound angry, and then at some expense to what remained of her strength, she made a loud thrashing in the water. Without Shriver kicking, the boat hardly moved, but she went on working, not daring to look at him. After a long time, she heard him begin to kick. But only with one foot—at least, that was the way it sounded. The soft little splash he made, like a twig dropping into the water, almost drove her mad. "Kick with both feet, you nut," she gasped. "You're supposed to be the strong one." But he did not even lift his head off the hull.

Then the other side of the *Dolly* butted into something solid, jarred, hung still, and began to rock as peacefully as a porch swing.

Very slowly, with heavy, paddling motions that had no connection with any stroke she had ever learned, Bay eased around the end of the boat. She saw the branch they had hit jutting like a horn out of the brown water. When she tried to stand, the soft mud sank away beneath her, and so she had to leave the boat and paddle farther in. When she had found a place where she could stand, chin deep in still water, she marked it in her mind and swam slowly back to Shriver.

"Come on. We're going in." She had to unbend each of his fingers to get him off the keel. "Swim!" But he hung, a dead weight, off her hands until she grew angry and said, "At least make an effort!" Finally she had to drag him the whole distance, hitched in the crook of her arm. Even then, he kept trying to slip away from her, stiff and unmanageable as a waterlogged piece of tree. At last she was standing and he was crouching beside her in the shallow water.

Presently she began to wring out her hair.

Shriver looked up, and she saw that his eyes were blood-shot from the water. "Can you make it from here?" she asked.

He nodded, and when she hooked her hands under his arms, he struggled to his knees and finally to his feet. Standing, he leaned his whole weight on her, and she felt, with surprise, his weight and his weakness. Then he leaned away from her and walked carefully to the bank and sat down. She followed and sat beside him.

After a while, she asked, "Why did you turn your face away when I was starting to swim for you?" She made it sound as though he had been rude.

He shook his head, knocking water out of his ears. "I was scared."

"I thought you could swim. I thought you told me that day on the pier you could swim."

"It didn't look like you were going to make it, and all I could do was hang on and try to push the boat toward you."

Bay began to shiver. Her fingernails were purple and her teeth clacked loudly in her head. "I'm too cold," she complained, and she kneeled and pulled off her wet slip.

Shriver took the slip and wrung it out. She looked at him. His khakis were pasted to him with water. She watched him wring out her slip and then she looked down and saw the top of her stocking and the metal hook of a garter.

"You're freezing," Shriver said, and he took off his shirt, which was soaking wet, and wrung it out and laid it across her shoulders.

She thought of saying, "It's late in the day for that."

"You're blue as slate yourself," she said instead when Shriver sat down beside her, and she took his hands and began to rub them. She had held his hand three times a week in the movies all that summer, but this was the first time she had noticed. She raised his fingers to her mouth as though to taste them and tasted instead the river water which was still falling from her hair. She caught his eye and smiled. For the last time, she noticed how big he was, blocking out her part of the sky, and then she put her hand up and brought his neck down like a twig, imagining that she heard the snap of bone as he kissed her.

THE ICE PARTY

Robin Winslow stood in the bay window at six o'clock on a winter evening and drummed with his fingers on the freshly painted white sill. Outside, beyond the glass which clouded with his breath, then cleared, the lights of the city were spread from the dark boundary of the river to the bay. For all its brightness, the city seemed to him to lie as peacefully below his window as a meadow or a rug or a tranquil inlet of the sea. He knew it well. When he moved his head slightly, the view of the city was replaced in the window by the reflection of his wife, a steamy essence, coiled in her bed.

The cold glass seemed to take only reds and whites, only the violence of her cheeks and the pallor of her nightgown. She was nursing the baby, and sighing.

"I do wish you'd go out, Robin," she said. "You make me nervous, standing there like a Christian martyr."

"Don't get nervous, you know what it does to the milk," he said. He spoke without emphasis, voicing her own alarms.

She shifted the baby so that his round, gleaming head appeared, reflected in the glass. "Sometimes I think you're just a little bit jealous," she said, attempting gaiety as cautiously as every afternoon she attempted to climb a few stairs.

He turned away from the window and stared at his son's bald head. "How's he doing?"

"He's doing fine—the pig." She looked down at the baby. Her forehead was broad and low and white, like a white linen scarf binding back her thick black Indian hair. "A pretty, practical face," Robin's father had said the first time he met her. Lilly sighed again, looking down at the baby pinned to her bare breast.

Robin went to his bureau and began to rummage around, sifting the day's mail that he had not yet opened. He shuffled it all together and put a silver brush on top. The surface of the bureau shone, reflecting the silver rims of his brushes and bottles and boxes. He felt a certain dreariness, looking at those things, all marked with his own or his father's initials.

"I suppose these will all go to him, one day," he murmured, touching the top of a silver box with his finger.

"Yes, they should. When he's twenty-one, you should give him some of those old things to go on the bureau in his first apartment."

Glancing at himself in the round mirror, Robin touched the points of his collar and straightened his tie. "Maybe I will go out, after all."

"You really should, you know," Lilly said, smiling. "It would be very rude of you not to go, when they expect you."

"You won't come?"

She shrugged, still smiling. "Honestly! Do you want me to go like this?"

"He'll be finished soon," Robin said.

"Yes, and I'll be finished too." Immediately after each feeding, she went to sleep, lying flat on her back with her hands folded on her stomach. She would sleep in that leaden way, her breath hardly stirring the fronds of hair which lay on her cheeks, until the nurse came to rouse her for the next feeding. Only in the middle of the day she stayed awake long enough to climb a few stairs and read the morning paper.

"It's preposterous, anyway—a skating party at dinnertime," Robin said as he went to kiss her.

"I think it's a lovely idea," she said, raising her mouth. Her lips were soft, very pale, with a scale of lipstick in the corners. She kissed him gravely, with passion. "I wish I was going!"

As he straightened up, Robin's lapel brushed the baby's head. Two or three fair hairs, so fine they were nearly invisible, stood up and waved softly. The baby's eyes were fixed, half-closed, and his whole face pouted to his mouth—like a pitcher, Robin thought. "I'll be back for the ten o'clock feeding," he promised.

"It would be a pleasure to have you, but don't feel we couldn't get along." As she spoke, she took the baby off her breast, with an unstoppering sound, and laid him against her shoulder. She began to pat his back, her mother-in-law's emerald flashing on her square, freckled hand.

The baby writhed once and gave a burp. "Good boy," Lilly said, taking him down from her shoulder. As she applied him suckerlike to her other breast, Robin turned and went out the door.

In the dark hall, which smelled of the scrod they had eaten for lunch, Robin met Miss Perkins, the nurse, catfooting along. She flattened herself against the wall to let him pass. He hesitated, looking at her, narrowing his eyes in the dim light. She was a scrawny middle-aged woman, yet he had once made the mistake of speaking to her too gently, too insistently ("I do appreciate what you're doing here"—was that it?) and ever since she had flattened herself against the wall when he passed. "I don't believe Mrs. Winslow has finished yet," he said.

"I'll just go along and see," Miss Perkins said, and she hurried down the hall with a rustle and slide of cold nylon layers.

Robin knew he should have stopped her. Lilly hated for "that woman" to come in while she was nursing. Twice when it happened, Lilly's face had flushed almost black, and she had shouted, "Miss Perkins! Wait until I ring!" She was not embarrassed; she simply couldn't bear to have the atmosphere diluted.

She heard Miss Perkins knock, very discreetly, on the bedroom door. Then she went in.

Walking on down the hall, Robin began to feel rather satisfied. There was something matter-of-fact about Miss Perkins that would put an end to the High Communion in that overheated bedroom. He went quickly down the stairs, pleased for the first time that day. Miss Perkins would take the baby away to change his diapers. "You have never changed his diapers," he would say one day to Lilly. Poor Lilly, who had tried so hard to keep that woman out of the house. "Why can't I take care of my own child?" she had demanded, drawn up in front of him like a battering ram, a month before the child was born. Robin had not expected that opposition.

In the hall, he took his jacket and gloves and opened the front door. The night air was cold and dry, stimulating after the staleness of the house, and he stood on the doorstep, buttoning up his jacket, and breathed in great gasps. He knew how he looked, gasping there on the doorstep like a stranded fish, his pale, gleaming, ungrained face rather gilled at the best of times. Yet he couldn't help it; it seemed nothing less than miraculous that cold weather prevailed outside a house which was so persistently overheated. He started down the street toward his car.

No, he had not expected that opposition. He had admired Lilly, of course, for sticking up for her rights; they were her rights, he knew that—had been from the days of the cave. But he had thought she was too tender, too spoiled, in fact, to want to do all that work. Certainly before the baby was born she had never put herself out, never cleaned a bathtub or pressed a shirt or done anything else to show. . . . Well, after all, this was different, he reminded himself, walking steadily along under the drooping streetlights. Yet it was such a change, so sudden, that he found it quite hard to accommodate himself. One morning she was lying in bed until eleven o'clock, and the next, practically, she was up at six, running for the baby, and wearing the same white wrapper. For her clothes had not changed, of all things. And yes, he did admire her, although perhaps not so much as his father, who when he came to call bobbed and scraped and pirouetted like one of the old park pigeons in springtime; positively danced in his highly polished black shoes. "A born mother!" he would cry, as though it was something rare. Of course, his father knew nothing about the difficulties of eating scrod off a tray at unseasonable hours or spending most evenings in an overheated bedroom. And then, since the baby's birth—and part of this, Robin knew, had been medical necessity—since the baby's birth, Lilly had kissed him so gravely, so passionately, but they had not once made love.

Eight weeks. He felt a quiver, at that, a touch of the desolation he had felt when he looked at his silver brushes. He unlocked his car and climbed in and turned on the heater. Cold air rushed up his legs. He sat for a while in the queer gaseous light from the streetlamp, pressing his gloved hands in between his knees. He felt cold and lost and a little ashamed, like a child who knows his misery is laughable to everybody else in the world. "What on earth is the matter with you?" his mother used to shout in a frenzy of common sense when he sat in a corner and mourned. That feeling, that lost sense of sadness and oppression, had not come to him for several years. Now, sitting in the car with the cold air rushing up his legs, he remembered crouching under the skirts of his mother's dressing table one day shortly before she went away. The organdy had tickled his nose, smelling of dust and starch, and his mother had said over the telephone, "Oh, what is the use! What is the use? That child doesn't need me any more than I need him." Her pink satin slipper had been thrust under the edge of the organdy petticoat, and he had reached out and touched the toe.

He started the car. The roar of the engine as he pressed down the accelerator made him feel almost gay. There was something rakish about starting out to a party alone. He was not the kind of man who made a habit of going out and leaving his wife; in fact, he could not remember a single other instance—except, if it could be counted, the night the baby was born. Lilly had looked at him through the flush on her face, through the dazzle in her eyes, and said, "Now Robin, you really must go out and see Evans or George or some of your other friends. I won't have you"—and then she had given a heave, with her whole body, as though she was pushing up a weight laid on her chest—"I won't have you glooming around here, making me feel responsible." All the time quite calm, quite rational, in spite of the flush and the dazzle on her face.

So he had gone out. He had not been worried, although his father had said, "She is old to be having her first child." He had not felt anything, leaving the hospital, except a numb, bleak sense of waiting, as though he was a child again, sitting in Dr. Bank's waiting room with the malaria print on the wall. Bessie Stokes, his nurse, had always plied him with candy and reassurances, but he had not been frightened. He had felt dull and empty, waiting to be filled with the pain of the booster shot—with the pain of the birth. But he did not feel the pain, in the end. He only felt the emptiness.

Evans Hill and Robin's cousin George had known exactly what to do with him. They had taken him to a bar and then to a restaurant and then to another bar, all new to Robin, who seldom went to Cambridge. At regular intervals, he had slipped away to telephone the hospital. They wouldn't tell him anything, they said that nothing was happening, and when he threatened to come and see for himself, the little night nurse, had said, "Now Mr. Winslow! Don't you go being a trial!"

He was bowling along the highway, by the edge of the dark, thick-looking river. He drove very fast, very skillfully, cutting in and out of the line of cars. It was something he enjoyed, for he knew he drove well, and he put his head back and laughed when he heard them honk behind him, heard them bleat behind him, wounded, angry, like lambs, because he had cut them off by turning from the wrong lane. Let them bleat, he thought—and remembered how Lilly had shouted when he had come to the hospital, finally, late, in the morning. He had looked terrible, unshaven, hangdog, the night like a scab on his face, and he had not been able to explain to her that finally he had given up telephoning, because they had made him feel like a fool. "I know where you've been— getting drunk, it's a sacred tradition," she had cried, looking so white and drained after the flush of the night. "I expected that!" she had shouted when he tried to explain. "But I did think you'd get back before the baby was born." The baby was four hours old—he had seen it, behind the glass; and he had known that she would never let him make up for those four hours.

Coming around a curve, he saw ahead of him, on the wide black river, the hive of lights that marked the party. He parked at the end of a long line of cars and got out. The wind off the river was tart-smelling, keen, with a kind of gaiety in it as though it had been whipping up the cheeks of pretty girls. Robin went around to the trunk of his car and unlocked it to take out his skates. He always kept them there, in case on one of his trips to inspect a venerable lady's collection, bequeathed to a museum, he had the good luck to pass a frozen pond. The skates were heavy and black, with dangling gray laces. He knotted the laces together and draped the skates over his shoulder, where they clanked companionably as he made his way down the bank. Once he stumbled—the rucked-up ground was frozen hard as iron—and caught himself with a gasp, frightened, as though in stumbling he had risked a fall that would have prevented him from getting to the lights. Then he hurried on, his skates thudding softly, and stepped out onto the ice through the dry rushes at the edge of the river.

At first, he walked cautiously. The ice was perfectly safe—Eloise Hill had made sure of that; the river was frozen three feet down. Yet Robin could not help thinking of the black, cold water moving sluggishly under the ice. He had never fallen through—and he had skated everywhere, on ponds and rivers all over New England—and yet he knew how it would feel to crash through the splintering ice and drop into the slow, cold water. He knew he would never have the strength to fight his way back up to the top. So he walked cautiously, pushing one foot in front of the other.

From the center of the river, the lights of the party threw long smears of color toward him across the ice. As he approached, he saw that they were flares on the ends of long poles which had been driven into the ice. The wind tore at the flares, tossing them about or forcing them down into their sockets. When the wind died down, they leapt up and danced a few inches above the wick. Beyond the flares, tables and benches were set out, and a great fire was burning slowly in a depression of melting ice.

As Robin came closer, he began to feel a little uncertain.

It was impossible to recognize anyone in that queer, shifting light. People with their backs turned to him were warming their hands at the fire. Others, skating, flashed in and out of sight, passing beyond the fire as bright and insubstantial as ghosts. Their voices sounded thin and faraway as they laughed and called to each other. Robin unslung his skates and sat down alone on a wooden bench to take off his shoes.

Immediately he was noticed, as though by entering the circle of light he had changed from a shadow into flesh. Eloise Hill rushed up to kiss him and to introduce the young men trailing after her. Evans, her husband, came to offer a pair of heavy socks, which Robin of course refused; he always brought his own. One by one, others came to speak to him, until he felt like a king or a chronic invalid, receiving on his bench.

He knew them well, for they were part of a group that had stayed together since college, a group that had been the seedbed of a dozen marriages, the alliances of college drastically shifted so that the mistresses of two roommates could, without any awkwardness, marry the wrong men. So he felt a warmth, an ease as they chattered which he did not feel with any other people in the world. They knew him with no disguises, they had even invented his excuses—for instance, the old lady benefactors who, they claimed, adored him. They were resigned to him, and he, accepting their resignation, applied it to his life, and then anything was bearable.

At last the chatter died down. "But where is Lilly?" Heather Scott asked after too long an interval, her bright voice reproving even while it endorsed the others' rudeness. She was a high-colored, slender girl, wearing a very short red skirt, and she stood poised gracefully on one skate, the other toed on its runner.

"She had to stay at home to nurse the baby," Robin explained, and understood from the slight rustle, the shifting of expectations around him, that this had been an odd thing to say. They were too determined, most of them, too sufficient to waste life on children.

By then his skates were laced, and he stood up and pushed his way out of the group. As soon as he heard the rasp of steel on ice, he felt an assurance that he did not feel when he walked down the street or climbed his own stairs. He had learned to skate very early. His father had bought him a pair of double runners, and together—the fair, fat child and the prim old gentleman, too old, they all said, to be left with such a small boy—they had scored most of the ponds in Massachusetts. A few days after Robin's wedding, his father had given him his own old-fashioned skates, but Robin had put them away, along with the cinnamon-colored knickers, because he had not wanted to overlay that particular section of the past. Now he skated quickly out of the cluster of people, out of the firelight, and felt on his cheek the steel chill of the ice, the breath of the frozen river.

He imagined that they called behind him—for they liked him, he knew that; he filled a certain chink in the pattern, providing an image of ordinary domesticity without which their scheme would have been incomplete. He remembered that several of the girls had sent presents when the baby was born. Heather Scott had sent a rather vulgar embroidered pink dress, obviously intended for a girl; it was her style to mock an obligation, even while she fulfilled it. Robin had been a little in love with her at college, and glad to be put off by her sheen, her clear, bright hardness. She was an exceptional girl, and she had remained undimmed by the ordinary events that had diminished the others' lives. She had not, even once, come anywhere near to marrying.

Robin skated on, slitting the fresh darkness, confident now of the ice as he heard it growl under his runners. Black ice. "The heart of winter," his father had called it. Robin circled, skated backward, and skidded to a stop, ice flaking up from his runners. His cheeks were burning, and his hands felt hot and malleable, like melting wax. His body was warm and sufficient, as though he no longer needed his clothes, his heavy layers of wool, to keep him warm. He stood still and looked back at the lights of the party. He knew it would be better not to go back. Instead, he would circle in the darkness, within sight of those lights, within sound of those voices, but alone, unseen and undiminished. Yet he needed someone to see how well he could skate—one of his insubstantial friends. Suddenly, he felt his father's scorn of them—that prim, athletic gentleman. "Your friends," he had asked, "why are they all so fat?" But Robin turned and skated back to them.

They were heating some kind of concoction in an iron pot on the fire, and he smelled cinnamon and cloves as he skated up. He stopped sharply, with a grating sound, just outside the circle. They all turned, startled, and he saw Heather draw herself together, as though he had been about to run her down. In spite of her poise and her little red skirt, Robin knew suddenly that she could not skate. He held out his hand with an almost wolfish smile. "Come skate with me." She hesitated—"I'm waiting for some of this cider"—yet she gave him her hand, limp and warm inside a woolen glove. He reached for her other hand and crossed her arms over her skirt, pinioning her. They started off across the ice.

He had been right. Her skates stuttered and she pulled at his hands, pleading, "Hey, slow down!"

"I thought you could skate," he said, with delighted malice. He liked to feel her whole weight dragging from his hands. Oh, she was an exceptional girl!

Her little nose was very red, a sharp red beak, when she looked up at him and said, "You know I can't skate or do anything like that worth a damn." Then she tried to disengage her hands. But he pressed her warm woolen gloves firmly. "Come on, I'll show you how."

As they started off again, he half-dragging her on her chattering skates, he knew that she was growing angry. "Haven't you ever skated before?" he asked her. She staggered, clutched at his hands, and then, recovering herself, turned on him in fury. "Is this the kind of thing you take seriously?"

When he saw her face, gleaming with irritation, Robin felt a little cowed, as he would have felt ordinarily, meeting her on the street. Humbly, he apologized, and then released her and stepped back, reached for her hands, and brought her slowly toward him at the end of her stiff arms. So they skated, facing each other, his runners cutting long, gradual curves over which she scratched, stumbling, flailing, smelling strongly of damp wool; but now beginning to smile. "You'll teach me yet," she said, almost cheerfully. Finally she began to understand, and the scratches she made on the ice smoothed and lengthened. Once more he took her hands and crossed them over her skirt, and they skated together, slowly and solemnly.

"But this is fun!" she cried, shining up at him, her hair tumbled and bright under the dark fur of her hat.

"I could teach you anything, I always knew that," he said, and he swung her in a wide arc around the circle of lights. Then he put his hands on her waist and pushed her backward, feeling her hips heave under his fingers. "There, that's enough; let me go now," she said.

He felt as though he could have skated with her on the black ice all night. She was becoming gay and malleable as he guided her, slowly, along the edge of the river, where the rushes hung their frozen beards, farther and farther from the swarm of lights. She leaned away and struck out boldly now, and he praised her with the words his father had once used: "That's the gallant one! That's fine! That's really handsome!"

She smiled at him, a little startled, perhaps, by his enthusiasm, yet touched. Finally he knew it was time for her to go on alone, and he undid her clutching hands. Then he stood back and watched her, slowly, yet with grace, waver alone down the ice. He liked her long legs in scarlet stockings and her little red skirt, and he leaned forward and plunged after her.

When he took her hands again, casually, he knew he could have done anything with her; and they began to talk. She told him, with little tosses of her head and sidelong glances, about the work she was doing — "Oh, it's with a bunch of fakes" — allowing him, finally, to extract the fact that she was the head of a whole department. "But it's just the art book department; there are four or five others," she protested.

"I always knew you were talented," he said, for once mastering the exact degree of cynicism which made the compliment palatable.

"Oh you," she said, "what do you care about talent?"

"My goodness, I'm in the talent game," he said, knowing she would appreciate the opportunity.

"You and your old ladies and their needlepoint!"

"It's not all needlepoint. Yesterday I went out to Weston to see a really fine little Corot."

"Yes, and tomorrow it'll be Norman Rockwell."

"You've decided I'm the common man," he said. "That's the only space you have to fit me in."

"You've got too much money to be the common man," she declared.

He laughed. "That's what Lilly says. She maintains I was corrupted in the cradle."

Lilly's name was like a draft blowing between then; for a moment, Heather did not answer. Then she said, awkwardly, "I hear you've got a mighty fine son." He heard the accent of her childhood, country-Southern, in those words, the accent she had long ago laid aside.

"Yes, he's a big boy," he said, rather vacantly. He never knew what to say about the child.

"Lilly must be crazy about him."

"Oh, a little I guess," he admitted, shocked that she had understood so well.

She looked at him and smiled. "I hear she's been devoured, body and soul."

He started to reply on the same level, "You people are so cynical." They could have gone on forever, then. Instead, he looked down at the ice and waited.

"What is it?" she asked, her warm breath brushing his cheek.

He turned and gave her the benefit of the blank, lustrous look which, a little earlier, he had bestowed on his son. "I supposed the whole thing has been a little hard on my vanity," he said with a laugh.

She did not laugh with him. Instead, she clung more closely to him, and her warm, supple flesh was applied to his side, healingly, like a poultice. She was all one piece, from the point of her shoulder to her slender, muscled thigh, and he felt her all one piece, warm and healing, against his side. "You've had a hard time," she said, and he noticed that she did not sound in the least surprised.

He let himself go. "If I'd expected this in the beginning — but you know, she was so lively, so interested in everything. And then, it's not as though she was a girl when we married; and I thought, somehow when you're twenty-eight a baby doesn't pop into your mind, automatically, as soon as you see an available man."

She laughed at his "available," but her humor was full of kindness and she did not loosen her hold on his hands. "I guess it depends a little on the woman," she said.

"But she was so lively," he protested against her unspoken condescension. "I could hardly keep her in the house. That first year, she was in and out, up and down, traveling — " He wanted Heather to be enchanted by that, by the gaiety of the life Lilly had offered him. For the first time, he had slipped out of Boston, once a month at least, casually, with no more thought of the hole it was making in his life, in his routine, than if he had been going to Concord with his father. They had gone to New York, to Italy, and everywhere, even on Beacon Street, she had seemed perched, eager to be off.

He understood from Heather's silence that this was not what she wanted to hear; not his happiness, but his distress was charming her. He caught a glimpse, then, of the labyrinth she lived in, where every conversation offered a thread, a way through devious corridors, a justification. It seemed strange to him that his vague, uncertain sadness should be spun into a long, shining justification for a single bed in a studio apartment and an icebox full of orange halves and the other sides of English muffins. He began to feel a little stale, as though he had revealed too much. "After all," he said gloomily, "it's not as though I didn't want children."

"I've noticed the change in you, Robin," she said, "everyone has. These last two months, you've been like a hunted thing."

"Well, not hunted, so much. Just bored."

"No." With her hand on the key, she would force it to turn. "No, I understand what you've been going though. A sort of moral desolation. You see, I know because"—and she looked up at him, her lips shining—"because my mother had a baby when I was twelve years old. My whole life, my existence was canceled out, just like that. So I know what you're going through!"

As he looked at her glistening, waiting face, he felt that he knew every cranny of her life and could imagine, even, how on Sunday mornings she washed her stockings and then went out to buy a special sausage at the Italian market. Inside the shell of her shining face, he thought he could see the kernel: the sullen face of the child who had crouched under the organdy skirts of the dressing table. "I'm not sure you understand, really," he said.

"Why do you say that? I do! I've been through it myself." He knew that soon she would begin to get angry, but at that moment, she would have slept with him to prove that she understood.

The smell of cinnamon and cloves blew toward them on the wind, and Robin noticed the dark shapes of other skaters crossing in front of the fire. Suddenly, he wanted to be rid of her, and he pried loose her hands, gently, as he had done once before. "I'll race you," he said as he turned away, leaving her stranded, and he felt the wolfish pleasure he had felt in the beginning. He skated off quickly, forcing his way though the wind, and slashed a path straight to the edge of the fire. Then he turned and watched her coming slowly, pushing one foot in front of the other, swaying, her arms outstretched. As awkward, he thought, as a steel pole; and he smiled. She saw that, and tossed her head and turned away, staggering, clashing her runners. Anything to be off in the opposite direction!

Smiling, quite consoled, he stripped off his gloves and stretched out his hands to the fire.

The Way It Is Now

AUGUST NINTH
AT NATURAL BRIDGE

I**T WAS THE HABIT IN THAT FAMILY TO CELEBRATE** birthdays—all birthdays, the parents' as well as the children's—
not with parties and paper hats and the bounty of friends,
but with expeditions. For all of them, it was easier. To have
invited friends to the house would have been embarrassing
for the children; no one they knew could have avoided staring, or drinking out of the finger bowls. Their parents had
many friends, but they were the same people who had posed
beside them in their wedding photograph, and it seemed
tactless to acknowledge the years that had passed since that

first occasion, years that had disfigured everyone except the
central characters.

Each of the children was allowed to choose the historic
shrine or state park where he would spend his birthday. The
list of possibilities within a day's drive, although not long, was
surprisingly varied. There were the limestone caves, Horse,
Floyd Collins, and the Blue Grotto, which were patronized
for the most part by ten-year-old Tom, who liked melodrama
and fakery and admired the milk-white body of Floyd Collins,
displayed in a glass coffin in the cave that had killed him. Then
there was the marriage cabin of Abraham Lincoln's parents,
which none of them cared for anymore—tourists and school
groups had begun to go there—and, farther east, the new
federal lake and the park at Cumberland Gap. These were
equally favored by Shelby, the youngest, who had remarked
on his first visit to the concrete Roman powerhouse at the
lake, "If this isn't beautiful, nothing is." Finally there were the
horse farms, foreign-owned, corrupt and flourishing, which
Vivian had chosen for the last three years because they were
only an hour's drive from home, meaning there was no excuse
to spend the night.

The children chose independently, even unpredictably,
according to the yearly change in their characters; but their
parents, who for reasons of emotional economy only celebrated one of the two birthdays between them, always went
on August ninth to Natural Bridge. By the time Vivian was
sixteen, they had been to the bridge twelve times, and each
time the drive up into the hills was the same, the Singing Pines
Guest Lodge was the same; even the numbers on their rooms,
which they carried around all weekend on keys jangling in
their pockets, were never changed. The manager of the lodge
had no trouble remembering how the Lysons wanted things
done, but sometimes a new waitress, bringing in the cake
with the single candle, would ask whether it was Mr. or Mrs.
celebrating this time.

There was no reason to be afraid, and yet Vivian had been afraid for three years of the trip, as though each time she exposed more of herself by submitting to the routine. Yet it did not occur to her to find a reason for not going; her father would have been hurt, and she could never have stood that. He had a way of looking at her with silent reproach and despair that prevented her from acting on most of her impulses; he clearly knew what was best and besides, he adored her. (Her mother had used that word for it once when Vivian had not been expected to be listening. She had been embarrassed, yet ravished by the appropriateness of the choice, and she had used it ever after that to herself: adore, adoring. She could not quite believe, however, in the adjective, at least in terms of herself.)

Finally her mother tried to excuse her. "I don't expect you'll feel like going, this time," she said. "You must be sick of that place after all these years, and someday (your father won't recognize it) we are going to have to break the habit."

"You know I wouldn't miss the trip for anything," Vivian said sparsely. Her mother's attempts to spare her made her angry. After all, it was her life, the only life she had ever known, for she hardly counted her nightly forays into foreign territory. She was in love, and given to committing treacheries between eight o'clock and her father's midnight curfew. Still, that could hardly be called an alternative.

On the day of the expedition, the dew had dried by eight o'clock and the katydids were churning by nine. Vivian's father read out the forecast—"a sweater"—with satisfaction. The more difficulties, the merrier; they would take two thermoses of lemonade. He told the boys to wear shorts, and he would have advised Vivian as well if she had not already gone upstairs to put on a pair of stockings. The stockings were new and they had her name taped at the tops to distinguish them from her mother's.

After she had dressed, Vivian closed herself in the back-hall closet and telephoned Steve. The clatter of the office behind him bothered her; his life would go on agreeably enough while she was drawn up slowly into the hills. At the end, she said, "I love you," and he said, "Have a good time," although she had never had a good time or even known what it was until he came into her life. She hung up the telephone and went down to the kitchen, where her mother was putting fried chicken into a wicker basket. "You can still bow out if you want to," her mother said.

Before Vivian could answer, her father came in. "Are you ready?" he asked, giving Vivian the quick checking look he gave her every morning when, to discourage suspicion, she crawled out of bed and went in her blue robe to have breakfast with the family. "Darling, you'll be fine as soon as you get that first cool breath of mountain air," he added and kissed her, gentler than her mother, younger and fresher-smelling too, with the lemon lotion on his neck.

"Daddy, what do you mean, smelling so cool," she said, and tried to catch his reflection in the tin sandwich box.

"That's enough, Miss," her mother said, whisking wax papers.

It was ten minutes past the hour their father had set when they drove away from the house. The two boys were in the back seat and Vivian was alone in the middle. In front, Mrs. Lyson began to clean out her purse, wiping a film of powder off her compact and cigarette case. Mr. Lyson drove earnestly, his shoulders bridging the view. Vivian had to look across him to see the road, which passed at a certain distance from Steve's house. To miss a Saturday night with Steve and in the course to drive with her parents so close to his house — that was an abuse of her willingness to come and go in other people's cars, according to their wishes. Vivian was glad to work up a little indignation. Her face, in the rearview mirror, looked as bland as lard. She craned to see Steve's chimney but lost it in the trees. His room was on the ground floor with its own entrance, and whatever his parents suspected, they never interfered; his mother looked at Vivian shyly when they met in the kitchen late at night. In the front seat, Vivian's mother turned her head as though she, too, were looking for the house, and Vivian stared at her neck, prodding her to say, "So that's where you go all the time when you say you're at the movies."

In the back seat, Shelby began his singsong for ice cream. His fathered ignored him, while his mother scolded, "Ice cream at nine o'clock in the morning!" Knowing how it would end, Vivian began to look around for a Humpty Dumpty.

Her father saw it first and swerved in across a line of traffic. Without a word, he jumped out of the car and went up to the ice-cream window. The boys were busily deciding what flavors they wanted when he came back with five vanilla cones. "I can't get something different for everybody," he explained, getting into the car and handling the ice cream back. Then he settled down to eat his own. Mrs. Lyson wrapped hers in a handkerchief and proceeded daintily, her tongue as pink and pointed as a cat's. But Vivian felt suddenly carsick and slid her cone out the window. It would have passed unnoticed except for Shelby, who began to complain about the waste. Mr. Lyson turned all the way around to stare at Vivian. "Are you all right?" he asked with a frown.

"Yes, I'm all right. Of course I'm all right!" she exclaimed, and wondered if she was going to be able to survive.

Before long, the open fields began to give way to patches of woods, and on the rim of the smoky sky, the first hills stood up. They passed a sign that read, "Welcome! Blue Ridge Parkway," and their father ordered the windows to be rolled down. Mrs. Lyson had fallen asleep; she put her hand up to hold her hair but she did not open her eyes. She did not even stir when the car began to halt, hitch, and plunge from one possible picnic site to the next while the boys hung out of the back window to jeer at the traffic honking and stalling behind them.

"There's the place!" Shelby shouted, pointing to a public picnic table, and Vivian wondered why her father put up with suggestions. The just system according to which the family was run produced in him a fury of self-righteousness, yet in the end it was always he who decided. Vivian sometimes heard him announcing these decisions to her mother: Shelby needs a summer at camp to take that fat off, Tom should learn to talk more, Vivian is old enough to look a little older. Steve never had any conclusions to offer, and when Vivian asked him why he was doing or saying this or that, he stared at her as though she had become, before his eyes, some kind of furiously functioning machine. "This is where we are going to stop and I don't want to hear another word," her father announced as he swerved off the highway and parked beside what was surely the ugliest view in the last ten miles: a heap of gravel and, downhill, a souvenir stand. Mrs. Lyson woke up and reached for the picnic basket.

Half an hour later, she was still chanting. "Chicken leg? Hard-boiled egg?" although they had eaten all they could, sitting in the noonday sun while the grass around them bent in the queasy wind from passing cars. The boys blamed the place on their father and he grew grave and refused to eat until Vivian handed him a chicken thigh. He looked at her gratefully and proceeded to devour the thigh and a breast as well. Afterward, he took the boys down to the souvenir stand, warning them beforehand that there was no money for buying.

Mrs. Lyson spread a newspaper on the gravel heap and sat down for the first time, stretching out her short legs. "This heat reminds me of the summer I was carrying Tom," she said and waited for Vivian to show some interest, but Vivian went on staring steadfastly down the hill. Her mother continued anyway. "I was sick as a dog every morning from January to June, never missed a day, and then that friend of your father's, Billy Lanaham, had the nerve to say, 'I never saw you looking so beautiful.'"

"I guess he was trying to be nice."

Mrs. Lyson sighed. "I know you think I'm terrible; you're at the age when everything about sex is supposed to be beautiful. I suppose the race wouldn't continue otherwise. Here, don't let those sandwich papers blow everywhere."

Vivian chased one and brought it back. "I don't see what there is here to spoil. Daddy always chooses the ugliest place."

But her mother said sharply, "Your father has had a long drive," and Vivian knew her mother had used up her stock of disloyalty on the remark about Mr. Lanaham. Angered, she threw the picnic basket into the car. "Temper!" her mother cried in the trim way that killed love. Vivian was relieved to see the boys running back up the hill. They had bought a plaster figure of a child on a toilet, inscribed, "The Best View in the Blue Ridge." Mr. Lyson had only to look at it to laugh.

An hour later, they drove up to the Singing Pines Guest Lodge, and the boys cranked open the back window and dropped out. Vivian remembered years back when she had led the exodus through the back window. Now, halfway between the bandy-legged troop of her brothers and her parents' stately march, she walked toward the lodge, pulling her damp skirt away from the backs of her legs.

Through wide plate-glass windows, the afternoon sun was scorching the daisies on the lobby upholstery. In one corner, a leatherette bench burned red as a coal. The electric fire was turned on in the fieldstone fireplace in spite of the heat; promotion for the lodge stressed the cool mountain air.

Behind miniature wooden privies and Vermont maple syrup, Mr. Lewis, the manager, was bobbing his greetings. When Vivian took his hand, he breathed out his "Long time no see" with the stale, irreproachable smell of pine mouthwash, which had frightened her since she was a child. Mr. Lewis smelled eternal, like the grave.

"Hello," Vivian said and blushed, suddenly aware of every physical change she had accomplished since their last visit.

Mr. Lewis seemed to be measuring the thickness of her bare arms. Actually he had turned his attention to her parents and was asking the questions about health and enjoyment which Mr. Lyson loved to parry. "As well as can be expected for a man my age," he said, causing the manager to throw up his hands and Mrs. Lyson to smile. Meanwhile the boys had gone to the windows and were exclaiming in false voices, "Isn't it beautiful!" They were not mocking; they had borrowed as best they could grownup ways of admiring. Vivian looked out the windows once. Beyond the boxes of false flowers, nothing had changed. The pine forest, browning in the sun, lay like a mangy hide over the hills, and higher up, Natural Bridge, a lump of stone, hung suspended in the glare.

"She is too old to share a room with two great boys," Mrs. Lyson was droning behind her.

Vivian turned around quickly. "Mother, you know I don't mind. I can always undress in the bathroom."

Her mother looked at her curiously and then turned back to insist, "No, it just won't do." Behind her Mr. Lewis was rubbing his hands with embarrassment.

"But we've always had the same rooms," Mr. Lyson said gloomily.

"Times change." His wife was signaling with her eyes.

Vivian said, "Mother, will you please stop?" But her mother's chin had begun to tremble, and Vivian was given her own room.

The change ruined the day, dislocated their expectations: Vivian had a number on her key that no one had ever held before. They all trailed along to see her room, and Vivian was mortified at the sight of the great sacrificial double bed. The boys said it was beautiful.

"Everyone put on a bathing suit, we're going down to the lake," her father announced hollowly, as though over a megaphone. The boys streamed hooting out of Vivian's room, and Mrs. Lyson, with a submerged sigh, went to get her bathing cap, her towel, and her suntan lotion, useless precautions against the heat and the mud of the manmade pond.

"I'm not going," Vivian said suddenly, fixing her eyes on her mother's back.

Her father stared. "But you must be hot, after that drive."

"I'm more tired than hot, and I never have liked that mudhole," Vivian said recklessly, taking off her scarf and shaking out her hair.

Her father was struck to the heart. "You always said you loved the lake."

Mrs. Lyson had turned around and was once again signaling to her husband with her eyes. "I expect Vivian has a good reason," she said.

"It's not the reason you think it is," Vivian exclaimed. Her mother often called upon their common female frailty.

Mr. Lyson looked perplexed. "Well, of course if that's it —"

"I'll be down as soon as I put my suit on," Vivian told him. Her father came close and took her elbows in his hands. "What's bothering you, honey? You don't seem yourself."

His grip was deceptively gentle, and Vivian knew better than to pull back. He had held her by the hand, the elbow, or the shoulder ever since she was old enough to think about getting away. "Let go of me, Daddy," she pleaded, her arms limp in his grasp.

"You've been upset since the first day of summer. What's happening?" he asked.

"It's just that boy," Mrs. Lyson said harshly.

Mr. Lyson did not hear. Placing his hand on the back of Vivian's neck, he pressed her head down onto his shoulder; barely pressed, for her neck bent easily. He smelled as he always smelled of lemon lotion and dry-cleaned seersucker, and Vivian found herself shedding two luxuriant tears on his lapel, tears for the unkind way she had been treated that summer, for Steve's rude forcing and the shame and the soreness of her giving in. Her father patted her neck between hot folds of hair. "Now listen, I don't want you to worry." Mrs. Lyson went silently out of the room.

"It's so hard, Daddy!" Vivian sobbed.

"It's a hard time of life," he said, and took her off his shoulder. "Now you get into your suit and come on down. You'll feel better as soon as you get into the water."

When he had gone, Vivian changed into her black bathing suit. She stood in front of the mirror to pin up her hair and stretched her elbows up like wings. Her small breasts rose smoothly under the black elastic and she could not help admiring them, as well as her bird-thin legs. She had a boy's body still, without an extra inch of flesh, except for the frills. The memory of her mother's legs, laced with thick blue veins, disgusted her as though it was her mother's fault that she had become ugly and old.

She went down the hall and knocked on her parents' door but they had already gone; her mother had insisted on that, Vivian felt sure, to give her a last chance to withdraw. She went outside and hurried down the concrete path to the pond.

It lay at the bottom of the valley and evening shadows had already stretched halfway across it. In front of the changing house, white sand had been spread on the mud, and her family were lying there in a close huddle. Beyond them, a band of local boys lay shoulder to shoulder; Vivian could tell they were locals because they were wearing tight, bright-colored sateen trunks. They lifted their heads to stare at her as she minced down the steps, and she drew her towel more tightly around her shoulders.

Her father had also looked up. "Isn't that a new suit?" he called when she was still some distance away.

"I got it last week."

Her father stood up and stretched, lean and elegant in his short white trunks. "Last one in is a dirty monkey," he shouted and sprinted down the beach. Vivian watched him fall full-length into the water, casting up a curl of spray.

"Vivian's it," the boys shouted, running after him. Vivian folded herself neatly onto a towel.

Her mother seemed to be asleep. Now and then, however, her eyelids quivered a little. She lay in a heap with her knees drawn up, as though she had been struck down.

"Next year I'm going to arrange for you to spend the weekend with Aunt Pat," she said without opening her eyes.

"I don't know why you should do that. I enjoy this, in a way."

"I'm not thinking about you. Your brothers need some attention and they never get any when you're around."

"That's not my fault."

"Nobody's talking about fault. I thought you were so crazy about that boy with braces on his teeth. I thought you didn't want to miss a Saturday night with him." Her eyes were still closed and the lids quivered rhythmically.

Vivian stood up, and at once the stranger boys lifted their heads. "I'm going swimming," she said coldly. Her mother was always hurrying her, pushing her out of the way, as though she prevented something from being accomplished or enjoyed. She stalked self-consciously down to the water, sucking in her stomach and holding her breasts high. The boys' stares hung from her shoulders like a train.

The water was warm and thick and gravy-colored; she waded in to her knees, then bent and splashed herself. Her brothers and her father were already swimming out to the raft, and after a minute she slid into the water and began to backstroke after them. As she swam, she heard splashing behind her and knew the stranger boys had come in.

Lingering along toward the raft, she almost allowed them to catch up with her. There were three of them; their round heads bobbed in her wake. Mountain boys, they hardly knew how to swim, and they thrashed the water vigorously and then stopped to gasp for breath. Vivian floated on her back and watched them. They did not exist for her except as mirroring eyes. Behind, her brothers were calling from the raft, and she turned over at last and began to swim slowly toward them.

Her father reached down and pulled her up onto the raft. "Better late than never," he said grimly.

Vivian did not answer. She stretched out on her back and closed her eyes, listening to the rippling water. The stranger boys were still swimming toward the raft, but they stopped a few yards off and began to duck each other. Their gruff shouts made her smile.

Her father sat down beside her, showering her face with drops. He was watching her brothers absently as they took turns diving into the water. "All right, that's enough," he said after a while, and Vivian was surprised to hear how slack his voice had become. "We're going in, it's getting late," he told her.

Vivian opened her eyes and watched him stand up. For the first time, she was not embarrassed to look at him closely; she even noticed curls of dark hair pushing out from under the elastic edges of his trunks. "I'm staying out here awhile," she said abruptly.

"It's late, the sun's going down, you'll need to dry your hair before dinner."

"I'll be in after a while."

He stood poised over her and then, at the same moment, she closed her eyes and he dove into the water. The waves he made knocked the raft one or twice, and Vivian heard her brothers calling. She lay very still until the ripples had died down. Then she sat up to look.

The stranger boys were six feet from the raft and swimming slowly toward her. She sat looking at them cautiously, feeling a little chill as the last light slid out of the valley. When they were almost to the raft, she shivered and lay down, closing her eyes again tightly.

The raft lurched and she heard the thud of bare feet.

There was a moment's silence and then someone drawled, above her, "Come on up. Nice view from here." The two in the water giggled.

"Asleep or dead?" he asked, and stubbed her arm with his toe. Vivian sat up quickly.

"I was just going in," she said.

He was a tall stark boy, rake-ribbed, his blond hair plastered to his skull with water. "How come I haven't seen you out here before?" he asked. "You staying at the lodge?"

She stood up, so close to him that her knees brushed his. Startled, she pulled back. "I'm staying here with my family," she said hotly, as though he had challenged her. Now that she was level with his face, she saw that his eyes were blue, but very pale, a strange color she had never seen before.

"Visiting from the big city?" the boy said and at the same time he shot his arm around her waist. His hand came up under her other arm and his fingers grasped her breast and molded it.

She stared into his pale blue eyes, stared and stared, as though waiting to hear him deny what he was doing. Then she began to wrench herself away. She felt each blond hair on his arm as she took her back away. Finally she darted to the edge of the raft and dove in. Coming up with a mouthful of water, she began, choking and spluttering, to swim to shore. She expected to hear them swimming after her; erratic, kicking wildly, she drove in. When she felt mud under her feet, she looked back. They were sitting on the raft, crosslegged, chattering like monkeys.

She ran up the false sand beach and snatched her towel, which lay abandoned beside her family's hollows. She wrapped the towel tightly around her shoulders as she ran, and at the same time, she began to sob. She touched the place where the boy had touched her and felt the cold wet elastic. Her breast ached as though it had been bruised. Steve had touched her everywhere, but he had never left a trace; afterward, going over her body, she could never find a mark of what he had done. She wanted to get back to that: to wash and dry her hair and dress in her summer cotton and sit down to dinner with her parents who would not know what had happened to her. She imagined telling her father and taking shelter in his outrage, but she was afraid he would ask why she had stayed on the raft. She was afraid he would say she had invited the attack. She stopped sobbing at that. The day might come when she would want it—the muddy water and the boy on the raft and the bruised tingling in her breast. She shivered and clutched her arms, staring up at the stone bridge that still hung in sunlight. It seemed to her that she would never be safe again.

THE WEDDING

On the way to New Jersey, Clare said she felt like throwing up and because he had been putting up with her for eleven months, Tom told her to go ahead.

She rolled down her window and put her head out, and the warm wind tipped off her hat and rolled it on the floor.

"I can't, now," she said after a minute and rolled the window up. "It's gone." She sat looking disconsolate, her hands folded in her lap.

"Your hat's on the floor," Tom said, already sorry he hadn't had the grace to stop the car.

She leaned down with her familiar swooping gesture, so sweet, somehow, nearly saccharine, as though she were scooping fledglings out of their nest: her way with newspapers, flowers, and waste baskets, an enthusiasm out of all proportion which usually turned at once to acrimony or tears. She set the hat straight on her head, like a platter.

"Look in the mirror." He tilted the rearview mirror toward her, would have taken her shoulder and tilted her toward the mirror if he could have stopped the car. Already her sweetness had soured and she stared at him balefully. "You think I don't know how I look."

"You know and I care," he said, distracted by her harshness.

"You care," she announced, beginning her sermon, "because you're afraid I'll offend. . . ." He did not hear any more for a moment, his eyes fixed on a large white airlines billboard beside the highway. The painted plane, winging south, had sunlight along its wings, yellow as honey. "I wish I'd come in my nightgown," Clare was saying.

"That wouldn't have offended them," he said, trying his mild humor, and realized at the same time, as so often happened now, that what he was saying was true: she was so pretty, wrecked, so bruised and appetizing, like a slightly overripe peach.

She reached up, flattered, he didn't know by what, and settled her hat at an appropriate angle on her head. "I hate your uncle," she chanted, "I hate your aunt and your cousins, every one of them. I hate the bride most of all."

"She's not a bride yet."

"I wish I could put a curse on her."

"You used to like her." He couldn't remember how long ago that had been; his cousin's personality had faded for him, too, becoming The Bride as soon as Clare started to call her that. How strange, how maddening, even, that Clare's peculiar point of view should have begun to bleed into his mind.

He had held off, for a while; her doctor's diagnosis made her seem remote and nearly safe. But after a while, her weirdness, so pleasant, so charming at times, had seemed to dress up his plain life, turning the subway stanchions into calla lilies, the watch shops on Eighty-sixth Street into dens of carnal delight, and the dismal plodding course of life into a cavalry. He had to remind himself that she didn't know hot from cold (at her worst) or black from white in order to remember that everything else about her perceptions was unacceptable. Yet he often wondered what difference it made — black or white, the hat flat or angled on her head — and knew, at least for the moment, that it made all the difference in the world. When her hat was flat she looked insane, and it was that look, like the steely rasp of her voice, which no one who cared about her could bear.

"And I hate the bridegroom most of all," she said sullenly, comparing her thumbnails like stamps, side by side.

"You've never even met him."

"I know about him, though. I know what he thinks he's doing." She glared at Tom. "He thinks he's going to start all over again, just go back and start over fresh! He thinks he can just cross out what's already happened."

"I don't know what he thinks."

"I know!" she went on raptly. "I knew as soon as I saw his face!" (When? Tom wondered, and had to take a minute to be sure that Clare had never seen William Borden at all.) "He thinks he can make it that he wasn't married before, he thinks he can just make her disappear. Quite a magician!" she added with her heavy, dragging irony.

"Aunt Lucy said his first wife was impossible."

She laughed. "Who's possible, I'd like to know? Except you." She turned, grinning, and he felt cold and smiled.

"I do take good care of you, Clare."

She snorted. "And that out there is the garden spot of the world." She gestured at the stinking marshes. "They should lie in those ditches for their honeymoon," she went on thoughtfully.

"Clare, do me a favor, don't say any more till you meet him."

"I'll say enough then," she promised and sang the rest of the way, a droning little song he had never heard before: "Fiddledeedee, fiddledeedee, the fly has married the bumblebee."

That was what other people could never understand, Tom thought as the song drilled his patience: what it was like to go out with Clare into the world, without protection, never knowing what she might say or do or, which was worst of all, if she would say or do nothing, simply sitting with her gnomic smile, her chin in her hand, until the sane people around her went mad with effort, aping, wisecracking to break her silence.

Yet Tom had insisted on taking her to the wedding, against everyone's advice; had insisted out of a stubborn refusal to believe that she was really impossible—a refusal he had not even known was there, since he had spent the last eleven months shielding her from every possible group or strain. She had come out of the hospital as fragile as a blown eggshell, and it had never occurred to him before to put her to any kind of test. Yet he had leapt at the wedding. It was as though the smell of stephanotis might bring her back; for she had been glazed and strained at their own wedding, five years before (but not this bad, of course—he would have known) and the flurry of the proceedings had shot her whole into his arms.

Or was it darker than that, his little motivation? He did not like his aunt, who had brought him up as a charity case; he loathed his broad unwieldy uncle; and he had loved their daughter too much, years ago, and been laid bare. Now the occasion would have to be taken seriously. No one who was normal could quibble at that, any more than choke on the imported champagne or vomit up the black Russian caviar.

The gravel in the circular drive whispered under their tires, whispered under the tires of the big car in front of them and sang a little refrain; Tom remembered listening to that lullaby as a child, in a bedroom upstairs, with the headlights wheeling across the walls. The lights and the song had seemed to be life itself, always put off, unapproachable. From the top of the stairs, the grownups in the hall below had looked like big bouquets, a blossom breaking off here or there—a lady in bright colors. It seemed to be their fault that, lately, the colors had faded.

One of the gardener's sons was taking cars, but Tom waved him on and drove to the big lawn; he did not want to go inside just yet. The grass was soggy from rain, and he felt the car sink in and knew that next day the lawn would be hopelessly rutted. He had not thought to bring Clare's boots, and he jumped out of the car and went around to lift her over the mud; but she was already out, sinking before he could get to her to the edges of her white sandals. He tried to lift her up in his arms, but she laughed and fought free, running with squelching sounds across the grass to the drive. There she consented to wait while he knelt down and cleaned her shoes as best he could with his handkerchief.

They went in hand in hand. The big door was opened by Nelly, his friend from years before, and he was glad to see that Clare remembered her. They walked on through the green-and-gray living room, the walls banked with flowers, out through the French windows onto the terrace. There were many people gathered there, and Clare's smile was not specific as he introduced her, naming names clearly in the dim hope that she would remember the connections, the details she had once relished. Old Uncle John, the seafaring man with his gold-buttoned blazer and cap, who really could sail and really did know the tides and the winds and yet was a bulbous drunk who put his hand up the parlormaids' skirts. Old Winny, his wife, worn down by trying. Old everyone,

Tom realized; they had aged in the year since Clare had been sick, their faces smoothly seamed or powder-caked under the bright lash of the spring sun.

Tulips were leaning out from the borders along the lawn, and he took Clare there for a moment. He had a sense of her limited elasticity which came mainly from her voice, rising so quickly out of the clear registers into the hard grating cry, seagull-like, of her rages. She picked up a red tulip and crushed it quickly in her hand, but carefully, holding it out of sight behind her dress. "Pick me a flower," he said, loving her for the childish angry gesture. She picked him another, pinching off the stem so short that the tulip sat like a pair of tongues on the palm of her hand. "When are the real ones coming?" she asked anxiously, and he led her to the birdbath and the altar, banked with smilax and white lilac.

Looking back at the terrace, he saw the people gathered there—his friends, his family—like a solid wall.

"What do you think of leaving now, we could drive out to the real country," he muttered, not expecting her to reply.

"But we must see the bride!" she cried, faint and far. "It wouldn't be right to leave without seeing the bride!"

He lost her after that, for a moment, having fallen into conversation with a friend he had not seen since college—not because he was absorbed in what the fellow was saying but because he saw in the smooth declining face the signs of time passing which he had not yet noticed in his own.

Her absence was like a cold breeze; he turned sharply. Aunt Alice, profound in her sense of duty, nodded gravely toward the house. Inside, Nelly, at the door, pointed him toward the downstairs bathroom and he knew from her expression that nothing had gone wrong yet. He stood by the door, his hand on the golden handle, and heard the toilet flush twice inside.

He opened it cautiously. Clare, her skirts up over her arms, stared at him with fury. "Can't I even—?"

He closed the door and waited. After another interval, afraid that someone was coming, he went quickly in. She was standing in front of the mirror.

"You have no business in here!" she called, her eyes on his reflection.

"Come on out. This service is beginning."

"But I'm pleading," she said.

"Pleading?"

"Bleeding," she pouted. "I didn't know it was time."

He knew from experience where Aunt Alice kept the pads and handed one to her, delicately, in its paper wrapping. He could not look at her, their five years together tearing across in the face of her disappointment; the lost months, the lost years, finally the lost child all washed away on currents of clear bright blood. "Is your dress all right?"

She turned around for him to see, but he could not get his eyes above her ankles, where two sharp bones pointed out, prominent as ears.

Aunt Alice would take her upstairs, he told himself as he led her out of the bathroom. Aunt Alice would give her something to make her sleep and have Nelly sit with her till arrangements could be made. Aunt Alice would touch his shoulder and murmur something that would, in spite of his ironies, move and console him. The family would fold around him if he could acknowledge his need. It was unthinkable. He took Clare to the terrace, and because the company had moved out to the smilax altar, they came along behind, conspicuously, scuttling ahead of the bridal procession.

Catching Clare's waist, he turned her toward the people coming, remembering how she had loved the pomp and display. The little flower girls, his young cousins, had daisies in their hair and tripped along in agonies of shyness. Behind, two older girls, bowed with large meanings, wore hats whose long streamers floated on the breeze. He was amazed by all their feet, light and quick as petals, and wondered what they

felt or if they felt at all. Behind, the real people came march-
ing stiffly, and he touched Clare's waist insistently. But her
face was turned, she was nodding and smiling, and he felt her
hair touch his shoulder.

"The bride," he pleaded in her ear, for she was nodding at
the row of tulips.

She turned, then; he felt her eyes align with his, felt her
rigidity as she watched that other girl in white. Cousin Lucy
was pretty that day, with the abashed radiance of a flickering
light; he had always loved her dovelike uncertainties and was
glad to see that her wedding had not reassured her. The flowers in her hands were shaking violently and she clung to her
father's arm (he was drunk, and walked mincingly) as though
it were a barrier against the flood. She did not dare move her
eyes from the minister's face, drinking his words desperately.

The man, William Borden, detached himself from the
crowd and came up front; Tom watched him carefully. He
was familiar, in his uniform and his careful self-control; it was
difficult to see beyond the reassuring details. Strong staff to
weak woman, the boy had laid aside his youth and looked
like a seamless grandfather. All his experience was gathered
in his round pale face: a lamp to the future. Tom felt a laugh
like an itch and at the same time heard Clare laughing; softly,
sweetly, like a dinner bell. He felt the quivers in her side and
held her fiercely, pressing down the laughter with his arm.
Fortunately the minister was possessed of a strong voice, and
the gentle even laughter was drowned. It was not so easy
to disguise the tears that ran smoothly down her cheek; the
other eye as far as he could tell was dry.

Someone behind him pressed a handkerchief into his
hand; he felt the monogram under his thumb.

At last music rang out from somewhere—trumpeters con-
cealed in the honeysuckle—and the pair marched off to the
house. The group broke up in merriment, and Tom thought
he heard the same hoarse hysterical cackle in their voices that

he had been afraid to hear in Clare's. She was holding the handkerchief to her nose, like a child asked to blow. He took it away and put it in his pocket.

A waiter came to them first of all, and Clare took two glasses of champagne.

"Put that down while you drink the first one," he advised her, but she drank one quickly and poured the other in the tulips.

It was easier, now, to disguise what she was doing; people were moving around freely, talking loudly, drinking, already losing track of what was going on. A tall white wedding cake had made its appearance, and the pair was coming out to cut it with a sword. Clare clapped her hands when she saw the shining blade, drawn with due reverence from its socket. "Oh, he has a sword!" she whispered. The cake was passed on little china plates Tom remembered from birthday parties. A pink sugar rose lay on his slice and he presented it to Clare and watched her gulp it in one large bite. "I'm hungry," she said, "get me another slice!" While he went quickly to get another, the toasting began.

He saw what she was doing in Willy Morris's eyes as Willy handed him another slice of cake; Willy Morris, who had served cake at birthday parties and had a perfected discreet ambivalent smile. But now his flat dark eyes were full of reflections as he looked over Tom's head, back toward the terrace. Tom did not turn until he had taken a silver fork and felt its coolness in his hand; by then it was too late and he turned, slowly, into the sound of Clare's raised voice.

She was standing on a wicker chair, the seat wavering under her feet, and Tom wondered who in the world had hoisted her up there.

She raised her empty champagne glass in one hand, her eyes on the clouds, her voice floating out in ribbons. "We have come here today to celebrate the feast of marriage," she was singing. People directly beneath her were watching cautiously, and as she continued, the ones who were farther away turned toward her until finally the whole group on the terrace was facing her, a wheel with her face at the hub.

"And yet the thing is, if we are to be honest and celebrate this thing the way it should be celebrated, the past has to be brought in; I mean, you can't sing to the flower without including the bud and stem and the root, even the mud around it, too. I want to make a toast to William, or should I say Bill, whom I don't really know at all: The Bridegroom." Before they could interrupt her with polite enthusiasm, before Tom could believe his relief, she was going on. "And to his first bride who is here today though nameless. To her hopes and her struggles and her tears and her despair. The stem must be recognized. And to the three children who are here today, too, although nobody knows their names. Children are the roots. Ignore the roots and what do you have? An empty ceremony. To William's children! May they grow up in bliss and sadness and come in the end to speak those things which are not spoken. To them!" She raised her glass and, realizing that it was dry, lost her lilt and hesitated; finally reached down and took the glass from someone's hand and drank it slowly. She was not in the midst of silence for more than ten seconds; then voices went up around her, "To Bill!" and every glass was raised to drown what she had said.

Tom felt his aunt at his shoulder before she spoke.

"Tom, you must. . . ."

"I know."

He felt her firm pressure, like a clamp, on his arm.

"If you need any help—"

"I won't need any, Aunt Alice. She's said what she came to say."

He left her to consider whether he had known about it from the beginning; the glitter of this little triumph faded as he began to make his way to Clare.

She was still on her chair, although everyone had moved

off and left her poised like a garden ornament. He touched her knee. "Come on."

She looked down at him, dazed, smiling, her eyes so bright with tears he thought at first she had been laughing.

"Help me down," she said, dropping the glass into the grass and then stretching out both hands to be taken.

"We'll start back now and stop on the way to eat. There's a place off the parkway. . . . It has a garden."

"Too cold for gardens," she murmured as she followed him across the terrace. He knew that certain people were staring and so raised his head, smiling, wearing their concern like a crown.

It was worth letting her have her way to find her, afterward, so pliant; he lifted her in his arms across the muddy lawn and placed her in the car and fastened the seat belt across her lap, feeling the warm body which was what had first drawn him to her: her limitless pliancy. Going around, getting in and starting the motor, he was driven by the sight of her profile, set, pale, and calm, a disobedient child, a hopelessly naughty child who tells the truth against all reason. He reached over to pat her and let his hand slide up her arm, cool and pearly, to the edge of her embroidered sleeve. "Clare, you really told them."

She looked at him thoughtfully. "I knew him for what he was from the time we met him at Malibu."

"When?"

"He took me on his lap there on the terrace and kissed my neck—a white kiss—and said he wanted to tell me about his troubles. Hypocrite, I said, it won't get you anywhere."

"I don't remember," Tom said dully, dropping his hand from her arm.

She went on for a little. He watched the road and the even woods that stretched far enough on each side to hide the houses; a limitless sense of open country was imposed by that half acre of spindly trees. The relief of money, its precious illusions. He thought of moving Clare out here, to a brick fortress or a Normandy château where her eccentricity could atrophy slowly and become, like topiary hedges, heated dog runs, and mahogany stables, simply another attribute of the rich. But he would still have to face her in the morning over coffee or at night when he tried to sleep through her whistlings and moaning — the nightmares that no medication had been able to erase.

Still talking, she moved closer to him and rubbed against his side, her set, rapt face discounting everything she was saying, and her warm arm, hot almost, fresh from the fiery oven, still the pale arm of a little girl who is allowed to make mistakes.

"I want to go to bed with you," she said, hot-eyed.

"Look at me, first." But she wouldn't, her eyes were fixed on the trees.

He wondered who she thought he was and whether he could persuade her to take her tranquilizers; he had them in his pocket and it was only a question of stopping somewhere for a cup of water. Usually he could persuade her to swallow them, especially when he held her in his arms and kissed her first, sliding the pills into her mouth after the kisses, sliding the edge of the paper cup between her lips and then kissing her again, for drinking.

He began to look for a place to stop to get the water. Before the throughway, he remembered, there was a diner. She was against him all the time, her thigh beside his thigh, and in the midst of worrying about her and thinking of the pills, he knew she had sensed his excitement. Bruised, rapt, and silent, she never knew who he was, in bed; her frenzies were mechanical; and yet he wanted her, in spite or because. . . . Because, because. . . . It rang in his head, for a moment, that she was mad and he was hopeless; but then he felt the smooth line of her leg, pressing though her filmy skirt, and saw the silver diner shining like a lost star through the trees.

RACHEL'S ISLAND

Since the beginning of hot weather, Jake had been saving the snapshot that his wife's sister had enclosed in her first letter from Nantucket. The snapshot was overexposed, and the summer house it showed seemed to rise through mists, fragilely anchored to the dunes by bayberry and scrub pine. To Jake, it seemed a clapboard castle, straining against the wind. He kept the snapshot under the socks in his bureau drawer, an unplayed card in the long hand of the summer.

Finally in August he wrote her that he was coming. By then, he was worn as thin as an old dime. The heat had done it, and the tedium of finishing his second novel in the midst of summer parties, summer outings, all set to his wife's fretful drone. Seallike, she surfaced now and then in the middle of his life, streaming complaints. My life is nothing, she would say; give me a child or I will die. I will leave my job, I will take a lover, I will claim the same rights as you. Usually she sank down again almost at once; Jake had potent ways of reassuring her. That August, she stayed above water a long time.

Yet when he told her that he was going to Nantucket, she did not protest. Their old rules still held and she told him with bitter objectivity, "Go, it'll do you good." He had not really decided to go, and he was irritated with Ann for reacting so predictably. He left the next morning on the bus for Woods Hole.

During the trip, his preoccupations paid out behind him, growing more tenuous as the city fell away. He sat by a window and watched the landscape flatten and bleach as they approached the ocean. After a while, the old man in the seat across the aisle leaned over and began to talk. He said that he had wanted to go to California since he was eight years old, and now he knew he would never go. Jake had nothing comparable to offer, and on an impulse, he told the old man he was in love. "With someone who don't love you," the old man shrewdly remarked, and after that, Jake sat peacefully under a gentle rain of advice.

The old man did not get off the bus at Woods Hole, and Jake had to face the ferry trip alone. It was beginning to rain, a sharp penetrating drizzle, and Jake regretted the trouble he was taking. It seemed to him suddenly that his sister-in-law was not likely to appreciate his visit, and he felt rejected beforehand, forlorn. The island, as the ferry approached it, looked bleak and unwelcoming. Jake had some difficulty finding a taxi, but at last the arrangement was made and he was driven, in the gathering dusk, down an empty highway. It was a desolate place in the failing light. Scrub growth covered the sand like a thick tight hide and the wind poured across from the ocean to the bay without a tree or a hill to stop it.

At last they turned onto a sand track and approached the house. It was much smaller than Jake had expected, with a shabby, summer-cottage air; the gray paint was peeling and the windows rattled in the evening wind. His sister-in-law came out onto the porch with the baby at her hip. She looked like a farm woman, Jake thought, with her coarse dark hair and her skirt wind-whipped around her. "Here you are," she said.

There was sand in the front hall and, on the stair landing, a wine bottle stuck full of reeds. Genteel poverty, Jake thought, prodding the thin mattress in his room. Except for the yellow jug on the table, it could have been the room where he had grown up: bald, bare, uncomplained-of, a room where nothing could happen. He took his typewriter out of the case and placed it on the table. Then he went downstairs. His sister-in-law had laid out a plate of cold chicken and a bottle of pickles; she walked up and down while he ate, jiggling the fretful baby. "He's colicky," she said.

During the night, Jake was wakened by a burst of rain shattering on the tree outside his window. A little later, the baby started to cry. The storm had had a certain natural grandeur, but the child's wail was another thing altogether, galling as a dripping tap. Jake tossed irritably. After a long time, he heard his sister-in-law go in, but the crying continued, winded and mechanical. At last she began to carry the baby up and down. The floorboards creaked as she placed her feet, solidly, calmly, with only a pretense of stealth, as though, Jake thought, she were stalking a sure prey. His sleep was her prey; she could not fail to know that. She could keep him awake until morning by tramping up and down. He had hardly noticed her before, she seemed so plain and neutral, but now when he sat up to pound on the wall, his fist fell back as though she had pressed her face, moon-smooth, unperturbable, through that section of matchboard. It was not her house, it was rented with her husband's money, she had no power to incorporate its elements. Thin light patched the windows, scoured the room of shadows, and still she walked. Below the bluff, the sea gasped and subsided and gulls clanged up and down the shore. At six, Jake went to sleep, his head under her feet.

Four hours later, he stumbled downstairs. The house was empty, the doors set open to the morning sun. Rachel's breakfast dishes, in the drainer, were already dry, and the baby's bib was pasted to the back of a chair. Jake made himself some instant coffee; it was very bitter, and he could not find the bread. It began to be clear to him that Rachel did not want him to stay.

Hurrying out of the house, he found a path along the bluff through the bayberry bushes. Presently, he looked down on her encampment: a blue towel and the baby's basket in the middle of the long empty beach. Leaving the path, he slid straight down the dune, filling his shoes with sand.

She was lying on her back with her hands clasped on her stomach. Long, gaunt, stone-colored in the clear morning light, she reminded him of the recumbent figures on crusaders' tombs. As his shadow fell over her, she opened her eyes. "Did you find something to eat?" She closed her eyes again without waiting for him to answer.

"As a matter of fact, I couldn't find the bread, or anything else much." He looked down at her defiantly. She was the other side of desire for him, with her knobbed shoulders and her raw working hands. He liked smallness and softness in women, and a ready response.

"I'm sorry," she said. "I meant to go to the store yesterday."

Jake sat down beside her and drew up his knees. The sand was damp from the night's rain and he felt uncomfortable and possibly ludicrous, sitting there in his city clothes. "I wish you'd told me not to come," he said.

"There's plenty of room."

"Maybe, but you don't want me."

"Oh, Jake!" She laughed. "Look, you're welcome to stay. I don't play hostess, that's all."

"I have the feeling I bother you."

"It would take a lot to bother me, right now."

The baby stirred and made a rasping sound. Jake glanced at the bald head, gleaming in the shade of the cot's canopy. "Does he cry every night?"

"No," Rachel said, sitting up and undoing the strap of her bathing suit. "Turn around."

Jake did not understand for a moment, and then he swiveled around in the sand. The baby began to cry and stopped abruptly.

"I don't want you to talk to me about Ann," Rachel said, as though he had already started.

Jake could hear the baby sucking. It was a strong sound, like water running down a drain. "I have no intention of talking about Ann."

"She's my sister and I love her, but I can't take on her problems."

"You might wonder why she's so upset."

"I expect she has a reason."

Jake turned around. "Look, she knew when she married me what it was going to be like." He stopped, staring at Rachel's breast, flattened by the baby's face.

"I know you make your own rules," she said.

Jake flailed around again. "Let's stop talking this way."

"All right."

Her smugness irritated him more than the hostility he thought he sensed behind it. He stood up, careful to keep his back turned to her. "I'm going up to the house, I have some work to do." At the bluff path, he realized she was not going to call him back.

He sat on the porch for the rest of the morning, going

over the first two chapters of his novel. There were many changes to be made and his thick-nibbed pen wore holes in the onionskin. Now and then he looked up. Finally, when she did not appear, he began to count, by twenties and then by tens and then by ones; the numbers drummed in his head while he read the manuscript. He had begun to count during the afternoons he had spent on the flowered window seat in the house where he had grown up. There had been twenty red roses in each row on the material, not counting the first and last roses, which were severed by the seams; he had never been able to decide whether to include those halves in the total he arrived at every afternoon.

At last Rachel came up the path with her paraphernalia. Jake did not look up, although the typed page faded in front of his eyes. As she came closer, he saw, without raising his eyes, the white line at her thigh where her suit had ridden up. "Do you like dusty miller?" she asked.

He looked up. She was holding out a small bunch of gray leaves. He touched them; they were sapless, pliable.

Smiling, she took the leaves away and put them in his room. He saw them in the yellow jug when he went up before lunch.

He knew then that he could stay. He had been dreading the trip back, and he looked gratefully at the dusty miller. He thought it was the nicest thing his sister-in-law had ever done, and in the course of comparisons, he remembered a girl he had known at college who had brought flowers—daisies, bachelor's buttons—to put beside his double-decker bed.

When he went downstairs, Rachel was fixing sandwiches. She had tied a ruffled apron over her bathing suit, which gave her an oddly coquettish air. Jake wanted to thank her for the dusty miller, but she seemed preoccupied.

They ate lunch together almost without speaking. Rachel's whole attention was absorbed in spooning mashed food into the baby. He pushed it out with his tongue and smeared it with both hands on his cheeks; as far as Jake could see, he did not swallow anything. "He certainly enjoys that," he said.

"It feels good, mashed."

"Isn't it because he doesn't have any teeth?"

"I guess that is the reason. Have you tried it?" With a smile that would have been coy in another woman, she held out the tiny tin spoon. Jake opened his mouth and she pushed in a mound, tasteless and soft as butter.

"I don't know," he said, confused, almost embarrassed. "I don't think I like it."

"That's all right," she said.

After lunch, she took the baby upstairs without a word to Jake about the afternoon. She seemed to expect him to work all the time. Presently he went to the stairs and called up, "Can I borrow your car?" She answered faintly, as though from the top of a tower, "Yes, go ahead." He had meant to ask her to join him but then he remembered the baby and its needs. He did not intend to drive that functioning breast along the public highway.

All afternoon, he rode the sandy lanes, skirting the bluff and the ocean. It was the kind of country he liked, dun-colored, flat, unpicturesque, and it reminded him of the cold marshes in France where he had spent two months finishing his first novel. He had always been happiest alone, free even of the demands of a beautiful landscape. Yet as he drove, he could not shake off a peculiar fusty forlornness, a self-pitying ache that seemed at once familiar and reprehensible, and he remembered the dusty roses on the window seat at home. His mother had not liked to know that he had spent the afternoon waiting for her, and so when he finally saw her coming, he would run to his room and pull down an armload of toys. Still she had often guessed that he had been counting the roses, and when he sat over his supper, his face reflecting her pallor and annoyance, she would scold, "Stop moping! What's the matter with you?" Later, when she washed her face, she scrubbed at that same expression, the desolate look of a woman abandoned and hopeless, a woman she could not bear.

For the next hour, he drove without thinking. The car fitted him closely, sweet with the smell of Rachel's things. There was a can of baby powder on the back seat, and an anonymous saturated cloth. Jake felt as though he were sitting inside her skin. He no longer noticed the threatening pastures, lined at the edge with gray sea and sky.

Driving back, he saw lights shining from the windows. The house, fully lighted, seemed to sail the dunes, like a great liner seen far out at sea. He approached it cautiously. Inside the front door, he smelled roasting beef and realized that for the first time he was going to be treated like a guest. He looked into the kitchen, where Rachel was standing beside the stove. She was wearing a dark dress and her hair was unpinned; it fell over her shoulders, limp as seaweed and with, Jake imagined, a brackish smell. "Did you have a good time?" she asked, glancing around.

"Very nice. I drove. . . ." He began to describe it to her, embroidering a little.

She was stirring something in a big tin pot. "I'm making spinach soup," she said, adding hastily, "It's mostly cream and sherry. And then there's roast beef—" she threw open the oven door—"and mashed potatoes and peas."

"What happened?"

"Oh, I took a nap this afternoon. I've been tired, with the baby."

"I thought you didn't like me," he said recklessly.

"Well, in New York . . . but here, you look as though you're starving."

"Hardly," he said uncomfortably. But he sat down at the table and tucked his napkin in.

All during the meal, she prattled happily and Jake watched her with surprise. She was pretty when she was flushed, and her body, which had looked so stark in a bath-

ing suit, took on a little softness from her dress. She seemed
to be flashing at him with her bright pale eyes and her big
teeth, set in her mouth like posts. He wondered what she was
thinking, what she was planning, and why she had hidden
the baby away.

"When do you have to feed the baby again?" he asked.

"Not until morning, if I'm lucky." She was heaping pink
ice cream on his plate and as she leaned down, her long hair
brushed his face.

He looked up at her and smiled. "Ice cream, too?"

"Yes, and chocolate sauce."

Jake dug a channel for the sauce and reminded himself,
quite calmly, that he had never made love to an independent
woman. She would be too proud to load him with her feelings;
she would remain, always, a little withdrawn. The family life
they shared would be more interesting after this—he imagined
glancing at her wryly over the Christmas turkey. They would
have made a secret pact against the ordinary strenuousness of
that life, against the gaping emotions, the endless demands.
He stared at her narrow legs as she went to get the coffee and
wished she had a little more flesh.

And then she went upstairs without saying a word. Jake
thought she might have gone to undress; it would suit her
to forgo the preliminaries. Time passed and he resisted the
urge to count by scrambling numbers in his head. Finally he
realized that she was not coming back. He got up and went
out onto the porch.

Even there, he was surrounded by her. A board creaked
somewhere, a shade slapped, and he thought he heard a
remorseless sucking. He went out onto the grass, preferring
the anonymous crepitation of the trees. The dew had fallen
and his sneakers were quickly soaked. He tried to believe that
she would come to him later and turned over images he knew
did not fit. She would not appear in tears to complain about
her husband, she would not lie in languorous positions on the

broken rattan couch. It began to be impossible to imagine her coming at all.

At last he knew that she had gone to sleep without him. Cold with resentment, he sat a little longer on the windy porch. He imagined her asleep, snuggling into her pillow, her dry lips parted by the tip of her tongue. At that, his anger drained away as though she had chided him—"Foolish! Foolish!"—as his mother used to chide, with equal pleasure and annoyance, when he plunged into her bed on Sunday mornings.

He walked upstairs on tiptoe and undressed stealthily. The dusty miller in the yellow jug amazed him with its false implications and he crushed a leaf between his fingers.

Next morning, he woke earlier than he had in years. Sunlight marked squares on the wall and the curtains, wind-lifted, hung suspended. Rachel was already up; he heard her in the baby's room. After a while, she passed his door and glanced in. "Awake?" she asked, surprised.

He sat up in bed and smiled.

"We're going to the beach. Do you want to come?"

"Yes!"

She shook her head. "What's got into you?" and hurried away before he could reply.

Ten minutes later, he met her on the porch and they went down the bluff path together, the baby swinging in his cot between them. At the beach, Rachel lay down exactly as she had before, her hands folded on her flat stomach. Jake stared at her. She was luminous, as though particles of light clung to the small hairs on her arms and legs. At last he stripped off his shirt and stretched out beside her. The air had been cleared, nothing they said or did would have the usual connotations. The plainness of the situation amazed Jake: here was his arm, here was hers, here were his expectations, clearly labeled, and hers were as recognizable. The solemn rotating demands of his life had moved off and hung in the middle distance, whir-ring, like planets. Meanwhile the baby dozed in his basket and the morning sun grew warm. Jake had brought a book but he did not open it; he lay touching the baby's basket on one side and Rachel's towel on the other. Far away, he heard the shore birds peeping; their cries merged with the baby's wakening cry. Finally he slept.

When he woke, Rachel was looking at him. "It's almost noon. Don't you have to do some work?"

He sat up, dazed. "I guess I can miss a morning."

"I don't mean to seduce you away from your work," she said seriously. "After all, that's what you came here for."

"I'll get started this afternoon," he promised.

After lunch, he brought his typewriter down to the porch. The wind stirred his papers and whirled them over the railing; Rachel helped him collect stones. The green and gray stones, sparkling with mica, held his attention on the pages, but when he heard her drive away, he gave up and spent the rest of the afternoon dozing and watching. Returning with a bag of groceries, she glanced at the papers and he thought she could tell from the position of the stones that he had not been working. He wanted to tell her that it did not matter, but he was afraid of destroying the excuse for his visit. Over supper, he talked about his work and she listened, vaguely, yet satisfied as though this was what she expected.

The next morning, he woke at seven and hurried downstairs to have breakfast with her and the baby. Everything they ate seemed predigested: the soft-boiled eggs, the liquid cereal, the white bread full of airy holes. The food slipped down his throat as easily as water and he knew that he, too, would soon be gaining weight. After breakfast, he put on his bathing trunks and followed her down to the beach. Since she did not object or even notice, he wore the trunks all day, even at lunch, spilling jelly and junket on his chest. That night, he put on a shirt and she let down her hair and they sat in the circles of light cast by the wine-bottle lamps. When the wind stirred a branch or when the foghorn moaned, he would go to the screen door; big moths were pasted there, feeling for the light. He too was at the source. From time to time, he had looked forward in his life and imagined the tangled objectives of middle age, but he had never before gone back, into the warm recesses before expectation or disappointment, and he felt as he had felt once a momentary certainty. "Spotted spiders, get thee hence," Rachel sang, rocking the dozing baby on her knee.

During the day, she had seemed either perplexed and silent or animated by a strange false glee, but now, Jake thought, she had settled. She had become what she had been before he arrived: a quiet presence, a floating shadow. Her wavering voice drifted up to him next morning when he lay watching the sunlight on the wall, and later, in the early afternoon, when he heard her humming in the silent house. "Dusty was the kiss," she sang, making peanut-butter sandwiches for their snack, "dusty was the silver, dusty was the kiss that she gave the dusty miller."

On the fifth day, it grew hot; the sun burned off the haze before eleven and at the beach, Jake turned over on his face. "Shall I do your back?" Rachel asked. It did not seem necessary to answer. Her hands worked across his shoulders, rubbing in the suntan lotion, and the touch which should have been merely sexual, seemed instead magical, caretaking, firm. After lunch that day, he watched her nurse the baby.

Milk sprang in a three-pronged fountain from her free breast, sank in drops onto the sand, and disappeared. She did not seem to notice the loss, her head bent over the baby, her shoulders hunched around him. Jake wanted to tell her that he had never imagined such bounty, he wanted to make her raise her face and stare, but he was afraid of arousing her smile. He reached out and caught one warm drop in his palm.

To stay, to catch what came, even to lie in wait, calmly, with the hidden assurance that in time all things would come. . . . He stretched himself on the sand like a cat beside a fire.

She was silent, she was withdrawn, the baby took everything, yet he felt her warmth lap over him, in wave after wave, until he was submerged, half drowned in her element.

That afternoon, he heard her sweeping the porch and came to take the broom out of her hands. She was looking tired and he told her to go and lie down, but she did not let go of the broom. "It's just one of my jobs," she said.

"Let me do it." He tried to take the handle but she held it firmly.

"You'll spoil me," she said. "I won't be able to get along without you, and you really ought to leave today or tomorrow."

He stepped back and she began to sweep again, with long strokes that grazed his bare feet.

"I don't want to go," he said.

She laughed. "You've liked it here, haven't you? I didn't expect it."

"Why should I go?"

"David is coming tomorrow."

"Can't we both be here?"

"He doesn't like guests."

"Guests!" he piped shrilly.

She laughed again. "That's what you've become, isn't it? Besides," she added seriously, "Ann will want you back."

"To hell with that!"

"Oh," she said, "you are stubborn, you really are stubborn, aren't you?"

The familiar injustice of her humor stopped his mouth. He knew what to expect if he kept on: the slight, gratified smile, the wheedling cruelty. "What time is the next ferry?" he asked.

"Six o'clock," she told him, surprised.

The rest of the afternoon lay between them like a bar. He knew that in some small way she was regretting his departure, and he sat in his bedroom grimly, waiting for the time. Next door, she was humming as she folded a stack of diapers. He got up once and went as far as his door, but the hall floor rose up against his feet. She passed while he stood there, walking silently, her face set forward like the carving on a prow.

At five-thirty, she went out and started the car. He heard the motor and came down with his suitcase. It seemed the last indignity that she had brought the baby, lying in a roll of cloth on the back seat.

The ferry left at the time when they should have been sitting down to dinner. "You can get something on board," she said as he climbed out of the car. "I won't stay to see you off, I want to get back to feed the baby."

"That child is going to be a monster when he grows up."

"I hope so," she said.

She had laid her hand on the edge of the window and he noticed, as he had at the beginning, that her knuckles were big and red. "Goodbye," she said softly, and he understood that now he could kiss her. He stepped back. She started the car and drove rapidly away.

On the ferry, he went to the bow, bracing himself against the salt wind. As the island fell away, tears came to his eyes, and he wiped his nose on his sleeve. "Cold!" a man said, passing. "Better get inside." As Jake turned to obey, he wondered why he was usually given advice and consideration, but nothing substantial, nothing with a taste. He remembered Rachel's bounty painfully. If he could have stayed on, quietly, never asking for more—but he remembered the roses on the window seat and the dusty forlornness of his need. It was a relief to get away from all that. He marched down the stairs to the saloon and looked around for the coffee machine. The paper cup was hot and he nursed it carefully, hoarding its warmth between his hands and putting off the time when he would have to taste it—coffee, only coffee, and thin and bitter at that.

Transgressions

APRICOTS

That June Caroline's apricot tree finally bore fruit. In the six years she'd lived in the house behind the tree, frost had nipped its buds every April and only a few dwarfed apricots had hung on the branches. Neighbors said the apricot was not native to northern New Mexico but came as seedlings in the saddlebags of the Spanish conquest; over the centuries they had not adapted to the harsh climate but neither had they died. All along Caroline's dirt road, dim conical shapes stood out in winter and, in a rare spring, were thickly hung with white blossoms and bees.

Living alone after a lifetime of living with other people granted Caroline time and leisure that had mystified and depressed her at first—where were the faces that used to surround her kitchen table, where were the feet that had pounded on her stairs? —but that lately had seemed the only real luxury life had ever, or could ever offer: to lie in bed late, dozing until the sun slid into her window and across her bed, a blade of hot brass; to eat alone off a tray in this or that corner of the house or garden; to fall asleep, sometimes, on the porch, while a summer storm rattled overhead, then gave way to stars and the pondering moon. To Caroline at sixty-three it seemed all the nature that surrounded her sustained her—the moon in its silver cycles, the pink-red geraniums and long flowing native grasses in her garden, and now the apricot tree itself with its bridal finery that didn't droop and was replaced, overnight, it seemed, with an astonishing crop. All pondered, all watched from within their private and separate existences.

At first she picked all the apricots she could and filled bowls and baskets where the fruit fermented, giving off a sweet perfume that reminded her of the candy shops of her childhood. She hated to throw out all that luxury, that unprecedented generosity, but at first she could not think of an alternative. For a few days she let the fruit drop from the tree and ground it under the tires of her car every time she went in and out; that was an unacceptable waste. Finally she remembered another scene from her childhood, of women sweating, chatting, bending over pots on a stove, and she decided to do some canning.

For a city woman, once a New York City woman, at that, the idea of spending a day in a hot steamy kitchen was, at first, unthinkable, but she remembered all the friends who would prize squat jars of apricot jam, and how a few of those jars would blaze on her pantry shelf in the depths of winter. And so she went out and bought four large, light aluminum pots, bigger than any pots she had ever owned, and after some searching, discovered that the cardboard trays of quilted jam glasses she remembered were still available, along with the white oblongs of paraffin needed to seal the tops.

But the task was daunting and Caroline soon realized she would have to have help. The steps in her mother's cookbook were complicated, especially the dry insistence on blanching the fruit to remove the skins, then processing them to prevent darkening. (Caroline was not sure why the fruit should not darken since she did not remember anyone in the old days caring what color it was.)

She pondered the situation for several days, meanwhile accumulating more bowls and baskets of apricots, which she kept in her refrigerator. Going out early in the morning to pick up what had fallen during the night, she would stop for a moment and stand with her hands on her hips, looking at the huge, glittering thunderheads already piling up in the west. Then she would bend to the task, feeling for a moment not like a sophisticated older woman released at last from unproductive demands but like a nymph loose in some glade in Arcady. Her yard and drive were not equal to that picture but she herself was, she believed, with her ocher-colored hair and long limbs and alert, unlined face.

Then it occurred to her that one of the young men in the class she taught at the local college might be willing to help. The class had not been a particular success, from Caroline's point of view; the students were listless and her attempt to interest them in the poetry of the Modernists largely failed. But there was one among them who seemed to have a spark of willingness; sometimes she caught young Charles Cooper's eyes fixed upon her as she lectured.

The semester ended shortly, and when she met with her students to hand them their graded finals and speak — she hoped — a few words of wisdom about the importance of E. E. Cummings and H.D., Caroline had made up her mind.

As the little group gathered itself to leave, she signaled to Charles who, as usual, was watching. He came to her desk promptly.

"I have a job I want to do—a domestic job," she added, realizing he would think it was something involving reading or writing. "My apricot tree is covered with fruit and I want to put up some jam."

He looked at her alertly. He was a slight, sharp-faced young man with brownish hair brushed straight back and oddly freckled green eyes. His hands and feet, she had already noticed, were small, but his legs were long and his arms, below the short sleeves of his shirt, were tanned and supple.

"Okay," he said, a little too quickly, she thought.

"Of course I'm planning to pay."

"That won't be necessary," he said, turning away. She had to call him back to explain that she needed a morning later that week, and to give him her address; as he listened, she felt sheepish. It was an unfamiliar sensation, not entirely unpleasant.

The day arrived with thunderheads, brilliant sun, and heat. Caroline got up early to gather the last windfalls; she now had seven containers of apricots, and her small kitchen soon filled with their sweet, narcotic perfume. She took a shower and dressed, then found herself, unaccountably, taking off her shorts and shirt and putting on a dress; she realized that if she had possessed such a thing as a housedress and apron, she would have put them on, not as a disguise (as she would have thought, even the day before) but as a proclamation of some kind. What the words in the proclamation were she did not know.

She filled the largest kettle and set it on the stove to boil water for the jam jars. As she took the jars off their tray, she felt their quilted sides and looked with admiration at the anonymous fruits that decorated their lids. The jars, which normally she would hardly have noticed, seemed like masterpieces of artistry to her; who could have devised the quilted pattern of the glass, or left such a cunning space on one side for a label?

Presently she heard a light knock, and went to let in Charles. She was struck by the fact that he came to the front door, obscured by walls and trees, rather than to the more accessible kitchen door. "That apricot tree is covered," he said by way of greeting, standing in front of her, poised as though to turn in any direction, or to leave.

"I've picked about all we can manage today," she said, gesturing toward the bowls. Charles put out his hand and picked up an apricot, which he slipped, whole, into his mouth. Smiling, he said, "That's the first one of those I've ever eaten. It's good!"

"Are you from around here?" It was, she realized, the first personal question she had ever asked him.

He shook his head. "Maine."

They set to the task at once; later, Caroline wondered if she should have offered him something first — coffee, or a glass of water. She knew young men usually jumped out of bed and ran out with no breakfast to whatever the day offered; she had raised three sons herself, and remembered their mixture of lassitude and spontaneity, which had so baffled her at the time. Charles, she assumed, was hungry; but when, later on, she asked him, he said he had already cooked and eaten a perfectly adequate breakfast.

They quickly sorted out the tasks, working side by side at the counter as smoothly, Caroline thought, as though they had been working together for years. She undertook the blanching (the jars were sterilized by now and laid out to cool on a linen towel), dropping the apricots by handfuls into boiling water, and then quickly lifting them out. Drained, the apricots went to Charles, who shucked off their skins; the pile of darkening yellow-and-orange skins grew by his elbow as the kitchen filled with the dense sweetness of the hot fruit.

"Do you really think darkening is a problem?" Caroline asked him as she studied the dog-eared cookbook, its cover a map of kitchen stains.

"They look better light," he said with authority.

He began dropping the peeled apricots into a solution of salt, vinegar, and water, and the piercing smell of the vinegar was added to the apricots' sweetness.

"Oh dear, I'm afraid I should have reheated them first," Carolyn said after she had read the recipe again, but Charles reassured her that the fruit was still hot from the blanching process.

Caroline stopped for a moment to watch him. His small, tanned hands moved regularly across the counter as he shucked the apricots and dropped them into the solution; he was frowning with concentration, lost in the task, she thought, until he asked, gruffly, "What are you looking at?"

"You. I never thought I'd see any of you young men in my kitchen."

"Why not?"

"I only know you in terms of my class," she said.

"I used to help my mother a lot," he explained, as though this was not the most interesting answer to the question she implied.

"I expect she's about my age," Caroline said, returning to her blanching.

"I don't know. How old are you?"

"Sixty-three," she said proudly. She had never stooped to lying about her age.

"Why did you never bother to get to know any of us?" he asked abruptly.

Caroline was startled. It had not occurred to her that anything she had done, or not done, in the class had had a consequence.

"You never even learned all our names," Charles went on. "Last week you called Todd Franklin Frank."

"I always mix up those names that could be first or last," she equivocated. Really he had embarrassed her and she wished suddenly that he would go.

"That's not the reason you called him Frank," Charles said. "You just didn't care enough to figure us out."

Caroline stopped what she was doing and leaned on her hands. Looking down, she saw the age spots rise from her skin like the spots on the back of a toad; she saw the little sacks of skin around her knuckles and wondered when they had come there. "I did the best I could," she said and knew, instantly, that it was not true.

"Taste one of these," Charles said, and he handed her a peeled apricot.

Without its fuzzy skin, the apricot looked small and vulnerable, like a naked part of a person that would ordinarily be hidden. Caroline slipped it into her mouth and brought her teeth down lightly; the soft meaty flesh of the apricot fell away onto her tongue. It was deliciously sweet, and hot.

"You have one, too."

Charles slid an apricot into his mouth and smiled at her. "I forgive you," he said.

Instantly she was angry. "For what?"

"Not caring."

"Do all your other teachers care?" she asked.

"Some do, some don't. But I always find a way to tell the ones who don't. For their own good," he added mischievously. "I could tell you were disappointed in the class; you might want to know why it didn't work."

"I thought it was the reading list," she said.

"There's nothing wrong with those writers." To prove his point, he quoted one of them, but Caroline could not identify the line.

"I'm sorry," she said.

Charles seemed satisfied. "Let's save some of these last ones to eat later."

She agreed, and they sorted out several handfuls of the cooked apricots and put them on a china plate. The china plate was decorated with a stylized bird and a farmer, in blue on yellow, and Caroline remembered with a shock (she had not thought about this in years) that as a child she had often eaten her breakfast off this plate.

At last they put twelve filled jars to sterilize in the popping, boiling kettle. The kitchen windows were blind with steam and the heat was overpowering. Caroline suggested taking the saved apricots outside.

She and Charles sat on the doorstep and ate them. One by one, they fed them into their mouths. At some point, without a word, Charles pushed an apricot into her mouth, and Caroline laughed with surprise. "Why did you do that?"

"Just to see."

She spit the dark, smooth oval seed into her hand and studied it.

They finished the apricots—Caroline anticipated an upset stomach, she had eaten so many—and went back into the kitchen. Charles fished the hot jars out of the sterilizer and pulled up the rack, and Caroline inserted the remaining jars. As Charles lowered them into the boiling water, a plume of steam obscured his face. Then he slapped on the lid.

"So masterful," Caroline said, laughing. In the back of her mind a sort of clock was ticking, telling off the details of the plans she had made for the afternoon: a visit to the post office to mail her sister's birthday present, some cleaning to pick up. The clock ticked and ticked but it seemed to have removed itself to some other part of the house.

Charles laid his hand over her hand on the counter. "I think you're very attractive," he said.

"Oh, honestly. I'm old enough to be—"

"Why do you keep harping on age?"

"Because it's the truth. Or part of it," she added uneasily.

His hand slid up her arm to her shoulder, bare under the strap of her dress. "You have an amazing body."

She was speechless. The feel of his palm on her bare shoulder reminded her of the texture of her own skin, which she treated now like a commodity, washing and drying it mechanically. She tried to remember other touches, other times, but it seemed that the years between had blotted out the memory. She flushed and breathed deeply, trying to regain her balance. "What are you doing, Charles?" she asked.

His hand moved from her shoulder to her waist as he turned her. "Kissing you," he said, and did.

Later Caroline remembered the flesh of the apricots, their slight graininess, the moisture that was not dripping like the sweetness of peaches but absorbed, contained. She remembered the woolly feel of the apricots' skins, and the smooth, shining brown pits. She even remembered the seam that ran up one side of each pit, and she also remembered the way the thick sweet smell of the cooking apricots had been cut by the tang of vinegar. And she longed to know what the apricots had meant, and continued to mean, even as she realized with dismay that her life was falling apart; the ticking of the clock had stopped and might never start again. With equal dismay and exhilaration, she remembered a line from one of the poets she had tried so unsuccessfully to teach her class that spring:

"that is why I am afraid; I look at you,
I think of your song,
I see the long trail of your coming."

That was said by an old poet of a young poet. Could it not also be said by an old woman of a young man?

BENJAMIN

On his flight to the West Coast, lunch has just been
served (Benjamin, who is ninety, has been quick to ask for the
last slice of pizza, leaving the more abundant grizzled chicken
salad to his seatmate), and the intercom is announcing that all
uneaten food items should be set aside for the homeless.

The intercom adds, with unction, that this airline has
instituted a new program, to cut down on waste and serve the
less fortunate; with the side of his fork, Benjamin mashes his
uneaten triangle of dark-berried pie.

"Please don't give this to the homeless," he says as he hands his tray to the flight attendant, whom in his mind he still calls a stewardess.

She glances at the mashed pie, makes a smile. "Oh, Mr. Price! I was just reading about your mural in that homeless center—where is it?"

"Detroit." He sets his lips. Now his seatmate is listening. "They have a big wall there. I had something I wanted to paint on a big wall." He does not treat the two women to a description of the squabble that followed when the center people refused to string a rope in front of his mural. Benjamin can imagine the effect of dispossessed shoulders and hands on his chalky rendition of the famous naked picnic, featuring local magnates—which had caused less stir than he had anticipated.

The flight attendant, clucking her refusal to be dismayed, moves on; she knows her celebrities, their disposition to be difficult. Nothing Benjamin can say or do, short of murder, will dim the glow she takes away from the encounter.

Benjamin's seatmate, a blond woman wearing snail-shaped gold earrings (she laid aside a roll, he's noticed, for the dispensation) glances at him uneasily.

"I don't believe in the poor," he says in his high, ratcheting voice. "I've always been poor—until very recently; it's a decent, serviceable condition. 'The poor are always with you,'" he quotes, betting she won't get it. "Why should we work against the Gospels?"

The woman looks at him sheepishly, as though she has a moral responsibility to upbraid him but can't think of the necessary words. Possibly she is sheepish because she doesn't recognize him. "My mother used to volunteer in a shelter," she offers.

"Either she was a fool or she had nothing better to do or both."

She turns the fixed jaw of pained dismay and looks determinedly at her magazine.

Missing her response, Benjamin remembers the years when Ida sat beside him and fended off the not-always unwelcome advances of strangers. Sometimes he'd take an aisle seat, leaving Ida the window, in order to engage in unauthorized talk with the person across the way. Especially if it was a woman. Ida was robust and charmless, a personal assistant addicted to the personal (she cleaned his ears with Q-tips, bought his boxer shorts in packages of six), who never aspired to the status such intimacy presumably confers. Which was why he'd kept her for eleven years until, tearful over her wasted youth, she insisted on departing; at that point Benjamin decided to make do with a grad student two afternoons a week.

In spite of all the commissions, his mail is decreasing, his phone rings less, and he is beginning to suspect his spectacular age is losing its ability to draw attention to his work. But he has all the mechanisms of avoidance in place: the answering machine, the fax, the computer with its self-satisfied digestion of unwanted data. He plans never to figure that one out.

Now the intercom announces that they are about to land in Los Angeles. His seatmate takes two Styrofoam cups from her enormous bag and sticks the open ends over her ears. All the way down to the ground, Benjamin watches as she shrinks into herself, closing her eyes and hunkering over her knees.

"What's with the cups?" he asks when they're taxiing and she's taken them down.

"I have earaches," she tells him with a dismissive shrug. "Terrible earaches! This way I create a vacuum."

Now the jetway is rolling out like a serpent bound to devour its prey and Benjamin feels the shortness of time.

"But what about the air already inside the cups?" he asks.

When she looks startled, he explains, "You can't suck the air out that's already in there, so how can you create a vacuum?"

She continues to look distressed, so Benjamin whips out his salvaged paper napkin and begins to draw one of her ears, in ink. The ear is clutching its earring. He signs the drawing, then passes it to her; she takes it gingerly, between two fingers, as though it might be infected. "Send that to Sotheby's if you're ever short of money."

"I thought you were somebody," she says, folding the drawing carefully and stowing it in a zippered compartment of her bag.

Then Benjamin follows her out of the plane, noting with pleasure that her butt is more shapely than her face has led him to expect.

She disappears into the crowd as the usual contingent comes forward to meet him. Benjamin leans away from the introductions, trying not to hear. Lately he's let the word go round that he's going deaf, yet refuses to wear one of those navel-colored hearing aids. In fact his hearing, like his eyesight, is uncomfortably keen.

They herd him through collecting his baggage and into a car.

He notices that the girl driving has a pretty neck, tendriled with dark hair. From the backseat (he has insisted on sitting there, claiming it makes him feel safer), he traces each tendril with his forefinger.

The girl reaches up as though to slap a fly; her boss, the museum director, shakes his head and she drops her hand. Benjamin can tell from the set of her shoulders that she is expecting the attention to go on — they'll be saying he's senile, next, giving him still more room to play — but he has become absorbed in watching the light change in the oily water running down the gutters. Apparently it has just stopped raining.

He finds the obscure tablet that opens the window and breathes the moist, fetid air. "I love the sheer unhealthiness of cities," he says, and has to put up with the museum director's comfortable chuckle.

Years ago, in his early eighties, with his first fame, his first money, Benjamin tried to explain that what he said, no matter how outrageous, was not said for effect. It made no difference how he scowled, or growled. He has become an old, harmless painter of great and safe distinction, a kind of greeting card, he thinks, offered to artists on the threshold of age. "Hold on awhile longer and this is what you'll get."

The museum director, an affable smiling blond man, whom Benjamin would have guessed scarcely out of his twenties if his title did not confer more age, lets him out at an old downtown hotel, a rookery refurbished now that the neighborhood is becoming prosperous. "For the atmosphere," the young man explains, hoisting Benjamin's suitcase out of the trunk. "All the old Hollywood stars used to stay here." He sees Benjamin through the signing-in process and the bestowal of the card that passes for a room key while the girl waits in the car.

"I like that young girl of yours," Benjamin says as the director is ushering him into a gilded elevator.

"She's not mine," the man says, handing him his suitcase.

"Then the museum's. I'm hoping she'll be at dinner tonight."

"The whole staff will," the young man says without emphasis. They are back on the flat ground of arrangements where, Benjamin thinks as the elevator glides up, no passion or appetite ever raises its head.

In his room, he lies down on a snake-colored bedspread and stares at the painting on the wall: a vast, naked-looking melon, poised like a threat over some harmless cherries. He remembers when he was grateful for such a sale, did not even wince when the hotel asked him to hang the piece, for free; remembers going into rooms like this, dank with emptiness, smelling in those days of the last inhabitant's cigarettes, scrabbling his hand along the wall for the light switch, blinking in the glare at the bald gray or green walls. Where to put the child of his invention, the hapless orphan of an eyeless world? He falls asleep studying the strange shine on the sides of the cherries. A sort of feverish, fruity glow.

Up in time to shave, again — he lets the fact that he still needs to shave twice a day provide the meaning he needs — shower, and dress for the performance. His evening clothes, folded haphazardly, are wrinkled, and he thinks briefly of muscling the ironing board out of the closet, and then abandons the notion. He likes his fluted purple dress shirt and polka-dot bow tie, and spit-polishes his patent-leather pumps with the tassels. Of course no one wears such clothes anymore, even to honorary dinners. Then he goes down to the lobby.

His old life returns as he waits in an armchair placed at an angle to a distressed-looking potted palm. In his twenties, he was night clerk in a hotel such as this one was a few years ago: plunging down into flophousehood. He'd been glad for the job, and turned it into a playground for his drawings of the inhabitants, which he kept on a sketchpad on his knees.

Then one night a distraught-looking man signed in late, and some instinct warned Benjamin of trouble; he went up to check and found smoke spiraling from under the door and the man half-conscious on his lit bed. It took a while for the local fire department to rouse its members. Meanwhile Benjamin doused the man and the bed with water from a paper cup, the only receptacle at hand. The man remained comatose, although not badly burned, and was hauled off to the local hospital; when Benjamin visited him there, a few days later, more out of curiosity — he had begun to draw him — than any regard for his welfare, the man told him with shame about the usual progression: a divorce, a job setback, the alienation of some minor children.

Well, it is always the same in the end, Benjamin thinks as his host comes through the entrance with a carnation in his buttonhole and another, the old painter knows, in the white box he is carrying; in the end heartbreak, even death, boils down to a few inevitable details: desertion, disappointment, all on the human scale.

He allows the young man to fasten the carnation in his buttonhole, noticing that his is red while the director's is white. "Red as the blood in my veins," he jokes as the young man holds open the door and scoops his hand under his elbow to help him into the car, then feels, unexpectedly, foolish: it is all too obvious. But the young man has scarcely heard and feels no need to reply. This time, he is driving.

In the vast hotel ballroom—another hotel; this time, one of a noxious chain—Benjamin looks around for the girl but does not see her at first. He pantomimes extreme deafness and distraction, holding his hand to his ear as a bevy of museum supporters is led forward and introduced.

They are all middle-aged women, handsomely dressed, and he knows how vital their support is to the museum, and how heavily their support depends on the success of events like this one. He believes these women have forgotten what it was like to ward off a man's advances, and he feels for them, briefly, and wishes that aging flesh, no matter how well preserved, did not ignite his uncontrollable disgust. He is a man of his times, after all.

Then he sees the girl in a becoming black cocktail dress, seated at the other end of the table—she is minor personnel, after all, and it would have taken a cosmopolitan imagination to place her near him. He waves his napkin and smiles, striking his dinner companion dumb; she has been carrying on about a trip somewhere, the art she has seen and absorbed, Benjamin imagines, as a great sea-going turtle absorbs the green contents of a wave. She is handsome as a sea turtle, too, in her smart green scaly dress, but he is beyond being polite and fixes his eyes, instead, on the discreet hint of bare breast the girl is displaying in her décolletage. She wears one of the official white carnations, pinned where it will draw attention to her charms.

She's conscious, then, he thinks with pleasure, of what her femininity can do, or could do, given the proper stage, which she assuredly lacks, and he is off at once, seeing her in silk lounging pajamas on the veranda of some gracious Tuscan villa, or striding out into the foam on a Caribbean beach. In his earlier days, women went for that kind of exchange, knowing that the less-than-satisfactory lover was likely to be replaced with the more-satisfactory at a plummy resort; accepting, he thinks, even now, after all the changes, that there was a fairness in spreading one's beautiful and accommodating legs in return for opportunities that were not wholly—never wholly—financial. But a young girl would be ashamed to consider that, now.

His companion has struck up her talk again—it appears that Rome, and Paris, too, are still to be got through—and he leans toward her with the transparent fatigue of the elderly. She sees this at once and pats his shoulder consolingly. They are both in the same shallow canoe, hurrying down a darkening river. But he will reach the end long before she will.

He notices the big diamond on her finger, and interrupts her soliloquy to ask about its purchaser.

While she details the well-memorized glories of her marriage, ended by the husband's death long enough ago to allow for the powers of reinvention, Benjamin doesn't take his eyes off the young girl. The swine on either side have not even bothered to notice her, being taken up with more important if less comely partners. Benjamin swallows his nearly-raw steak, bit by bit, and imagines opportunities.

The after-dinner toasts pass rapidly and he is only required to nod and smile, not to respond—another advantage of his age. It is presumed that he is exhausted from the long flight and the change in time, which in fact he has scarcely noticed. He allows waves of congratulation to pass over him while he drinks his coffee, well-laced with sugar and heavy cream. He has scornfully turned down someone's kindly suggestion that he might prefer decaf.

Now he feels his heart pounding, as it will do in spite of all his efforts to avoid noticing it, at the end of the day, after a lot of food and drink. (The champagne is a good French vintage and he has not stopped at his usual two glasses, even rising to clink and say something foolish about the honor.) As he pushes his chair back from the table, he feels his heart leaping like a demon under his purple shirt and stops to steady the leap with his palm.

Immediately the young director has his hand under his elbow and is suggesting a swift trip back to the rookery, and rest.

Benjamin shakes him off and makes a beeline across the room to the girl, chatting colorlessly with another woman.

She feels his approach as one might feel, Benjamin thinks, the approach of a heat-sensitive missile, and turns, her hand already up, palm out. He takes that as the greeting it is not and places his own palm against hers. How warm her skin is, how limpid.

"Drive me back to that hellish place and I'll buy you a drink," he says, hearing the thickness he hasn't felt on his tongue.

She glances at her boss, across the room, who must be nodding approval, or even insistence, then makes her manners to the various functionaries and tells Benjamin she will meet him at the front door.

Still he is not sure of her—they are slippery, these girls— and while the director is helping him into his overcoat and outlining the next day's heavy schedule, Benjamin is thinking of various face-saving devices. But then she is there, outside, sitting a little bowed in what is apparently her own car, a tiny red coupe, so low Benjamin has to double himself to get in. Once seated he straightens and fastens the belt as though he is girding on a sword.

At the click, the girl begins to drive, her pretty profile pointed forward like the figurehead on a small, stately yacht.

"I like you," he says, at once—there is no time left, in the whole world, it has run out to the last few grains in the hourglass—and without anticipating her response, he reaches over and fondles her breast. "I was admiring you all through that ghastly dinner, in that low-cut dress."

She has her instructions, and although she is not responsive, she does not shrug his hand away. He wonders, suddenly, if she is ambitious. Her black dress might suggest as much.

Then he feels her nipple harden under his fingers—ambitious, for sure; she is not wearing a bra—and crows his delight.

Of course she can't help it, she is driving, and also under instruction of some kind. Still he lets his fingers nuzzle the stiffness, and feels to his amazement, a corresponding liveliness in his crotch. This is so rare now as to provide another crow of delight.

He keeps his hand on her nipple as she turns and glides the car through the downtown streets. When she draws up in front of his hotel, she does not cut the motor but remains staring fixedly straight ahead. "Come upstairs with me," he says, adding, "I'm a harmless old man, there isn't much I can do."

"I doubt that," she says, still staring straight ahead.

"Well, there may be a little, with your help. Have pity on a fellow sufferer," he adds, kissing her cheek. Her skin has the texture and taste of a slightly green apricot; it will be a few years before she reaches her full bloom. At the thought of her perhaps near-virginhood, he is aware of resources at the bottom of his spine he thought long ago dried up. "It isn't so often these days I can get this, just from touching a pretty girl's breast," he says, loosening her right hand from the steering wheel and guiding it to his crotch.

To his amazement, to his eternal delight, she turns, smiling slightly, and says she will go upstairs with him.

Later, in the grim light from the bedside lamp—she has wanted the dark, but he needs to peruse her—he is unable to remain hard long enough to enter her and lies, finally, on her frail, subsiding body, sobbing. His tears fall into the hollow at the base of her neck.

"I'm a stupid old goat," he tells her later as she is dressing, and tries to think of a way to cheer her. "You'll have so many men in your life—so many accomplished, adoring lovers. You'll forget this unfortunate business right away."

"But you're a great artist," she says, pulling up her hideous panty hose. How they disfigure her hips and distort her ass as she turns around to step into her shoes.

He laughs then, at the thought that she has imagined a great artist as a great lover. "I expect you'll have another great artist," he reassures her, "one young enough to satisfy your expectations."

"You could have used your mouth," she says, with a glance.

He sees in her glance everything he has ever wanted. It is only an instant, and then she is gone, closing the door with a nurse's dispatch.

His sleep that night is both deep and deeply disturbed. In the morning, in spite of a fierce headache, he goes out into the street to look for a fancy jeweler, but the neighborhood is only slowly emerging from decades of decay and the shop he finds specializes in pawn.

He goes in, but the grimy rhinestones and battered turquoise express a despair that sends him fleeing.

Then it is time for the luncheon, and the unveiling of his painting.

Somehow he makes it through the smoked salmon and capers, through the vichyssoise and crabcakes; he is waiting to see if the girl will reappear. But this is a select group of big donors, and she is not high enough on the totem pole to be included.

Then, staggering a little from the wine and the coffee, he is escorted into the throne room, as it were, of the museum:

the glacial marble gallery where his painting is hanging, hidden under a piece of golden damask.

He manages not to hear a word that is spoken and to fend off the looks of concern that are beginning to wing his way; he knows he is very pale, and he wipes his forehead on his sleeve. His perspiration feels cold as it dries, a clamminess that alarms him. But he will make it through, somehow; the girl is standing at the edge of the group. He is able to notice her Chanel knockoff, her neat navy bow.

Then a heavy gold tassel is placed in his hand, and he knows he must pull. He doubts that he has the strength, but the gold curtain is flimsily attached and comes down with a single tug.

And there it is, the painting of his prime.

First, he is shocked by the display of mastery—the fireworks of the painting itself—as though (and this he would prefer not to believe) he has never until now believed in his ability. The painting dazzles him as, apparently, it dazzles the others; there is a moment of silence, and then a gasp. He feels his own breath filling out the gasp and says, under his breath, "How did I know that much about how to. . . ?"

Someone asks, avidly, for the end of the sentence, but he is beyond finding it. The maze of the past is winding its web around him—the jeweled streets of his youth spun now to spidery gold.

He steps closer, peers. The others draw in. He realizes for the first time that he can't see as clearly as he supposed; the vermilions and greiges swim as the oily water in the gutters swam on the drive from the airport.

He takes another step and realizes his nose is only inches from the painting's surface.

Now someone is at his elbow, subtly resisting his forward lunge. But he shakes the fellow off—is it the blond young director?—and closes the gap.

His eyes float across the surface of the painting that he has not seen or thought much about in thirty years, and he relishes each detail, each successful brushstroke, as though a fundamental doubt about his life is being resolved.

But when he steps back, finally—and he senses a sort of relief blooming around him, knows his reputation as a wrecker has preceded him and at least one person has feared he will actually harm his own work—he sees the painting as a whole, and whispers, "She never wanted me to paint her."

Now the girl is nearby—he can smell her light lemony fragrance—and he turns blindly in her direction. "She told me if I painted her, it would be the end," he says. "I didn't care much—I wanted the painting. I wanted the painting a good deal more than I wanted her, even at the beginning," he admits, with a dry laugh. "I don't think she knew that."

"I expect she did," the girl says, cupping his elbow.

He would like to shake off her unneeded support but cannot summon the strength. His elbow squats like a toad in her warm palm. He continues to examine the portrait, noting the details of the gilded lace fichu—Madeleine had insisted, once she'd finally agreed to the sitting, on dressing herself as a turn-of-the-century Philadelphia heiress—the sparkler attached to the red velvet over her small breast. Seeing that, he shapes his crabbed hand to the memory of that breast, its responsive nipple. Even when she was sobbing, or excoriating him for some imagined or real misbehavior, he could rouse her nipple with a single touch. "I liked her breasts," he tells the girl—the other people seem to have drawn away, or else he is simply, now, freed of being aware of them. "Her breasts were the best things about her."

"Were they," the girl says.

"Her breasts, and her hair," Benjamin goes on, squinting through the reeling darkness at Madeleine's black, piled hair. A stray curl is arranged, carefully, over her temple. He can't see her face—that wistful smile; her features are, mercifully, blotted out by a flesh-colored cloud. "And she had nice skin." Dead and gone these many years.

"These are pearls that were her eyes," he adds, looking at the dazzler that tops her puffed hair; a sumptuous diamond, as large as an egg yolk. "She was very proud of that diamond," he says. "Her second husband. I heard she kept it, after the divorce. She was between marriages when I met her," he adds.

"What was her name?"

As he turns to answer her—proud that he remembers, proud, that he has known her name all his life—Benjamin feels something tear. It is as though the fabric that has bound him tightly for so many years has at last given way. He hears the rent, feels something entering.

"Madeleine," he says, hoarding his breath so that he can say more. For he knows what must come next: he must tell the girl how he looked for a jewel, for her. He must ask her name, so he can remember.

THE HUNT

HEIDI WAS CHARMED BY THE COURTSHIP. Not one of the
many men she'd known, including her long-ago husband, had
gone to the head of her family to ask for her hand, or even
been able to imagine such a term. And although it pained her
to laughter to admit even this one time that her older brother
Harold was now, as he had always desired to be, the head of
that amorphous tangle even Heidi acknowledged as family,
she was deeply touched by what had happened. The ancient
form, adhered to in all its outdated quaintness, seemed to set
her at a very high price.

Of course Larry had not been asking to marry her. No one married, these days, except the very young. He had been imagining, and outlining (so Heidi believed), a long-term relationship, something with little of whim or impulse in it. Harold's understanding and eventual acceptance was needed because, as Larry reminded Heidi, who grimaced, she would not be happy with a man her brother found unsatisfactory. Larry perhaps had been too tactful to mention—or perhaps, being Larry, he'd never thought of it—that Heidi was dependent on her brother's generosity to keep her little house in Santa Fe and her relatively carefree life.

When she was disgusted with that life, which did not give her much to chew on, as she sometimes said, since she was retired from city government and not interested in volunteer work or aimless socializing, Heidi liked to imagine that primordial scene between Harold and Larry.

It had taken place on a Saturday morning, six months earlier; Harold generally spent Saturdays going over his stamp collection or attending to his assortment of firearms. So Larry would have found him occupied, perhaps down on his knees in his library with cans and rags and newspapers spread out and the gun cabinet standing open and half-empty behind him. But even that task, which he adored, would not have prevented Harold from looking up at his visitor and understanding, at once, that serious attention was needed.

Harold would then have stood up—with ease, for a seventy-year-old—dusting off his knees and offering the man he'd been calling "Heidi's beau" a softly-upholstered armchair.

From that point, Heidi, even at her most animated, could not imagine the scene. Harold might have sat in his desk chair, although he would certainly have pulled it out, first, from behind the mahogany partners desk that had been their father's; Harold did not depend on gestures and positions to communicate his authority, which had been his like a birthright, Heidi thought, since he was seven years old and claimed all the stars in heaven on a summer night, as well as the moon.

"You can have the evening star," he'd told a tearful Heidi, who had already understood, at three, that her brother took what he claimed. There may even have been a time or two since, she knew, over the many years, when she had been grateful to be allowed to have the evening star.

But what the two men, so different, and cast in such different roles in terms of Heidi, could have actually said, she was not able to imagine. Larry had been reticent on the subject, merely saying that the talk had gone well and that Harold had seemed to understand. But what the texture, and the details, of that talk and that putative understanding had been, Heidi realized she might never know.

Now—six months after the conversation—Heidi and Larry were going to spend their first weekend with Harold and Laura, a cold weekend in November; the aspens had lost their leaves and the piñon nuts had fallen and been gathered. Harold and Laura lived twenty miles southeast of Santa Fe in the family house where Heidi had spent summers in childhood; as soon as he was released from his Michigan university, at retirement age, with a good pension and many honors, Harold had packed up a slightly-protesting Laura and driven out to Pecos to reopen the house and occupy it year-round.

According to the terms of their father's will, the house was to be for Harold's sole use, and he was responsible for its considerable expenses. However, Heidi knew her father had intimated that she should be invited to share the old place as often as possible. For five years, Harold had honored that agreement scrupulously, inviting his sister to Thanksgiving and Christmas and to all large parties. But she had never before been asked to spend the night. Nor had Larry been included, until now.

That in itself was significant, Heidi thought as she sat beside Larry in the front seat of her Jeep. Larry was driving with his usual concentration and thoroughness, as though nothing else could be happening in the world—which was the reason he considered the radio an annoying distraction. As they rode along the throughway in the humming silence, Heidi told Larry she felt they were being invited to spend two nights—not one, but two—because of the way he had approached Harold to ask him for his permission. Heidi felt full of generosity when she made such concessions.

"I wasn't exactly asking for permission," Larry said with his journalist's exactitude, which annoyed and delighted Heidi about equally. "I just wanted to give him a chance to tell me what he thought."

This was a new view of the situation, and not a very satisfactory one. "I guess if he'd expressed some reservation, you'd have just given me up," Heidi said.

"Maybe for the time being. I know how important Harold and Laura are to you. But I'd have asked him again," Larry said.

That felt a little better. It was one thing, Heidi thought, to hang in the balance—she had been hanging in one balance or another her entire life—and another to feel her brother's hand on the scale. "I should hope you wanted me enough to try again," she said. Already, she seemed to be a habit of Larry's, along with not eating meat, volunteering at the animal shelter, and protesting, gently enough, to women he met wearing fur coats. To Heidi, habits were prunelike facts, shriveled and hard, with very little juice left after the long drying of practice.

Larry answered something automatic, then saw her disappointment and tried to improve on what he'd said—or what he hadn't said. Meanwhile Heidi concentrated on the pale blue sky unfolding over the mountains; the early-morning clouds were clearing and the sun looked out. "Maybe the dripping will have stopped by this afternoon," she said, remembering the fringe of ragged pines around the old house. It had always held fog and damp and rain and dew long after the surrounding fields were dry.

They turned in at the green gate, which hadn't been repainted in Heidi's memory, passed the big mailbox on its stick, bent almost to the breaking point years earlier by a reckless mailman, and proceeded down the sandy rut that could hardly be called a drive. Part of the reason the house was kept in a state of permanent decrepitude was that Harold had always feared being labeled ostentatious; he had spent his life grubbing (as Heidi thought of it) in the literature department of a mediocre state university when he might have retired early and cultivated all kinds of pleasant habits.

Even Laura, his wife of so many years — Heidi was astonished when she thought of the sum — had spent most of her forties and fifties, after their five children were grown, laboring away at the city hospital, passing out books and holding hands; the couple had seemed, during those decades, so hard-pressed and so benevolent that Heidi had shrunk from the comparison. All those years she'd traveled, painted a little, tried modern dance, taken up all kinds of habits and hobbies and nurtured or dropped them. The song of her freedom seemed a reproach to the dull drone of her brother's responsibleness, not to speak of Laura's, who had always seemed an admirable but pathetic martyr to Harold's way of life (including, Heidi would have liked to intimate, five children and now all kinds of grandchildren with their escalating demands).

Heidi, all those years after her divorce, had stayed single, sampling men cautiously but with a kind of ease she knew she'd have lost, once and for all, if she'd married or had children or pursued some solemn career.

Larry parked her Jeep under one of the dripping pines and sat for a moment, studying the house's long brown façade. "Such a big place for two people."

"In the old days, in the summertime, when our parents and their generation were alive, every bedroom had at least one body in it." Heidi reached for the door handle. "Get my suitcase, would you?"

Then she stood waiting while Larry took out their two suitcases, or rather, hers, and his backpack. Heidi had given up suggesting that he join the adult world and buy himself a wallet, a suitcase, and some leather shoes; he had principles that prevented such compromises, and Heidi was well on her way, laboriously, to appreciating his honesty.

She walked up the broken brick path ahead of him and saw the outline of Laura's head inside the screen door. As her sister-in-law opened it, Heidi stepped forward with a spurt of her old enthusiasm and kissed her.

Heidi didn't introduce Larry; of course Laura knew him—at least, she had met him several times. Still, it was an omission, for Heidi, of a grace note she valued because she felt such efforts smoothed the path for Larry, who had no family of his own and sometimes seemed almost in awe of hers.

That was an uncomfortable notion, which Heidi dismissed at once. She did not want her lover to be in awe of anything or anyone. If he cherished a bit of reverence for her, that was more than sufficient, especially in the heat of their intimacy. Stepping into the dark porch, Heidi remembered the embroidered lingerie-covers her mother had used on trips to cover her stockings and girdle when they were left, briefly, on a hotel bedroom chair. "Your father shouldn't be exposed to that sort of thing," she'd said.

Laura and Larry were chatting behind her, and Heidi admired her lover's easy way.

At the end of the long hall with its jammed bookcases and mounted heads of elk and moose, Harold was waiting, his finger in a book. His tall frame was propped against the doorpost as though, Heidi thought, he was posing for his portrait, one of those moody brown-and-tan full-length oils their father might have commissioned, years ago. *Boy with Book*, something like that.

As she kissed him, however, Heidi realized that something had changed in her brother's skin. His cheek was as dry as the heel of a loaf of bread.

She looked up at him inquiringly. Harold's pale blue eyes seemed to be examining her from a distance, as once he had examined his extensive collection of butterflies. "Are you all right?" Heidi asked, and managed to include Laura in the question.

"Just getting old," Harold said, and turned to shake hands, heartily, with Larry.

Heidi was perplexed. Although she was only four years younger than her brother, and exactly the same age as Laura, she had never felt old, or even thought much about it. When occasionally the clerk in the grocery asked if she qualified for a discount, she laughed as though such a question was preposterous, and, once in her car, quickly applied more lipstick. "Age is such a tricky thing," Heidi would sometimes say, or "It's all in the eye of the beholder."

Yet her brother's cheek felt old. And Laura, if she was not sick, looked old—faded and shrunken. Something had changed with the change in the weather; when they were last together, it had been Indian summer, and they'd sat out on the lawn shelling peas and telling stories. At a time like that, the distance that separated Heidi and Harold from their shared, contentious childhood had seemed so slight Heidi could have bridged it with her little finger.

"Moth is here," Laura confided as she led Heidi to her old bedroom down the hall. "We didn't expect her, she just showed up."

Heidi was instantly alert. "Trouble?" This niece was unpredictable.

"Her father says she won't go back to school."

"Well, Robert and Tiny encouraged her all those years to do just exactly what she wanted to do," Heidi said, taking her suitcase from Laura and dumping it on the narrow, lumpy cot. "I guess this is the outcome anyone could have predicted. Remember when she threw fits over going to nursery school and Robert and Tiny let her stay home?"

"Moth was awfully young and shy," Laura murmured, protecting her youngest son and his wife from criticism. She stood with arms akimbo as Heidi unsnapped the locks on the suitcase. When Heidi threw back the lid, a faint scent of roses filled the room, and the bright-colored clothes in the suitcase seemed to levitate.

"Let me help you," Laura said as Heidi began to take out her clothes, and with an impulsive gesture that felt like generosity and caring, Heidi thrust a bunch of orange-and-yellow lingerie into Laura's hands.

"You have such pretty things," Laura said as she folded the lingerie and laid it in a drawer. Heidi would have liked to hear a note of sadness, of jealousy, even — Laura wore the kind of white cotton underpants that are sold in packs of three — but she failed to detect more than the slight curiosity of a relative who already knows all she needs to know.

"Are you supposed to persuade Moth to go back to school?" Heidi asked as she lined up her cosmetics on the frayed bureau scarf. The mirror was tarnished, and as she peered at her reflection, she might also have been seeing the ten-year-old who hoarded her first lipsticks on that same scrap of linen.

"Oh, I'm out of it," Laura told her with relief. "Harold is going to handle it."

"How?"

Laura smiled, turning from the bureau. "I don't really know. You can ask him," she added, as though conferring an honor.

But in fact there was no opportunity, for Moth was with them from the next moment on.

She was a pretty seventeen-year-old, Heidi decided after watching her sitting motionless and silent at the dinner table, not eating a thing. Her dyed blond hair was cut very short, with ragged points over her temples, and her square child's hands, when she laid them on the table, were decorated with bright blue nail polish. The jeans and tight T-shirt she wore might as well have been a uniform, and even her air of dismay and scorn was familiar from countless videos and advertisements. She'd been formed, Heidi guessed, more by the currents she swam in than by her parents, conscientious Robert and his hardworking spouse, the oddly misnamed Tiny. Moth was their only child, and Heidi remembered protesting when she heard they were going to give the baby that name. This outcome might have been expected, even then.

Larry, to his credit, was laboring to make conversation with Moth, who was seated on his left. His newspaper had recently inaugurated a young people's corner, or page—Heidi couldn't remember which—and Larry was soliciting Moth's reaction to its contents. Predictably, she hadn't read it, or anything else in the past year, Heidi guessed, and she answered his inquiries with a pouting grimace, as though to say, What fool is this that thinks I could possibly be interested?

Laura came to the rescue, offering Moth something else to eat since the roast lamb didn't seem to be to her liking. The girl brightened up at once and soon devoured the bowl of spaghetti Laura produced—spaghetti absolutely plain, as Moth had decreed, which was the only way she could eat it.

Heidi expected Larry to ask for some spaghetti, too, and then saw with astonishment that he was already eating his lamb.

The rest of them were also enjoying the lamb, which Laura said she'd been marinating for days. Heidi glanced at

her brother, wondering if he remembered the great quarrel
that had erupted, four or five years before, when she'd asked
why Laura was forced to spend so much time in the kitchen.
After all, it would have been perfectly possible, and appropriate, for Harold to hire a cook. She remembered with some
pleasure that her brother had nearly snarled at her — "We like
to do our own work" — and that Laura, with a piteous look,
had asked her to change the subject.

But, truly, if it was not ill-health that made Laura look
so diminished, it was certainly, Heidi thought, forty years
of servitude. Harold never asked for it, perhaps never even
expected it; service was simply what his authority inspired.

Heidi wondered, as she had so often before, where
the root of his authority lay. Harold was not particularly
handsome or physically impressive, and age was wizening
him, but even so, he had instead of the appearance of a retired
professor the air of an aged magician. Harold had little humor
or imagination which meant, in Heidi's estimation, that he
had no great intelligence, yet now, when he looked at Moth,
she instantly straightened in her chair and returned his gaze.
There was not a child or an animal or a woman who could
resist Harold's glance, Heidi thought, Harold's call to instant
attention. He had it from their father as a gift — unearned, she
felt.

She glanced at Larry, sitting across the table, and saw
that his gaze was fixed on Harold's face, a half-smile lingering
around his lips as though in anticipation of a particularly deli-
cious bite of food. When he saw that Harold was bending his
attention to Moth, Larry dropped his smile and began listening seriously. It was as though, Heidi thought, Larry believed
Harold would want to know his impressions, later — over
brandy and cigars. In that house, even brandy and cigars
were possible, along with a separate time, after dinner, for
the men.

As Harold continued to prod answers out of Moth about

her school (although "prod" was scarcely the word for his delicate thumbing), Heidi remembered the horror of those dinners when her parents were still alive: the stilted conversation on approved topics, directed by her father; the dead vegetables; and her mother's anxious molelike face, which seemed to quiver with apprehension around the nose—culminating in a dismal retreat by the women to her mother's bedroom, where they sat around on the bed and smoked cigarettes. When finally Heidi's mother would announce that they could go back to the living room, they would troop down like a herd of depressed sheep, hearing, on the way, the men's loud voices and laughter as they lingered in the dining room.

Now Laura was serving baked apples with, as a concession to decadence, a small pitcher of heavy cream.

When they had finished eating, Harold stood up and beckoned to Larry, who started away from the table, dropping his napkin. Laura bent down and picked it up. "We're going to the library," Harold said over his shoulder as they walked to the door. The three women in the dining room sat silently glancing around, as though they had found themselves deposited in a foreign airport.

Then Laura said, "If we all pitch in, we can have this cleaned up in half an hour."

Moth and Heidi followed her to the kitchen.

A little later, up to her elbows in soapy water (they did not believe in dishwashers, for a reason Heidi couldn't remember), Laura asked, "How are things going with Larry?"

"Pretty well," Heidi equivocated, glancing at Moth, who was strangling a wineglass in a tea towel.

"You two fucking?" the girl asked.

"My goodness, Moth," Laura demurred.

But Heidi was not taken aback. "Of course," she said. This was just the sort of question she would expect from a girl like Moth.

"You getting married?"

Again, Laura murmured a reproach.

"I don't believe so," Heidi said, and heard with incredulity something that sounded almost like a whine. "I never wanted to get married, not even the first time."

But Moth was not satisfied. She set down the wineglass with a clang on the counter and grabbed a fork, which she wrapped in the tea towel as though savagely swaddling a baby. "So what are you going to do? Live together, or what?"

"We don't want to live together," Heidi said circumspectly, although she had never discussed the issue with Larry.

"Hush now, Moth—that's enough," Laura said, tipping cold coffee out of the cups.

"How am I supposed to learn?" Moth asked reasonably. "Or do you just want me to repeat your mistakes?"

"What mistakes?" Heidi asked before Laura could stop her.

"Living with people you don't like," Moth said judiciously, filing the fork in a drawer. "I don't think it matters whether you're married or not. Either way, it just goes on and on."

"Young lady!" Laura exclaimed. "Whatever got into your head to imagine—"

"I have eyes, don't I?" Moth asked. "Ears, too. I heard you and Grandpa Harold arguing last night."

"We were having a serious discussion."

"You were crying," Moth said. "Remember? I saw you afterward, in the hall."

"I expect the men are ready," Laura said hastily, leading the way back to the living room.

In fact Larry and Harold didn't emerge from the library for another half hour, and when they did, they were laughing. Harold had flung his arm over the younger man's shoulders. "Larry's going with me tomorrow," he announced. "We'll have to get started at dawn. Coffee at five-thirty," he told Laura.

"Where are you going?" Heidi asked.

"At the last minute, Gus called to say he can't go hunting—

his wife's down with a bug, and they have grandchildren on their hands—so Larry said he'd fill in," Harold explained, going to the fireplace where he began to adjust the logs. "Get me the matches, Moth. They're in the kitchen. First fire of the season!"

Moth hurried out of the room. Laura, sighing, sat down under a reading lamp and began to fish around in her basket of mending. "I hope it won't rain all day tomorrow the way it did today."

Heidi was staring at Larry, or rather, at Larry's back. He was kneeling at the fireplace, crushing up handfuls of newspaper. Harold directed him where to put them, pointing to gaps in the structure of the logs.

Then Moth came back with the matches, and Harold let her light the fire. It blazed up quickly, bathing the dark room in light. "Good dry piñon," Harold said. "Cured all summer in the woodshed."

Heidi was still looking at Larry's back. Finally he stood up and turned around. She saw the same waiting half-smile on his face she'd seen at dinner. "I'm afraid I don't have the right gear," he told Harold.

"We'll fix you up," Harold said. "Early to bed, though. We need to be off before light to get up the mountain in time."

A few minutes later, after a round of good nights, Heidi followed Larry down the long hall to her bedroom. Once inside the door, she closed it firmly and stood with her back to the knob, studying him. With careful casualness, Larry sat on the edge of the cot and began to unlace his sneakers.

"I can't believe you agreed to go," Heidi said.

He glanced up at her. "Harold doesn't want to go alone, and the other guy dropped out. I couldn't very well refuse."

Heidi felt the doorknob in her back. She pressed against it as she said, "You told me you'd never in your life kill a living thing."

"That's right," Larry said, "but there's no chance I'm actually going to hit anything. I'll just keep Harold company."

"The first time I spent the night with you, your cat dragged in that dead squirrel and you spent almost an hour shaking the ants out before you'd bury it, so the ants wouldn't be buried alive."

"I do the best I can," Larry said, "to stick to what I believe, but sometimes circumstances—"

"Circumstances, hell," Heidi said, leaning into the door-knob. "It's not circumstances, it's Harold."

"He's my host." Larry stood up and unfastened his belt. "Now how about we drop this and go to bed."

"It's not a bed, it's a cot," Heidi said.

Half an hour later, on the floor, he had unlocked her hands and her jaws and her knees, and she was hearing the sounds of her enjoyment.

Then he bit her shoulder, and she cried out sharply.

In the morning, Larry was up and dressed and gone before Heidi opened her eyes.

Laura had breakfast ready in the warm kitchen—a basket of scones, jams, and butter. The plates from the men's breakfast were already scraped and soaking in the sink.

Laura offered her the scones. "I'll just take some tea," Heidi said. She was unwilling to swallow anything solid, as though, like the pomegranate seeds, crumbs would seal her imprisonment in that house. "When will they come back?"

"Harold promised Moth he'd take her out with the shot-gun late this afternoon," Laura said. She was sitting across the table, peeling potatoes, the skins spiraling over her thin hands. "That means they'll be back by five, I expect."

"Moth wants to learn how to shoot a gun?"

"You're damn right," Moth said, coming into the kitchen. She was wearing a pair of cutoffs and an inadequate T-shirt.

"Maybe you ought to concentrate on graduating from high school first," Heidi said.

Laura interposed, "Oh, Moth's going back home tomorrow, to get ready for school. It's all agreed."

"Why in the world?" Heidi stared at the girl, who had at last surprised her.

"Grandpa Harold's going to buy me a Thunderbird," Moth said. "The day after graduation. Any color I want." Seizing her advantage, she went on, "He was up in arms about the noise you made last night."

Heidi glared at the girl. "What in the world are you talking about?"

"Caterwauling like an alley cat in heat," Moth said. Then, sensing from the two women's faces that she had gone too far, she added, "That's just what Grandpa said, at breakfast. I didn't hear a thing. But then, my room's at the other end of the house."

Heidi was dumbfounded. Something like shame began to creep into her eyes, shrouding them with tears.

"Just ignore her," Laura said, reaching across the table to pat her hand.

Heidi snatched her hand away. "It's all very well for you to put up with everything—"

"Moth, go put the laundry in the dryer, I just heard the washer stop," Laura said.

Moth sauntered toward the door to the laundry room.

"Ears in the back of her head," Laura said with pale humor. "Now, what's going on with you, Heidi?"

"You put up, and put up," Heidi astonished herself by saying. "I've watched you for years. You let Harold tyrannize you."

"I don't call it tyranny," Laura said, picking up the next potato.

"You gave up a promising career. . . ."

"I didn't have the talent to be a professional dancer. My goodness, Heidi, that was so long ago!"

"But you were so alive then! I saw you! Dancing what was it, Stravinsky, at the armory?"

"It was *Singing in the Rain*," Laura corrected mildly.

"Whatever! You were alive, then. . . ."

Moth came quietly back into the room and sat down at the table. "Can I listen, Grandma Laura?"

"No!" Heidi said.

"If you cross your heart and hope to die you won't repeat anything you hear," Laura answered.

The girl crossed her heart. "I just want to learn," she told Heidi. "I mean, the four of you are so fucked up—"

"That's enough," Laura interrupted, "or I'll send you to your room. Heidi and I are having a serious conversation."

The girl nodded. "Go on, Aunt Heidi."

"You've been a martyr all your life," Heidi told Laura. "You let my brother make all the decisions, enslave you for his comfort. He couldn't begin to live this way"—and she gestured at the warm kitchen, all its appliances lined up and waiting— "if he didn't have your free labor. You know it's not fair! He's never done a thing for you! He doesn't even listen to you!"

"But I love him," Laura said. "I like doing things for him. I always have. Didn't you notice how much he enjoyed my roast lamb last night?"

"Oh, I give up, I just give up," Heidi said, pushing her chair back from the table. "You are never going to change."

"Are you?" Laura asked.

Already halfway turned to the door, Heidi turned back. "I'm changing all the time!"

Moth looked at her fixedly, then turned her gaze back to Laura.

"I don't see any evidence of it," Laura said, getting up to throw the potato skins into the composter. Then she dropped the peeled potatoes in the sink and began to run water over them. "Remember, I've known you more than thirty years. And I've watched you do the same thing, time after time—oh,

Harold and I have talked a lot about it. That's why he was so glad to see you'd finally found a decent man."

"So that's why he gave his permission. I wondered exactly what quality—"

"His permission, as you call it, is conditional."

"Conditional on what?"

"On your seeming happy and well-taken-care-of. And you do seem happy—we've all noticed it."

"Of all the damned gall—"

"What's gall?" asked Moth.

"And now you're going to wreck this relationship, too." Laura turned from the sink and stood leaning against it, her arms folded. "I could tell last night you were ready to skin that poor guy."

Moth laughed, then covered her mouth.

"Larry's a pacifist," Heidi said. "He's been that way all his life. He was planning to go to Canada during Vietnam but then the war ended. He never has eaten meat that I know of till that damned lamb, last night." For an instant, it seemed that had been the whole problem—the mouthful of meat Larry had politely swallowed. "He could have asked for spaghetti, like Moth—"

"It wasn't all that great," the girl said.

"But no. He had to do what he thought Harold wanted him to do. And now this." Heidi clenched her fists.

"Just walking on the mountain with a shotgun," Laura reminded her.

"Larry's never handled a gun in his life; he won't be able to shoot an elk."

"Just keeping Harold company."

"It's the principle," Heidi said. "How can I respect him if he sacrifices an important principle? Just to keep Harold happy?"

"I guess he likes him," Moth said judiciously. "Last night at dinner he couldn't keep his eyes off him."

"That's enough, Moth," Laura said, and she stepped toward Heidi as though to embrace her. Heidi moved quickly out of the way. "At least give this one a chance, Heidi. Remember that poor guy at the university—the one you kicked out in the street because you said he had a 'drinking problem.' A couple of beers was all I ever saw—"

"Passed out in front of the television at seven every evening!"

Laura went on quickly. "And that Mike—he took you abroad, bought you that gold and diamond necklace—"

"Wow," Moth said.

"I never wore it, I didn't even want it!"

"Then you drove him away because he had children he needed to visit every other weekend."

"He was enmeshed!"

"And on and on," Laura said gently, reaching out to touch Heidi's shoulder. "And on and on and on. None of us is that young anymore, Heidi. You need to think about your future. It can be pretty lonely, getting old by yourself."

"I can't love a man I don't respect," Heidi said.

That ended the conversation. The afternoon passed in fits of rain and long periods of silence. The three women avoided each other, smiling when they passed in the hall or met in the kitchen. Eventually Moth retreated to the television in the library, and Laura announced she was going to take a nap. Heidi knew how rare that was—once, she had asked Laura if she might have chronic fatigue.

Around five o'clock Heidi took her book to the window seat in the living room. Rain streamed down the panes, which felt cold to her fingers. She found herself tracing the path of the drops, her book open on her knee. Somewhere, a clock struck, and the light began to fail. Laura passed on her way to the kitchen to start dinner.

Then the old wooden-sided station wagon hove into the drive. It swayed and crashed through deep puddles, its windshield wipers sawing. From the front hall window, Heidi could just see the faces of the two men, behind the wipers.

On top of the station wagon, a dark bulk was roped. When the car pulled up, Heidi saw the white antlers.

She ran to the front door. "Who shot it?" she shouted across the wet yard, where the men were slowly approaching. "Who shot the elk?"

Harold was grinning, his thin hair pinned to his head with wet, his slicker streaming. "Would you believe it, this tenderfoot here — "

Heidi turned and ran to her bedroom. She lay down on the cot and buried her face in the pillow.

Larry came in and began silently to take off his wet clothes.

Heidi looked around at him. "The uniform of forgotten armies," she said as he piled the wet fatigues on her chair. "I never thought the day would come."

"Hush, honey," Larry said. "You're making a mountain out of a molehill."

"No, Larry. That's what you did when you told me how strongly you felt."

"A long time ago — "

"Five months!"

"Can't we let this go?" He stood stalk-thin in his underwear, looking at her with annoyance.

"Yes — if you want me to believe nothing you say matters."

Quietly, he said, "That's not the point, Heidi. The point is, I owe Harold."

Heidi sat up. "Just tell me what you mean. Tell me in simple words."

"You know what I mean," Larry said, going to his backpack.

"No one gives permission for me," Heidi said. "No one."

Later, while the others were eating dinner, Heidi packed her suitcase and let herself out of the house. The keys were still in the Jeep's ignition, and she started the motor and drove down the sandy road, bumping and splashing through puddles.

Back in her little house, she dropped her suitcase and began to turn on all the lights: the sixty-watt bulb in her mother's painted china lamp, the harsh fluorescent strips in the kitchen, the tarnished globe of the bridge lamp jettisoned from the old house. When all the lights were on, the small rooms looked pitilessly bare. The rain drummed on the flat tin roof and pinged in the bucket she'd set under a leak.

She opened the refrigerator, wanting to be hungry, wanting to cook something small and special for herself.

Her eyes fell on the plastic container where Larry had stored the casserole he'd made two nights before. She stared for a long time at the neat way the top of the container fit the bottom; she could see Larry's long fingers sealing the edges. "For Sunday," he'd said, "after we get home from your brother's."

Heidi began to cry. They were simple tears, like the rain on the flat roof that pinged from time to time in the bucket.

She was sitting at the kitchen table when Larry knocked on the door. He knocked, and waited, and knocked again, although she knew he could see her through the glass.

Finally he opened the door. "Your brother drove me back."

Heidi did not answer.

"May I come in?"

Heidi stared at the wall.

Larry stepped inside, closing the door behind him. He shrugged off his backpack and let it fall to the floor.

"Heidi," he said, "I'm sorry."

"You don't understand," she told him, and for the first time it was not a complaint or a demand but a simple statement of fact. She took some comfort from that.

Red Car

RED CAR

CAR MAY NOT BE THE WORD. *Automobile* is long outdated and *car* seems to be going or to have already gone the same way, although it is perhaps still appropriate for this particular vehicle, a red '59 Cadillac convertible with a front seat wider than a porch swing, a cumbersome white top, and the makings of history in its various grilles, bumpers, fins, and chrome ornaments.

To tell the story of this car is to tell the story of marriage; not their marriage, not the marriage, but marriage as it generally happens: a state, a place, a condition that gives rise to certain thoughts and attitudes, certain conclusions. Marriage equals the red car.

March: the red car has been parked for a year in front of a pretty frame house in Florida. It sits at the curb like a claim, loud and clear, to the pretty frame house, an exclamation point in that quiet neighborhood.

The wife rode in the car for the last time in March. She had eaten dinner with her husband in a restaurant they visited on the way back from the airport, on the way to the airport, and often in between, a lively little place with a bar overlooking the ocean.

They both dreaded going back to the house. There's a silence particular to the end of a marriage, when there are no words, not even any actions to convey the despair, the listlessness, of the approaching end; and the broad white bed in the big bedroom is no longer even a hope or a possibility but another item on an endless list of disappointments and regrets.

So when he said, "Shall we take a drive?" she thought it was a good idea, to put off that end.

They drove out along the bay where the houseboats are snubbed up against the highway and the lights from the strip developments waver in oily darkness. He pulled her in under his arm and drove with his left hand and she wondered why, once again, she was allowing him to drive her when he was drunk, and why, once again, their past seemed to have returned: the one-handed driver, the broad seat, the woman shivering in a light cotton dress under the heavy arm of a man to whom she appears, against all reason, to belong.

They stopped to look out over the water for a while as, a few months later, they would stop in an overgrown field to look for the last time at a pair of circling hawks. The power that held them in the palm of its hand arranged these last times carefully: the beautiful golden field leading to massed sycamores at the edge of the creek, the beautiful expanse of the Atlantic at the edge of the built-up town. Last times have a certain weight, a smallness and density; they stay in memory, like pebbles at the bottom of a child's pail.

Driving back, she remembered the way the red car had come into their lives. A son, turning sixteen, bought it for one hundred dollars; the car barely moved, but the body was beautiful and the design recalled a vanished elegant life.

This son spent a desultory summer poking around under the hood with the help of a wisecracking handyman who knew something about machines. But the process was slow and before long the handyman had taken over; he knew what to do and he worked in the cool early morning before the young owner was stirring. So by the end of the summer the car was running, but it no longer belonged to the boy who had paid one hundred dollars for it. It belonged to the handyman's master, who had paid for parts and labor and who now had the car repainted a brilliant carmine red.

The boy did not protest when his stepfather took the car. After all, he had paid for the parts and the labor. The handyman drove the car down to Florida that winter and parked it in front of the pretty frame house.

As the marriage began to slide, the family seldom went to Florida; the trip was expensive in more ways than one, and no one hoped, any longer, to be able to enjoy spending time together. A few incidents had ended all expectation of that, substituting a brittle atmosphere where no one laughed or cried.

So the red car gathered dust and leaves outside of the pretty frame house. Passersby sometimes noticed it and wondered about its history.

In June the handyman's master, the husband and stepfather of the family, began to come down to Florida alone. He enjoyed driving the red car to restaurants, and when he met people there, he drove the car to their apartments. He liked to take the car that had been his stepson's (but not really) and in which his wife had sat, silent, under the weight of his arm, to little spots in Old Town, little apartments above bars, respites and hideaways where the young women who worked the bars and restaurants lived with their clutter of makeup bottles, their fleets of sandals, their blue jeans patched and faded, their collections of T-shirts, and here and there a snapshot of a mother back at home in Indiana.

Soon one of these young women laid claim to the red car. She had been taken to restaurants in it and she had put her comb in the glove compartment and her feet up on the seat as she curled in under the driver's arm. She felt sorry for him—another fortyish married man who groaned when she stroked him—and she liked the car, and so one Sunday night when she drove him to the airport, she asked for the keys and he gave them to her.

Now she drove herself to work, parking the red car outside the clothing store where she was about to become assistant manager. It was hardly fitting for an assistant manager of a store that had outlets in Miami and Fort Lauderdale to come and go on a battered Schwinn.

After that the husband let the girl know what flight to meet on Fridays and she was always there, freshly showered, in a clean T-shirt and shorts.

It seemed a paradise, to both of them: the pretty frame house, paid for by the wife (who never came to Florida anymore); the pretty red car, which everyone noticed and admired, and which had belonged to the stepson (but not really), and the picture they made in it: the handsome fortyish husband and the girl who was assistant manager and knew her worst days were over.

The car seemed to lengthen; it seemed to take up more space at the curb.

Then one night there was trouble for the husband back East, and two men came down to Florida and began in an unobtrusive way to look for the red car. They were skillful professionals and no one would have noticed them except that their clothes were dark; they did buy themselves "Last Plane Out" T-shirts but that did not blunt the edge of strangeness that made people look at them twice.

They went first to the pretty frame house. The car was not there and the young woman, who by now was living in the house, did not appear to be there either.

They discovered the car parked in the bushes at the airport. They looked it over carefully and found a comb in the glove compartment.

Late one night they watched the young woman step off the Miami puddle-jumper and walk to the red car. She had a little suitcase that she threw into the back seat, and then she released the chrome hooks that held the top in place (with which the wife, who never came to Florida anymore, had often struggled) and pushed the top back. She pulled the car out of the bushes and started down the highway along the ocean, going at a good pace, and the two professionals drove along behind her.

First she stopped at a large expensive house and knocked on the front door. A Cuban woman (or so the professionals dubbed her) came out with a small child. All three got in the red car and drove rapidly to a pet store which, since it was night, was closed; however, someone was waiting inside behind the bubbling fish tanks and the parrots on swings, and the three went in, emerging a few minutes later. They drove to another pet store on the other side of town and repeated the sequence. Then the young woman took the older woman and her child (if it was her child; the professionals couldn't tell, although she seemed protective of the little boy, holding him by the hand) back to the expensive house.

Next the young woman drove to an old house that was broken up into many small apartments. After she had been inside for a few minutes, a fancy foreign car drove up; the driver hopped out, went inside briefly, and came out again.

That was all that happened. Something had been claimed, exchanged, or given away; certainly, the professionals knew, money had been involved. But they couldn't find a reason to ask questions. Young women do come and go.

The red car, which had belonged to the sixteen-year-old boy, which had passed through the hands of the wisecracking handyman on its way to the fortyish husband who was about to become single again and in which he had driven his wife for the last time, was parked outside of an old house broken up into many apartments, where young women kept their clutter of makeup bottles, their fleets of sandals, their collections of T-shirts, and here and there a snapshot of a mother at home in Indiana.

Did it all begin with the boy's silence when the car, as was only just, passed out of his hands? Or with the handyman's silence when the car, which he had fixed, passed along to the owner? Or with the silence of the wife when she sat under the weight of her husband's arm?

Or is there another silence, the silence of night ocean and south wind, combing the darkness while these sleepers lie under the secret verdict of the future?

SAGESSE

In Normandy that summer just after the war, the weather was cloudy and gray. Sarah thought it matched the beach, which had suffered during the Invasion.

The new governess warned her, "Be careful, Sarah. You don't know what you might find. A boy digging in the sand blew his arm off."

"Blew his own arm off?"

The strange Mam'selle didn't smile. "He found a grenade, still lively." She seldom made a mistake in English but when she did, Sarah did not correct her. Mam'selle had been hired, Sarah knew, for the beauty of her French accent, which the three American children were meant to acquire during their summer abroad. Small mistakes in word usage did not matter.

"She's not a servant," Sarah's mother had explained, which meant that Mam'selle was to be treated differently from the sighing cook at home in St. Louis, or the maid who made up their beds in the hotel.

Mam'selle came from a good family, had married into it, or was related in some other way. That family was gone, wiped out by the war, and so she was working as a governess for Americans. Sarah had learned this from her parents' conversation.

Her lost family had left Mam'selle a set of fine possessions. The possessions were few, but of the best quality; she carried them in a stout black leather suitcase, worn, but very clean. Its peach-colored silk lining smelled of sachet.

Sarah had looked in the suitcase cautiously when it was lying open on the foot of Mam'selle's bed. That was the first day of her employment, and she had been hanging the contents of the suitcase in the armoire, next to Sarah's and her two little sisters' clothes.

Mam'selle had arranged a series of peach-colored satin bags on the armoire shelves. What was in the bags Sarah didn't ask; instead, she studied Mam'selle's gestures, folding and tucking precious things away.

Sarah's family had brought eighteen pieces of luggage to France. When they traveled—and they traveled a great deal—all kinds of clothes were needed, as well as books, photographs of kin left back in the States, writing materials, and her mother's enormous dictionary.

Yet things didn't matter, Sarah thought, except for the moment when they were brought out of their boxes, smelling of newness. Soon enough, the girls' dresses, bought for the trip, the dolls, patent-leather slippers, and hair bows in every color lost their new smell and became encumbrances to be put away as quickly as possible, in the big armoire.

Mam'selle's things smelled of other times. The tiny gold binoculars (Mam'selle called them opera glasses), the soft long white gloves, the crisp black veil—all of them smelled of old times, sweet, if a little musty.

After Mam'selle had settled in, Sarah's parents left for Paris, and the three girls began to grow accustomed to the routine of hotel life.

Sarah ordered Sole Meunière every other night (every night, Mam'selle told her, would be extravagant), learned to drink bottled water instead of boiled milk, and ate hard-crusted bread with sweet butter that came in little pots.

On rainy days, they walked across fields to a farm where a woman gave them sour yogurt with a crust of cream at the top. Mam'selle and the woman talked, and Sarah began to pick up a few words of French.

On sunny mornings, Mam'selle took Sarah and her two little sisters to the beach. They were allowed to swim, but not to dig in the sand. Alice and Sarah wore dresses, at Mam'selle's insistence, with smocked bodices and puffed sleeves, which they had worn to the country club, back home in St. Louis.

The youngest girl wore a romper over her diapers and spent the morning lying on a shawl, protected from the sun by an open umbrella.

Mam'selle arranged their things in neat piles—sandals, sailboats, pails, and towels—near the slatted wooden dressing hut the parents had rented for the season.

Later, inside the hut, Mam'selle helped the girls change into their bathing costumes (as she called them) under their dresses. At first Sarah protested, but then she became interested in the way this was accomplished.

First, she stepped into her damp woolen bathing suit and pulled it up over her thighs, under the full skirt of her dress; then Mam'selle lifted the dress over her head while Sarah, at exactly the same moment, pulled the bathing suit up to her chest. Finally, she slipped her hands through the straps as the dress flew off.

At the end of the morning, the whole process was reversed, which meant, Mam'selle explained, that Sarah and her sisters did not have to submit to the indignity of wearing wet sandy bathing costumes when they walked up to the hotel for lunch.

Something precious was being protected in this way.

Sarah was reminded of the saint's thighbone that lay inside a gold box in the village church. On special days, Mam'selle told her, the box was taken out and paraded through the streets, but it was never opened. No one would have been equal to the sight of the naked bone.

Mam'selle did not possess a bathing costume. On the beach, she wore one of her black dresses, which were not quite uniforms — there were differences in detail, a lace collar, an embroidered yoke. When they came back from the beach, she took off each laced-up black shoe and shook out the sand.

Sarah was embarrassed by the sight of her feet, curled like kitten paws inside her black stockings.

At meals, Mam'selle taught Sarah a few more words of French. Her sisters were too young to take an interest, but Sarah practiced her new words on the waiter, redheaded Eduard, who laughed, and on the mouselike maid, Henriette, who did not seem to understand.

Eventually Sarah learned what to call the articles in the bathroom she shared with her sisters and Mam'selle, a room as dark as a chapel. *Comb*, she would say, *brush*, and think of the governess's thick braid of black hair, which she let down every evening.

Mam'selle taught her how to differentiate between the other children and their governesses at the hotel. Sarah might talk to the English and the French, but never to the German. There were only two Germans, a sad-looking elderly lady with a dispirited boy, who sat in a remote corner of the big white dining room.

One morning at the beach when Alice was playing at the edge of the water and the baby was asleep on her shawl, Mam'selle began to talk about her life. Sarah was an eager listener, and after that Mam'selle always talked to her when the younger children were out of the way.

First, she told stories about her childhood in the precious time before the war.

In her village, there had always been enough to eat — this was a cardinal point.

Then there came a shady period when Mam'selle said she had been "moins sage." Sarah thought she meant the herb they used at home with roast chicken, pronounced oddly. At that time, Mam'selle confessed, she had gone about the streets in short skirts.

But at last in a blaze of light and white lilacs, she was married, and spent happy years in a city in North Africa where her husband pursued his military career.

With the war, shadows and silences fell. It was not only the defeats, the deaths, although Mam'selle told Sarah about all of them, omitting no detail. It was what she called "the loss of heart."

Sarah began to mourn then for something she had never known: Mam'selle's youth, blown up to the blue North African sky along with sand and buildings.

As to what had happened to her young husband, Mam'selle indicated that he had been killed in one of the early engagements. "One must go on," Mam'selle said at the end of the story, stretching her black skirt over her knees.

When Sarah asked questions, Mam'selle became discreet or distracted. So the stories lacked the explanations Sarah was used to from the time her mother had told her about the three little pigs; here was no straw house to be seen as a symbol of the pig-builder's laziness, no brick house, proof of his brother's foresight. There were only the stories themselves, endlessly unfolding.

The evenings were long after Alice and the baby were asleep and Mam'selle retired to the bathroom for her ablutions. Usually Sarah lay on her bed, reading books her father sent down from the British bookstore in Paris. There were novels about the Crusades, and Robin Hood, and one about Saint Joan and her great war.

One dismal afternoon when they were walking back from the yogurt farm, Mam'selle took a shortcut through a park, as she called it. It was not a park in Sarah's view but a vast lawn leading to an empty gray castle. The Germans, Mam'selle said, had pillaged it, and the family no longer came.

At the edge of the lawn, they saw a small chapel with a stained-glass window that showed a woman holding a lily and a shield. The door had been forced, and Mam'selle allowed Sarah to step inside.

Under the stained-glass window, there was a stone tablet on which two names and four dates were carved.

When Sarah called out the dates, Mam'selle explained that they recorded family deaths: two generations, father and son, had been killed fighting for France. Sarah read the inscription aloud—"Mort pour la France"—and looked at the stained-glass lady with her lily and her shield.

On the way back to the hotel, they passed another engraved stone tablet, set into a wall. Mam'selle explained that it commemorated another kind of death, at the hands of a German firing squad. "We were not all shameless," she said.

On their next visit to the yogurt farm, Sarah realized she could understand some of the conversation. The farm woman, hands stuffed under her apron, was telling Mam'selle about a child, or children, who had spent the war years hidden in the hayloft.

Mam'selle listened without comment. At the end of the story, she embraced the farm woman with unusual warmth.

And then a great weekend arrived: the parents were coming down from Paris. Alice, waiting, ran back and forth to the hotel's front door. Sarah waited more discreetly. When the parents finally appeared, with boxes of presents and suitcases, life began to move.

Bicycles were rented in the village, and everyone except Mam'selle rode them to see a nearby castle, not the gray empty castle in its park, but one with furniture, and a guide. In the evening, Sarah's father started a new book for her by reading its first chapter aloud; it was about a Frenchman who went to America to fight in the Revolution.

But what Sarah remembered most clearly from the frantic two days was a moment with her mother in a roadside flower garden. Her mother insisted on stopping the car, and in her limited French, she asked the man hoeing there if she could pick some flowers. They were orange and pink nasturtiums, and when Sarah smelled them, she remembered that her mother had a row of nasturtiums outside the side porch at home.

"Are you homesick?" her mother asked when she noticed Sarah's face. "Do you want to go back to St. Louis?"

"No," Sarah said. "I'm learning French."

In September, after most of the other guests had left the hotel, Sarah finished the last novel in her father's box, a romance about the days of the knights.

She went to Mam'selle, who was sitting on the bathroom stool, holding Alice on her knees.

"I want to be honorable," Sarah said. "Like the knights, fighting for something."

Mam'selle took her request to heart and meditated on it while she waited for the thermometer in Alice's mouth to register.

"You will face challenges when you are older," she promised. "Now it would be wise for you to get a little air."

Sarah was never allowed to go out of the hotel alone, but now Mam'selle wanted her to walk to the village to pick up some medicine the doctor had prescribed. Alice was not gravely ill but she had a cough that made the doctor frown.

Mam'selle folded up several francs in a piece of paper and put it in Sarah's hand. "Go to the pharmacy and come right back," she said, in French; by now Sarah could understand every word she heard.

She felt important and serious as she started out, her old winter coat buttoned to the chin.

Walking along the sea wall, she watched the curl of low waves as they broke over debris left in the sand. Further along, she passed the smashed concrete bunkers the Germans had built, their evil eyeholes aimed at England. She hurried past those dark openings.

When she reached the village, she stopped to look at sailboats in the toy shop window, then hurried on, remembering she was too old for such things.

At the pharmacy, she handed paper and money to a man who stood above her, behind a high desk. The man smiled at her, and gave her change in thin coins she couldn't count.

Going back along the sea wall, she noticed a ray of sun on the water and decided to walk the rest of the way on the beach.

As she walked, she saw a boot in the sand. It looked almost new, and it was still laced to the top. She turned it over; the other side was torn out. She wondered if the sea had done that, grinding the boot against a rock. Or perhaps an exploding shell had shattered it, and the foot of the soldier; but why was the boot still laced?

She hurried on.

Three men were approaching her from the other end of the beach. She walked with her eyes on the tips of her shoes, her hands in her pockets.

The men passed quite close to her, and then one of them said something, and she felt a hand reach under her coat and skirt and touch the back of her naked thigh.

She slipped quickly away.

As she ran, she stumbled over more debris—rusted chunks of metal, and wire caught up in tattered cloth.

In the hotel lobby, she stopped to catch her breath. The concierge behind his desk was watching her.

Then she climbed the two flights of stairs to her room and went in and lay down on the bed, without taking off her coat or emptying the sand out of her shoes.

After a while she remembered Alice's medicine and carried it to Mam'selle. As she handed her the medicine, Sarah apologized for taking so long.

"I know you were wise," Mam'selle said, looking frightened. She used the French noun that sounded like the herb.

Sarah looked at her shoes.

"Why are you sad?" Mam'selle asked.

"I'm always sad after I finish a book," Sarah said in French. It was her first whole sentence.

Then, in spite of herself, she began to cry. "There is no honor," she sobbed.

"It is the war," Mam'selle said.

"But the war is over," Sarah said, in French, using words she hadn't known she knew.

"You are speaking French," Mam'selle said.

That evening after Alice and the baby were put to bed, Mam'selle took out a crochet hook and a ball of silky white thread and showed Sarah how to make the chain stitch.

As she worked, Mam'selle talked about her wedding dress, which she had sewn herself in the town in North Africa, crocheting lace onto a hem that swept the ground.

"We thought it would be all right, after the war," she told Sarah, "after the Americans came."

Then she added, quickly, "At least now we can eat. Do you understand what that means, Sarah, you who have never been hungry?"

"Yes," Sarah said, "but it is not all right, and it is not going to be all right."

Mam'selle was silent, pressing the point of her crochet hook into another knot of white thread.

Then the hotel was emptying, and it was too chilly to go to the beach. The parents came down to take the children to Paris; they had found the perfect house.

Mam'selle was packing her black suitcase when Sarah went to tell her the news. "Five bedrooms," she said, "which means a room for each of us."

"I will be returning to my village," Mam'selle said, and now she spoke the frozen English of their first weeks together. "It is better so."

"It is not better so!" Sarah cried, and she ran to her mother to demand an explanation.

When she saw her daughter's flushed face, her mother shook her head. "You must learn to control yourself."

"But why—?"

The head shaking continued, the slight motion like the one used to shake salt over food. When Sarah continued to demand, her mother said, "Mam'selle was all very well for a summer vacation, but not for Paris. She is not suitable."

Walking back along the hotel corridor, Sarah remembered the short skirts Mam'selle had worn at the time when she had been "moins sage." That adjective was not yet in Sarah's vocabulary, but she knew it had something to do with the war, something shameful, like the touch of the man's hand on her thigh.

When everything was packed up and loaded into the car, Mam'selle gave Sarah the little opera glasses. "Everything will all be right in time," she said, "when the years pass."

And then she was gone, with a small flourish of her gray skirt as she climbed into the taxi.

SWEET PEAS

AT A CAFÉ NOT FAR FROM THE SORBONNE, a couple is sitting in the August crowd. They are Americans—anyone can see that—comfortably if casually dressed, their hands folded around their demitasse cups in the proprietary way Americans have. They are wedged in at their small table—both are tall—by the knees and elbows of people at the adjoining tables placed along the narrow stretch of concrete.

The woman reaches out during a silence in the conversation and touches the ordinary bright red geranium blooming in a wooden planter at her knee.

The silence is not long, it is not profound, it is the silence that occurs when two people have spent a month together. This silence is made up of the moment before dawn when one of them woke and, turning, found that the bed held the other; a moment not of seeking, yet not of satisfaction, for the body that is found at dawn in the bed is always the body of a stranger, no matter what may have transpired the night before. This silence is also the silence of waiting on train platforms, in airport lounges, where a tinge of anxiety gives the silence texture; it is the silence of waiting to be noticed in the far-too-expensive restaurants they feel obliged to try.

It is his silence—Roland Boyd's silence—when his companion begins to speak French (she speaks well, this Madeline, he admires her for it, yet silence is his only resort at such times since he speaks no French at all), and it is her silence when he reads the *Paris Herald* and seems to disappear. They are old enough, and wise enough, to have arranged various separations, strategically located during their long trip; they do not want "to wear each other out," as Madeline says, "to get dull and staid," as Roland says—they have a horror of the way other Americans travel, or seem to travel, alternating irritation and numbness.

Neither of them would call this trip their honeymoon— they are not married, have no plans to marry, have never even discussed marrying, except obliquely, in terms of other people's mistakes—and yet an impartial observer might assume as much, because of the careful, quiet way Madeline has dressed, even on this hot August day, because of the way her hand strays, now and then, to Roland's on the white table-cloth. And she has, the observer would surely have noted, offered Roland the little white cup of sugar lumps, would—if she hadn't restrained herself—have taken a lump out with the tongs and dropped it in his tiny cup, because he loves sugar and often denies himself.

Madeline, however, does not make this mistake—not

this morning, not this hot August morning in the café near the Sorbonne—because she is finally coming to understand that her gestures do not summon his, as for a long time she thought or felt they might.

She remembered this when they sat down at the little round table, jammed in with its neighbors, because of the way Roland stared out at once into the street. She knows him so well, this keen observer, that she no longer needs to ask him what he thinks or how he feels. (Sometimes he volunteers this information.) He sat down in the chair, fatigued—they have been walking the neighborhood all morning—with the obliviousness that, she knows, is key to his survival. He has loved once, he has loved deeply—so he has told her—and he does not expect to love in that way again.

Madeline, a realist whose husband left her early in their marriage, knows that when a man says something about love or the lack of it women should take note, for if a man knows anything at all, he knows his capacity to love, or not, as he knows the interior of his car's engine or the contents of his wallet. Other statements may be open to question—how and why a child rebels, for instance, or what is a suitable way to greet a lover after a breakup—but on the question of love, men are exact. So she has taken note—took note, in fact, the first time they had dinner together—and is always in the process of wrapping her feelings around his. She likes the starkness of his lack because she can festoon it with her own luxuriant emotions, growing morning glories to cover his absence.

She has had, though, an odd moment an hour or so before they sat down. It began when they were walking through the vast church whose name she has already forgotten, when they were admiring the great golden balloon, several stories tall, which some modern artist has placed in the nave. The great balloon reflected on its golden surface the high windows in the chancel; it was beautiful, Roland said, the most beautiful thing he'd seen so far in Paris, and Madeline objected that it was beautiful but so out of place, taking up the entire nave where once people prayed.

"Oh you Catholics," Roland said gently, and since it was a topic they've agreed to avoid, she said nothing.

But the moment stretched itself like a small, sunning snake all the way to the table on the sidewalk. Without that moment, Madeline knows, she would never have noticed the sweet peas.

Paris is full of flowers—it is one of the things she loves about the city—and the sidewalk florist they passed just before they sat down was nothing special, nothing even particularly attractive: a torn canvas awning, a few tubs of flowers, a woman scaling off leaves behind a counter. But in the tubs set closest to the sidewalk, there were sweet peas— lavender, white, and pink.

"Sweet peas!" Madeline said, and Roland, a step or so ahead, nodded without turning around.

But Madeline stopped and leaned down—bent double, almost—to smell the closest bunch. It was pale lavender, the small blooms tied tightly together, the stems swimming in water. A few drops of water clung to the blooms, and Madeline tasted one drop with the tip of her tongue. The water tasted only of coolness but when she breathed in, the sweet pea blossoms had the sharp, small scent that was exactly what she needed, exactly what she came to France to find.

"Sweet peas," she said, again, as she lifted her head but Roland was already negotiating for a chair at the café table.

She hurried then to find him. There was a sweatiness in the air, the city air of a long summer, a confusion of people and cars and slightly leaning three-story buildings; the sky seemed blocked, or was it only pale, so pale it could hardly be seen? She did not know as she took the other chair at the table and saw Roland staring at a wall, or a car, or someone else—she did not know, it did not really matter. His eyes were averted.

Now she summons the waiter in her precise, educated French, the accent not quite right, she knows, but still intelligible, and he brings them two more demitasses of thick coffee which he places beside the cup of sugar cubes and the saucer of lemon rinds.

Then, without being asked, she hands the sugar to Roland and suppresses the impulse to take out the sugar cube and drop it into his coffee.

There are ways and ways of coming to understanding, she will think later, when she reflects on that morning, but surely the moment of understanding that has the highest polish takes place in Paris, derives some of its luster not so much from the place itself—a big city on a hot morning—as from the memories and assumptions that cluster around it.

Roland doesn't thank her for passing the cup of sugar. He is used to her ministrations, as he calls them. Usually she doesn't notice his failure to thank her—how absurd it would be to hold someone who knows her so intimately to such a formality—but today, because of the sweet peas, she does notice. "Why didn't you thank me?" she asks, as frankly as a child.

He replies with a stare and something dismissive. It doesn't matter, she knows, exactly what words come to him at that moment; they are the words that have been waiting for a month like pebbles at the bottom of a well.

"I asked because of the sweet peas," she explains, "and my mother."

She has told Roland, as she tells all her close friends, the story of her mother, which is dim and gray as, it often seems, her mother, who worked hard, who saved money, who had no time, was dim and gray; but the sweet peas are from another compartment, one she's never opened. "She took us to France, one time; it was the only trip we ever made together."

Roland is interested because this is new.

"We couldn't afford the cities so we stayed out in the country, at a dreary beach place on the Normandy coast, in a family hotel with bad food and smells in the hall. We didn't like it particularly because there was nothing for American children to do and it rained all the time. But one day when it rained we took a walk and we found this garden where an old man was growing sweet peas."

Now Roland may be listening — it is not clear — or he may be drinking his coffee and thinking about something else. In any event, Madeline falls silent, not out of discouragement but because she does not feel capable of describing what she saw that day: her mother bent in the garden, her face in a mass of lavender sweet peas.

"The man cut a big bunch and gave them to her, and when she opened her purse to pay, he waved it away. And then," Madeline says, and now she is talking to herself, "she cried."

Ordinarily she would have added that her father had been gone for a long time, that her mother had no friends in France, that the boys were being difficult, but now these explanations seemed irrelevant. The sequence — her mother burying her face in the flowers, the man giving her a bunch, her tears — is enough. No interpretation is needed.

"I'll be back in just a moment," Madeline says, getting up and almost falling over the knees of the man at the next table. She expects Roland to ask her where she's going but he says nothing and she finds herself oaring her way through the hot, fume-laden air.

It occurs to her that perhaps the florist's stall was a dream, that it will have vanished like the witch's hut in a fairy tale, but there it is, prosaically occupying its few feet of the sidewalk.

She heads straight for the tub of lavender sweet peas and seizes a bunch — yes, seizes, that is the word. Then she smells them to make sure the scent is there — it is — and hurries to the counter to pay. The sweet peas cost, as she quickly figures, five dollars in American money; she counts out the change and refuses the woman's offer of a paper to wrap the stems in. She barely notices the woman, which is strange since all during their trip she has been recording every detail.

She is remembering the way her mother's pretty face

crumpled. Madeline was only twelve when that happened, and she thinks at first she had been embarrassed—she must have been embarrassed!—but then she knows with certainty that she had not been embarrassed, that she had felt for her mother at that moment, and perhaps only at that moment, love.

For of course there had been disagreements later and separations and they had both faced each other finally like knights on horseback, holding their lances and shields.

Now Madeline sits down at the table and Roland glances at her as she holds out the bouquet. "I bought myself some sweet peas," she says, and tries to remember whether she has ever bought herself anything before. Of course she has, she is comfortably off, she has bought acres of clothes and furniture and dishes over the years, yet somehow that is not the same and she knows it is not the same because all those things had no link to love.

"Smell them," she says, and wonders again if she's ever said anything so direct. Roland leans forward a little and sniffs the bouquet.

"That was the only time I ever saw my mother cry," she reminds him, and a dry choking starts in her throat as though something is lodged there.

"Yes," he says, patiently.

She draws the flowers in close, inhaling their scent. "I never told you I loved her then," she says, "just the way I love you now. My two loves," she adds.

"That's nice," Roland says.

Now she knows what she wants to ask. "Why didn't you buy me the sweet peas?"

"I didn't think of it," he says.

"What do you think about?" she asks, gliding into deep, cold water.

"What kind of a question . . ."

"No kind of a question," she says. "I don't know if you love me."

"You know I do."

"No, I don't know," she says, and she shifts the sweet peas to her other hand. Their stems are growing warm; she doesn't know how she will preserve them.

"Well, I've told you," he says, and she looks at his beautiful face, the brown eyes she adores, the pallor and the charm that will always win him the hearts of women. "Yes, you've told me," she says, "but I've never believed it."

"Maybe you should wonder why."

She weighs that carefully, staring at the way the sweet pea blossoms are fastened, fragilely, to each stalk. Perhaps she caught her mother's sadness long ago, like a germ.

But finally she says, "I don't believe it because it isn't so," and the café and the city around it drop away.

That sentence has freed her not from Roland—she never wanted to lose him—but from the tyranny of the past. She has loved twice in her life, and lost twice. She loved her mother, once, and the rest of what passed between them is irrelevant; she loved Roland, she will probably always love him, and the fact that they do not see each other is irrelevant.

The sweet peas, of course, did not last through that long hot day.

SALLIE BINGHAM published her first novel with Houghton Mifflin in 1961. Since then she has published four collections of short stories, four novels, and a memoir. She was Book Editor for *The Courier-Journal* in Louisville and has been a director of the National Book Critics Circle. She is the founder of The Kentucky Foundation for Women, and the Sallie Bingham Center for Women's History and Culture at Duke University.